Praise for Faith Martin

'Brilliant characters that leap off the page' *The Sun*

'Faith Martin has created a wonderful Wodehousian world of intrigue and suspicion and a tricky puzzle to solve'
Helena Dixon, author of the Miss Underhay Mysteries

'Amuses and intrigues in equal measure... a splendid start to what promises to be a long-running series' *Daily Mail*

'All the ingredients of a classic mystery – engaging characters and an impossible crime. The story races along like a runaway locomotive... enormous fun'
Orlando Murrin, author of *Knife Skills for Beginners*

'We devoured this whoddunit in one sitting!' *Bella*

'The perfect village mystery. A golden-age world with an energy that is totally contemporary'
J.M. Hall, author of *A Spoonful of Murder*

'With murder, intrigue, and ghostly happenings, this will satisfy cosy crime fans' *Heat*

'A charming and clever take on a locked room murder that left you guessing how and why the victim snuffed it! I enjoyed the clever plot, original ideas and the idyllic setting very much!'
Sarah Yarwood-Lovett, author of The Doctor Nell Ward Mysteries

'Her knowledge of the genre and easy writing style makes this an effortless and fun read' *My Weekly*

'A clever mystery' *Woman's Own*

'This engaging and energetic mystery hosts an abundance of engaging characters and is great fun' *Platinum*

Also by Faith Martin

The Ryder and Loveday series
A Fatal Obsession
A Fatal Mistake
A Fatal Flaw
A Fatal Secret
A Fatal Truth
A Fatal Affair
A Fatal Night
A Fatal End

The Val & Arbie Mysteries
Murder by Candlelight
The Last Word is Death

A DANGEROUS TRAIN OF THOUGHT

FAITH MARTIN

ONE PLACE. MANY STORIES

HQ
An imprint of HarperCollins*Publishers* Ltd
1 London Bridge Street
London SE1 9GF

www.harpercollins.co.uk

HarperCollins*Publishers*
Macken House, 39/40 Mayor Street Upper
Dublin 1, D01 C9W8, Ireland
This edition 2026

1

First published in Great Britain by HQ,
an imprint of HarperCollins*Publishers* Ltd 2026

Copyright © Faith Martin 2026

Faith Martin asserts the moral right to be identified as the author of this work.
A catalogue record for this book is available from the British Library.

HB ISBN: 9780008738433
TPB ISBN: 9780008738426

Set in Meridien LT Std by HarperCollins*Publishers* India

This novel is entirely a work of fiction. The names, characters and incidents portrayed in it are the work of the author's imagination. Any resemblance to actual persons, living or dead, events or localities is entirely coincidental.

All rights reserved. No part of this publication may be reproduced, stored in a retrieval system, or transmitted, in any form or by any means, electronic, mechanical, photocopying, recording or otherwise, without the prior written permission of the publishers.

Without limiting the exclusive rights of any author, contributor or the publisher of this publication, any unauthorised use of this publication to train generative artificial intelligence (AI) technologies is expressly prohibited. HarperCollins also exercise their rights under Article 4(3) of the Digital Single Market Directive 2019/790 and expressly reserve this publication from the text and data mining exception.

Printed and bound in the UK using 100% Renewable
Electricity at CPI Group (UK) Ltd

For more information visit: www.harpercollins.co.uk/green

ENGLAND – SPRING 1926

CHAPTER ONE

Sir Bayard Cherville, resplendent in his royal-blue dressing gown, stood gazing out of his open bedroom window and breathed in deeply the fresh spring air. It was the last week of April, but already the weather felt more as if they were in the middle of May, and the perfume from his gardens below bore the unmistakable mix of wallflowers and narcissus, bluebells and hyacinths.

Beyond the formal gardens of Cleeves Lea Manor spread the rest of his grounds and estate, set in the gently rolling acres of south Yorkshire. Over six miles away lay the coast, just far enough that the salt in the air didn't affect his crops but close enough for him to keep his yacht and enjoy sailing her, whenever the weather was right and the mood took him. At five feet ten, with grey hair and eyes, he was getting a little solid around the middle now, but still considered himself to be a fine figure of a man.

He turned from contemplating his fiefdom, and far more critically regarded the woman lying in the four-poster bed behind him. She was propped up against the cushions and studiously pretending to attend to the tea and toast on the tray which her maid had just brought in and had carefully positioned over her knees.

Lady Sybil, at thirty-two years old, was a pale, slender

woman, exactly twenty years younger than her husband. She possessed a fine length of ash-blonde hair (currently caught up in a becoming bedcap of pearl-coloured silk and lace) and startling aquamarine-tinted eyes. Her husband often said that it was his lady wife's eyes that had first captured and then hopelessly ensnared him, when he'd first been introduced to her at some soiree or other in Wimbledon five years before.

The youngest daughter of an impoverished son and lord, she had accepted his proposal of marriage six months later, reluctantly conceding that she was in dire danger of becoming an old maid if she didn't. And even more reluctantly facing the fact that, despite her beauty, breeding and charm, her lack of any dowry worth its name meant that she would almost certainly never be able to make a better match.

It was the truth that Sir Bayard might lack the sophistication she would have preferred, for he came from a generation of landed gentry that were first and foremost farmers, but in Cleeves Lea Manor, at least, a lovely Georgian house with wings stretching back to Elizabethan times, the new Lady Cherville had no cause for complaint. Better yet, wool had made Sir Bayard's ancestors wealthy enough to keep all successive Cherville brides in silks and pearls, and although the Great War, taxes and the changing times had nibbled into the coffers somewhat, the family were still a name to be reckoned with throughout this part of the county.

It hadn't taken long, however, for Lady Sybil to chafe at such isolated country living and she had quickly taken to prolonged visits to town, forcing her husband, over the last few years, into hosting rather lavish weekend parties so that he might keep her entertained, whilst safely under his watchful eye. Not by nature a gregarious man, Sir Bayard was nevertheless proud of his home, gardens and estates and liked showing them off well enough and so he bore these proceedings stoically.

So, on this Thursday morning, he found himself contemplating the arrival of the first of his guests for the latest gathering, and his lips twitched in a rather evil-looking smile as he observed his wife making a show of nonchalantly buttering a slice of toast. She studiously avoided the jar of Oxford marmalade, as she watched over her svelte figure with a ferocious regard that had once intrigued him but now only amused him. For he knew well enough why she wanted to stay young, slim and beautiful.

'We've got a mixed bag coming up this time, haven't we, m'dear?' he murmured, stuffing his hands into the pockets of his dressing gown and wandering casually back towards the marital bed.

His wife eyed his approach warily. 'Well, darling, whose fault is that?' she retorted crisply. 'If you will go and invite an extra person behind my back at the very last minute and not even let me know in good time. . .' She shrugged a slender shoulder to indicate her displeasure at such behaviour.

Sir Bayard affected a look of innocence. 'But I thought you two were such good friends?'

Sybil felt herself tense and forced a bored smile onto her face. 'That's not the point, Bay, and you know it,' she chided, careful to keep her tone light now. 'A good hostess picks and chooses her guests carefully, so that they can complement one another, and we can make the most of them. It's an art, you know, choosing houseguests who can rub along well enough, whilst at the same time, sparking off each other, thus amusing everyone concerned. I had a perfectly balanced group, and then you go and tell me now, this very morning, that you're bringing in someone who'll upset the whole—'

'Nonsense,' Sir Bayard interrupted her bluntly. 'You fuss

too much. I think this weekend party will go with a swing and probably prove to be one of our best yet.' And so saying, he turned and headed back to the window again, before tossing a final comment over his shoulder. 'And I, for one, intend to enjoy it enormously.'

And he would too, he thought, his somewhat anticipatory smile quickly falling away as he stared out over the awakening countryside. Oh yes, the Lord of the Manor mused, watching a pair of blackbirds patrolling the well-manicured lawns for early-morning worms. He intended to enjoy the coming long weekend very much indeed. But not everyone, he suspected, would get as much satisfaction out of the things that he had planned for the following few days.

Lying in bed, Sybil watched his back thoughtfully. After four years of marriage, she'd come to know her husband very well, and she was sure that he was up to something. In some ways he was rather childish, and like some children, he could show a definite cruel streak when the mood took him. Uneasily, she put the tray to one side of the bed and swung her feet to the floor. 'Well, I'm off to have a bath,' she said, as casually as she could manage.

But as she made her way down the landing towards the nearest bathroom, she was feeling anything but casual. *He couldn't know, could he?* The thought made her shiver uneasily, and she told herself crossly not to get a case of the collywobbles. *Of course* he couldn't know – there was no way he could possibly have found out. She'd been so careful. They had *both* been so careful. This unexpected little twist of fate just had to be one of life's odd little coincidences, that was all. It was all very annoying and everything, but they only needed to keep their heads for a few days, after all.

In the bathroom, where her maid had already half-filled the tub, she poured some of her favourite scented French bath salts into the gently steaming water and settled in with a small sigh of pleasure. But her mind couldn't rest easily, as she tried yet again to convince herself that she was worrying over nothing. After all, Bayard did sometimes invite people to their parties that she'd rather he didn't. Take silly Agnes, for instance. He'd put his foot down over inviting her this weekend because the last time they'd enjoyed her hospitality she'd brought the son of a Duke to table, which was always something of a coup, and he insisted they owed her.

Still, her guilty conscience insisted, asking the annoying, fussy, old maid that was Agnes Warren to come was a far cry from inviting. . .

Suddenly, Lady Sybil sat up in the bathtub with a quick cry of distress as another realisation swamped her. For once, though, her thoughts weren't solely concerned with herself and her own woes and worries, but with someone else's.

'The Rowes!' she yelped, appalled. Good grief, she simply must stop the Rowes from coming! With a splash, she clambered out of the tub and awkwardly tried to don her silk dressing gown. Of course, she was so wet that it stuck and clung annoyingly to her form, preventing her movements, and with a near sob of frustration, she had to stop and dry herself with a towel first, all the time wondering what time it was.

Perhaps, if she was lucky, they wouldn't have left for the train yet? But coming all the way from Oxfordshire, they'd be sure to be setting off early.

Cursing her husband roundly, she all but ran down the landing and the stairs, some locks of her damp, long hair flying free from under her bath cap as she headed for the telephone in the hall, quite scandalising Jardine the butler, who was on his way to his pantry to polish the breakfast silver.

*

In their Woodstock home, mother and daughter Elizabeth and Bernadette Rowe, known as Betty and Bernie to their closest friends, surveyed the large trunk standing in the hall with somewhat shamed faces. They closely resembled each other with their big blue eyes, their short but shapely figures and the shade of their brown hair – though Bernie favoured the more fashionable bobbed hairstyle of the day, whilst her mother kept her locks long, if swept back and up-rolled into a neat bun on the back of her head.

Widowed young, Betty had raised her late son Marcus and her daughter single-handedly. The two women had always been very close, and after the tragedy that had rocked them both last year, they had taken to clinging to each other more tightly still. Now they looked from one another and then back to the trunk, sighing almost simultaneously.

'We *are* only going for a long weekend,' Betty said fretfully. 'Do you suppose we should. . .?'

'Absolutely not,' her daughter said instantly, not needing her mother to complete the sentence to know what she was about to propose. 'We have to hold our end up amongst Lady Sybil's glamorous set, don't forget, and besides, we don't have time to go through it and prioritise our outfits into two suitcases instead.' She glanced at the grandfather clock standing in the hall, ponderously ticking away the minutes. 'We'll miss the train for sure, and who knows when the next connection will be? Yorkshire is all well and good, but Cleeves Lea is the very dickens to get to.'

'At least they have their own private halt,' Betty pointed out. 'And Sir Bayard will send the Rolls to pick us up.'

'That's true – oh, what it must be like to have private railway stations and a gorgeous manor house to live in,' Bernie said dryly. 'I must say, Mother, your best pal really does have a knack of coming up roses. I've never known someone so jammy as her ladyship.'

Betty gave her incorrigible but beloved daughter what she hoped was a stern look. 'I do wish you wouldn't say such things. I know you moderns think it's very funny and all that to be disrespectful to your elders, but I for one don't like it.'

'Sorry, Mummy,' Bernie said meekly enough, although her blue eyes were twinkling.

Betty sighed inwardly, but in truth, her heart really wasn't set on defending her old friend too stalwartly. Even as the youngest child at their boarding school, Sybil had quickly acquired the irritating habit of always being able to get what she wanted. Which was something that Betty, even at almost six years her senior, had never managed to acquire.

'I think that's Mr Draper here with the taxi,' Bernie said, hearing a car engine rattling along outside. 'I do hope he can manage that humongous trunk!' In fact, it took the former blacksmith Mr Draper very little time or effort to affix the trunk to the back of his rattle-trap car, and within minutes they were heading noisily for the station. Betty, vaguely watching the splendour of Blenheim Palace recede in the distance, gave a little sigh. It was always nice, of course, to get away and visit old friends, but there was no place like home. Then her smooth brown brows puckered into a little frown; home hadn't really felt like home for some time now.

She was only too aware that it was nearly a year to the day since their whole world had turned upside down – so perhaps it was just as well that they had been invited to spend such a dark anniversary far away from Oxfordshire and all that was so familiar. Perhaps in the depths of the beautiful, rolling Yorkshire countryside, the painful memories wouldn't be so bad.

'I do hope the other guests are going to be a gay crowd,' Bernie said wistfully, as if reading her mother's mind. 'Sir Bayard hinted that he had a real "celebrity" lined up. I wonder who it is?'

'As long as he's not a magician, I don't mind,' her mother said firmly. 'I really can't abide magicians. All that "pick a card" business and juggling about with those poor doves and rabbits. I'm sure the poor things can't like it.'

As the two Rowe women contemplated the sad fate of luckless doves and rabbits, back at their house, their housekeeper answered the telephone to a distressed and rather breathless Lady Sybil, and had to inform her ladyship that, alas, madam and Miss Bernie had already left for the station.

At Cleeves Lea Manor, Sybil hung up with a string of frustrated swear words that made the parlourmaid, scuttling past on her way to the morning room, squeak in alarm and turn a vivid shade of embarrassed puce. Just wait until she told the little tweeny about the mistress's latest goings-on! The in-between maid had always looked up to her so!

*

In Harrogate, Miss Agnes Warren was enjoying a much more leisurely and stress-free start to her day. It wasn't that far for her to travel to dear Lady Sybil and Sir Bayard's place, and she had already arranged for a private car, due to arrive in a few hours, to take her all the way to the front door. She did find rail travel such a chore. Even in first class you never knew just who might take a seat in your carriage, did you?

Aged forty-seven, she was a slender woman of five feet seven or so, with brown hair rapidly turning grey, hazel eyes and a good complexion, but she somehow gave the impression of being much older. It was perhaps her clothes, which tended to be dowdy and dull, or perhaps her air of trying to blend into the wallpaper. An only child who had lived with her parents until their deaths, she knew herself to be unsophisticated, and had never quite seemed to discover the trick of how to overcome such self-knowledge. This left her inevitably feeling socially awkward and nervous in company. Paradoxically, however, she knew herself to be lonely and craved the company of others – but wished she could learn the trick of winning their approbation.

Her large Victorian house, which she'd inherited from her wealthy and beloved parents, overlooked a small park and one of the spa town's many first-class hotels, but for once the tranquil and rather splendid scene outside her window failed to soothe her. Indeed, as she ate her grapefruit half and drank her herbal tea, she was so excited that she found it difficult to even sit still.

For something wonderful had happened to her recently, something so utterly beyond her wildest dreams that she still wasn't quite sure that it had actually happened at all. But of course, it had. And whilst she had been persuaded to keep it a secret for now, after this weekend everything would have to change. Wouldn't her friends have something to say when they found out. . .

At this point in her pleasurable daydreams, her maid, Clara, came in and asked if she wanted some toast. Clara was, like her employer, in late middle age, but there any similarity between the two women ended. Practical, easy-going and intelligent, the maid regarded Miss Warren with her usual mix of affection and exasperation.

Something had put the little duck into a tizzy and no mistake, Clara thought now, but as her maid of many years' standing, she'd learned to take it all in her stride. For it didn't take much, she'd quickly realised, to upset her employer's equilibrium – which was never exactly robust at the best of times.

'Oh Clarrie, have you packed my book?' Agnes instantly asked, for the sixth – or was it seventh? – time. Patiently, the maid assured her that her precious book had been duly packed. As had all her medicines – and extra bottles too, just in case. And her best beaded shoes. And her spare reading glasses.

'Well, don't forget my gloves,' Agnes reminded her. 'I want the white linen pair, then the pale blue silk gloves with the lace, the long black pair – oh, and my kid gloves in case the weather turns chilly.'

'Yes, ma'am.'

Agnes quickly waved away the idea of toast and with a bird-like glance, dismissed the maid with a little twitter. It was only after she was sure that she was alone that she went to the cupboard and withdrew several small paperbacks and hid them furtively in her voluminous handbag. These 'penny dreadful' murder mysteries were her main indulgence, and her addiction to reading them was a foible which she fondly believed she'd successfully kept secret from her household and friends for many years.

Of course she had done no such thing, and many a time after she'd left a bridge party or a WI meeting, her former companions had laughingly wondered what tale of murder or wrongdoing she was about to go home and avidly devour next.

In the kitchen, Clara and the cook were discussing their employer over large cups of tea. The cook, a huge behemoth of a woman who had an undeniably light hand with pastry, began to munch on the rejected toast that she'd already prepared and sighed. 'Is it just me, or is the old dear all of a flutter about something? More than usual, I mean,' she added, as Clara paused with her cup halfway to her lips.

'No, it's not just you. She's been on edge all week. It'll be this weekend party she's going to, I expect.' Clara rolled her eyes. 'You know what she's like.'

The cook did indeed. 'If she quotes to me once more from that dratted book of hers about how I can improve my way of living, I might just brain her with it,' she said, not meaning a word of it.

'It's just her latest fad, it'll be over soon,' Clara comforted her. Before someone in her sewing circle had introduced Miss Agnes to *The Art of Harmonious Living* by Dr Randolf Schuber, it had been the tarot. Before that, it had been some sort of diet. And before that . . . what had it been now? Oh yes, origami. She had almost driven Clara mad by leaving little paper dogs and cats scattered about. 'I know what you mean though – and if she quotes that silly Doctor Schuber fellow's nonsense at me one more time I might just scream myself!'

The cook sniffed. 'It'll be nice to have a bit of peace and quiet around here for a few days, without having her constant twittering and fussing to deal with,' she said, and Clara couldn't help but agree. There probably wasn't a more generous or kind-hearted mistress that you could wish for than Miss Warren, but sometimes she did get on one's nerves so!

*

At that moment, not far away in the historical city of York, Bill Endicott watched his man making a neat fist of packing his case and felt a sense of profound satisfaction. He hadn't always been able to rely on the services of a valet during his scapegrace existence, but right now things were coming up roses all right. And what could a fellow do but enjoy it to the fullest?

Just turned thirty, he was a tall man, standing an inch over six feet in height, and was endowed with a head of fair hair to go with blue eyes and a rather square face with a strong jaw. This Adonis athleticism had allowed him to squeak into Oxford, where he'd rowed and played amateur tennis rather more than he'd ever studied, although his natural intelligence (despite his lazy nature) had allowed him to scrape by with a more-or-less-decent second-class degree in history.

He was leaning nonchalantly against the mantel of his fireplace. He had recently taken rooms in the attic of a large

Victorian pile that had not long been turned into a rather smart set of flats. In his hand was a letter, smelling of violets and written in a flowing feminine hand, the contents of which were causing a rather rakish smile to play about his lips.

His valet, a somewhat sobersides sort of man by the name of Hatchett, pretended not to notice this. At nearly forty, he'd long since learned to pretend that all his 'gentlemen' were indeed gentlemen, even when they clearly weren't.

'Shall I pack the diamond studs, sir?' he inquired gravely.

'Eh? Oh, yes, I suppose you'd better,' Bill agreed airily, but his eyes glinted as he contemplated this latest gift from his 'little woman'. It would make old Sir Bayard's eyes bulge a bit to see those little beauties glittering in his shirtfront all right! And it would do the old duffer good too, to be put out of sorts for once. His way of looking down his nose at you, all superior and haughty, could really niggle at a chap.

Whistling a ditty from the latest song doing the rounds at the music halls, he took out and glanced at his pocket-watch and nodded absently to himself. Yes, he had plenty of time to make the journey towards the coast. It wouldn't do to be late.

The thought somewhat sobered him, and he abruptly stopped whistling.

For, in truth, he wasn't much looking forward to the weekend party at Cleeves Lea, and he would be jolly glad when it was over and done with. But then he shrugged philosophically. Sometimes in life you just had to grit your teeth and grin and bear things.

*

Also living in York, but in a far more genteel neighbourhood of the cathedral city not far from the Minster Close, two others also contemplated Sir Bayard and Lady Sybil's weekend party, but with a great deal more pleasure. And since they would not be travelling there until tomorrow, they were not concerned, just yet, with all the preparations that surrounded spending time away from home.

Roger and Daphne Potts-Gibbon, however, had very different reasons for looking forward to this small break from their domestic norm.

Daphne, the daughter of a former archbishop and a mother who had been the offspring of an earl, was a handsome, rather than beautiful, woman, with red-gold hair and distinguished grey eyes. Tall and slender, at forty-two she was three years older than her husband and was hoping that the coming weekend party would provide her with some bridge players worthy of her time and effort, and that conversation over the dinner table wouldn't include either business or golf. For, it had to be said, much as she was generally happy with her lot and with her choice of spouse, she did sometimes miss mixing with people who understood her.

A gentle and genteel soul, she loved her garden and her dogs and her husband – probably in that order.

Roger was a different kettle of fish altogether and regarded her now with much affection as he reached for his hat and prepared to leave for his office. Balding and running a little too fat, he'd been born in London to academic parents who regarded his more practical-minded and money-making propensities with a mixture of vague dismay and reluctant pride. A self-made and now very wealthy man, he had, he knew, very definitely married 'up' when he'd bagged Daphne, and he was inordinately fond of her and very grateful that she'd ditched the rarefied world of her upbringing to take him on. It would have been nice if they'd had children, but he wasn't about to let that intrude too much on the pleasure he insisted on taking out of life.

'Daphers, old girl, would you mind awfully buttering up old

Bayard for me a bit this weekend?' he asked, checking in the breakfast-room mirror to make sure that his club tie was straight.

At this, his wife lifted her elegant head from her contemplation of a seed catalogue and regarded him with an amused eye. 'Oh? And just how much butter, exactly, do you think I should apply?'

Roger grinned. 'Oh, you know, just get him in a good mood and all that. I want his name and title to adorn the board of directors for this new subsidiary I'm starting up. And there's nothing that inspires confidence in investors more than a solid, long-standing title on the letterhead.'

'I can't think why,' Daphne murmured dryly, thinking of her mother's rich and indulgent set in particular. 'Most of the finest houses in the land have more black sheep in their lineage than Sir Bayard's flocks of prime Herdwicks or Wensleydales or whatever it is he runs over all those square acres of his.'

Roger grinned. 'Darling, if your sainted father could still hear you talk sometimes, he'd probably pop out of his gaiters in shock.'

'Daddy would have done no such thing,' Daphne corrected him amiably. 'He'd almost certainly have agreed with me.'

'Do you know who else is coming to this bash of the Chervilles?' Her husband, satisfied with the knot in his tie, regarded his jowls with a scowl. He would have to start reducing soon, no doubt about it. But not until this weekend was over, obviously. Sir Bayard did keep such a fine table.

'No,' Daphne answered with a small sigh. 'I expect there'll be the usual mixed bunch, with some "name" or other, for our delectation. I just hope there won't be too many young people though, insisting on the gramophone and dancing the Charleston all night long.'

'Oh, I'm sure you can trust the Chervilles on that score,' her husband said confidently, and popping an absent-minded kiss on the top of her head, he reached for his hat and left her to her spring bulbs.

*

The next day, Friday, dawned as warm and sunny as the day before, and by mid-afternoon it was positively balmy. Sitting in his first-class seat in a comfortable pullman carriage, Arbuthnot Lancelot Swift, having dined on Dover sole and a very nice parfait, sat replete and dozily content, looking out over the ever more glorious rolling hills and wooded dales as the train headed steadily northwards.

He had no idea that he had been cast as the celebrity, or 'name' for the Lord of the Manor's upcoming bash but wouldn't have minded much if he did. He was a happy-go-lucky enough chap, and nobody could accuse him of having a notably swollen head or an unwarrantedly high opinion of himself. He was simply looking forward to doing a spot of fishing in the nearest river, indulging in a bit of cricket perhaps, the playing of a few games of billiards with some like-minded cove and making the most of whatever fine dining was on offer.

Then his eyes met those of the young and beautiful blond-haired girl seated opposite him, and his spirits fell a little, as he realised that he'd have to include doing a bit of work in this itinerary as well. A certain Miss Valentina Coulton-James would make sure of that!

'So, what chance is there of a proper ghost this time, do you think?' that young lady asked him now, all business. 'Our last two were total washouts.'

Arbie (or 'that young fool Arbie' as he was commonly known to friends and relations alike) sighed and shrugged. His second volume of *The Gentleman's Guide to Ghost-Hunting* had been published a few months ago and had been met with as much rampant acclaim and success as his first effort. Primarily a holiday guide for those with an interest in spooks and spectres, the humorous and self-effacing accounts of his attempts to unearth fresh spectres and ghouls to delight his readers now meant that he'd been plagued by his publishers into signing a contract for yet another book.

This, naturally, was something that he had tried desperately to avoid, for not only was he inherently lazy, but after having been orphaned young and left a considerably legacy by his late parents, he had no financial impetus to bestir himself into unwanted labour either.

No, the sole fault for his current need to investigate yet more holiday destinations (and local ghosts) could be laid firmly at the door of his old friend Val. Having grown up in the same Cotswold village together, the vicar's daughter had terrorised him since infancy, and through a process that still baffled him completely, had somehow taken to calling herself his 'literary assistant'. And, as might be expected of a vicar's daughter, her work ethic was the exact opposite of his own.

Hence this acceptance of Sir Bayard Cherville's invitation to attend a weekend party at his manor. Not only was the area a prime holiday spot, being so close to the coast and possessing a most picturesquely ruined abbey, walking paths and other such attractions, it also came with its own ghost – thus making it a prime candidate for inclusion in his next tome.

'I can't say that I have any more high hopes of our ghostly signalman, Jethro Hoskins,' Arbie responded dampeningly, 'than I had of the "lavender lady" or the "crying child". Just as we never caught so much as a whiff of our lavender-scented and allegedly murdered lady of Boresmouth Priory, nor so much as a muffled sob from the tragic tot of Totnes, I daresay our chances of catching a glimpse of a ghostly signal lamp at our destination's end is just as unlikely.'

Val regarded her companion with a displeased eye. 'Well, if that's going to be your attitude, I can't imagine the next book will sell more than a dozen copies! Come on, old bean, buck up! We need a really good chapter to get our readers' blood up. Maybe this will be it. A fateful and tragic train accident when Victoria was still sitting on the throne and the hero who died trying to prevent it. Sounds to me as if the reading public will lap it up. Aren't you the least bit excited?'

Arbie, who felt as excited about his latest chapter as a plateful of cold leftover bubble-and-squeak, could only offer a weak smile as he consulted his pocket-watch. 'Well, we'll be arriving at Middle Stratton soon, anyway. I do hope the other guests won't turn out to be too grim,' he added anxiously. He still had nightmares sometimes about a weekend party that he'd attended just before his twenty-first birthday, when he'd been stuck with an overseas missionary, a teetotal duchess, a deaf professor of physics and the dreariest lot of wilting wallflowers a chap could imagine.

At this further evidence that the so-called celebrated author had pleasure rather than business at the forefront of his mind, Val gave him another disapproving glance. 'All you want to do is loaf about and have a jolly good time,' she accused.

Arbie, though, had by now acquired more than enough sense to let the remark pass without comment. Not only was it accurate, and thus indefensible, he knew that arguing with Val about anything was pointless. A tall, splendid girl, she often put him in mind of one of the Valkyries, and as such, he as a mere mortal knew his place.

'Ah, we're slowing down. I think this must be our stop,' he said, as the steam train's puffing wound down to a mere asthmatic wheeze. As the train came to a halt, they could hear the conductor's reassuring shout carrying down along the platform.

'Alight here for Middle Stratton and Cleeves Lea Manor. Alight here all for Middle Stratton!'

As Arbie opened the carriage door and started hauling out

their luggage (for he doubted that the middle-of-nowhere spot included the services of a porter), he noticed one or two other doors opening further down the train. And after clambering down and holding out an arm to Val to assist her onto the platform, he regarded his fellow travellers with interest.

One or two were clearly village women returning from the nearest market town, easily identified by their laden shopping baskets, and one was just as clearly a farmer, who set off at such a brisk pace towards one of the surrounding hills that Arbie suspected he had miles to tramp before he got to his steadings. But the three others who alighted were of a vastly different type.

One, an elegant and rather handsome woman with a chic chignon of red-gold hair, caught his eye at once. She was accompanied by a man who, judging by his solicitous treatment of her, could only be her husband. A shorter, fatter, balding individual, he was dressed as expensively as his spouse. Fellow guests of Sir Bayard, Arbie mused, or he was a Dutchman's uncle. (And he wasn't.)

Unfortunately, the last passenger to uncoil himself from the train reminded Arbie of nothing so much as a snake-oil salesman, and his heart sank a little at the thought of spending the next four days or so in his company. Tall and lean, with black hair made to look almost like water by the application of too much pomade, he had black liquid eyes to match. Worse still, he was dressed like a fop.

So when, after glancing around to get his bearings, this individual followed the sign pointing to the footpath that led to the nearby village, Arbie heaved an audible sigh of relief.

It was at this point that Arbie caught the eye of the rather handsome woman and saw her smile faintly at him. Thus encouraged, he approached her diffidently. 'I say, you aren't by any chance going to Sir Bayard's bash too, are you?' he asked affably.

Daphne Potts-Gibbon regarded the handsome youth briefly. Somewhere in his mid-twenties, he had copious amounts of dark brown hair and a rather agreeable square jaw and chin. Dressed in Oxford bags and wearing an Oxford college tie that she vaguely recognised, he had an engaging smile and rather fine grey eyes. 'Yes, we are. I take it you are our fellow guests?' she replied, her gaze taking in Val also, as she came to a halt beside Arbie.

Arbie agreed that they were. 'Mr Swift, and this is Miss Coulton-James,' he introduced them. 'How do you do.' At which point, the man beside her spoke.

'Roger Potts-Gibbon and my wife, Daphne. How do you do.'

There followed that moment of awkward silence which often occurs after strangers make themselves acquainted without the benefit of a third party known to them all. It was into this hiatus that a man stepped onto the now deserted platform. Dressed in a chauffeur's bottle-green uniform, he regarded them respectfully.

'Party for Cleeves Lea Manor?' he asked politely.

Everyone concurred that they were, indeed, for Cleeves Lea Manor, at which point the chauffeur obligingly began to ferry their luggage to the end of the platform, where a rather rudimentary road played host to a magnificent Silver Ghost Rolls-Royce.

'Well, this bodes well,' Arbie said quietly in Val's ear as he regarded the sumptuous automobile. 'If Sir Bayard has as good a taste in port as he does in transport, looks like we'll be in clover, old thing.'

Val couldn't help but secretly agree with this pleasant assessment, but of course, nothing of that showed on her face, and taking the hand offered to her by a polite Roger Potts-Gibbon, she allowed herself to be helped into the car's luxurious interior.

CHAPTER TWO

Inside the car, Val regarded Mrs Potts-Gibbon closely, so much so that when the lady noticed it, Val felt herself blush. 'I'm so sorry, but I'm sure you look familiar to me. Have we met before?'

Daphne regarded the young blonde woman with a thoughtful smile. 'It's possible,' she conceded. A quick inventory of her fellow passenger's perfectly respectable but hardly couture outfit informed her that she was unlikely to have come across the rather lovely Valentine Coulton-James at one of her high society affairs. There was also something so very wholesome about her manner that Daphne felt confident of placing her in the right camp. 'My father was an archbishop, and before my marriage, I often accompanied him on his various trips to conferences and other dioceses. Is your father. . .?'

Instantly, Val's eyes cleared. 'Oh, of course – yes, now I remember! My father is the vicar of Maybury-in-the-Marsh, and we met at an Oxford Synod occasion once – oh, yonks ago now. I was probably still in pigtails at the time.'

Daphne laughed. 'I'm sure they were perfectly delightful pigtails. Tell me . . .'

Arbie let their chatter wash over him, but as he watched the two women strike up a friendship, he couldn't help but feel a little relieved. Not unnaturally, Val's papa hadn't been best pleased by his daughter's determination to launch herself into Arbie's literary world. Both he and his good lady wife much preferred that Val direct her considerable energies towards finding some suitable man to marry.

As the vicar had lectured them, 'gallivanting around the countryside looking for ghouls and legendary black dogs and whatnot' was no activity for a circumspect young lady. And in this, Arbie had whole-heartedly agreed with him, but even their combined powers of persuasion had failed to dent Val's enthusiasm for her choice of 'career'.

In the end, even the Reverend could find no objection to her coming to Yorkshire with him on his latest 'research trip' because, naturally, there could be no breath of scandal arising from his wayward offspring attending a weekend party at the home of a respectably married peer and his equally respectable guests. And now the inclusion of an archbishop's daughter was bound to soothe the parental breast even further, once Arbie relayed the news to him.

Although he hadn't told Val this (naturally), he had high hopes that her status as his assistant was going to prove to be a very temporary one indeed, for he fully intended to make the next chapter of his book something so outlandish that Miss Coulton-James would not be allowed anywhere near it. He hadn't quite figured out what that could be yet – but he would. It had to be something that no father would countenance for even a minute, and he had been periodically racking his brains to come up with the answer.

As he was doing now.

Miners killed in a cave-in perhaps, and said to haunt the bowels of the earth somewhere? There wasn't a ghost of a chance that Val's papa would allow her to go down a mineshaft! (But selling a dirty, disused mineshaft as a choice holiday destination to his readers and editors might prove a bit ticklish, what?) So, failing that . . . hah! He had it! It was perfect. A haunted friary.

That was just the ticket – no women would be allowed in *there*. The good brothers themselves would insist on that.

And so, as they travelled the short distance to Cleeves Lea Manor, Arbie made a mental note to look up any all-male ecclesiastical residences within hailing distance of a nice little seaside resort somewhere, feeling much more relieved in his mind and confident of a future sans Val.

Opposite him, Roger Potts-Gibbon, having ascertained how his fellow passenger earned his crust, began to engage him in a gentle fishing expedition concerning the famous author's investment portfolio. The name of the odd literary illuminati on one of his boards couldn't hurt, after all.

Some five minutes later, Arbie, having successfully fended off the predatory businessman with some waffle about his accountant 'mucking about with all that sort of thing', caught his first glimpse of their destination and gave a sigh of contentment. For there, nestled in a charming little valley and set in a garden beginning to froth with colour, was a delightful country house of the sort that made you proud to be an Englishman.

As the car glided majestically to a stop at the front door, the butler greeted them with a polite nod of his noble head and snapped his fingers at various hot-and-cold running footmen who began to collect and disperse with various portmanteaus and cases into the country mansion.

In the hall – a high-ceilinged affair with the prerequisite suits of armour, old clocks, sweeping wooden staircase, sparkling crystal chandelier and almost mandatory black-and-white tiled floor – were their host and hostess, waiting to receive them.

'Roger, good of you to come, old man,' said the individual who could be no one other than Sir Bayard Cherville. Dressed in shabby tweeds and walking brogues, he had a fine English setter standing beside him, tail a-wagging, and on his other side, a stunningly beautiful wife. As Sir Bayard and Roger exchanged hearty handshakes, Arbie blinked helplessly at Lady Sybil.

She responded immediately to this sweet if unsophisticated compliment by stepping forward and putting out a slender, beringed hand, not for him to shake but so that she might lay her fingers gently on his arm. 'And you must be our wonderful man of letters, Mr Swift?'

She was dressed in a flowing moss-green dress that was fastened in a velvet bow low down on her left hip, and silver slippers that drew attention to the delicate ankles exposed at the hem, which terminated just high enough on her shin to be provocative. Her ash-blonde hair was swept up in an elegant chignon, which a silver hair clip, adorned by a peacock feather, kept in place. But it was her large blue-green eyes that held and fascinated him – like those of a most fabulous cat, the kind which had almost certainly been worshipped in ancient Egypt.

Arbie gulped audibly.

'Lady Sybil, how nice of you to invite us,' Val said politely, moving up to stand beside Arbie and placing a firm hand of her own on his other forearm.

Arbie blinked again, and gulped again, but this time for very different reasons.

With a somewhat wry smile, Lady Sybil let her hand fall away. 'You must be Miss Coulton-James,' she remarked. 'Mr Swift's secretary?'

'Literary assistant,' Val corrected her sweetly.

It was at this point that Daphne deemed it necessary to step in. 'Sybil, my dear, Miss Coulton-James's father is an old acquaintance of Daddy's,' she said, not perhaps very truthfully. 'Isn't that a lovely coincidence? We were just talking about the time we all met up in Oxford. Valentina's father is the vicar at Maybury-in-the-Marsh,' she added gently – and pointedly.

Sybil's smile widened. 'Oh. How lovely. Darling, did you hear that?' she remarked to her husband.

Sir Bayard smiled avuncularly at Val. 'Splendid, splendid. It's a small world, what?'

'Come on through to the drawing room – it has the best sun at this time of the day,' Sybil suggested brightly. 'Tea, please, Jardine.' She nodded at the butler, who moved silently away to do her bidding. 'Or would you rather go to your rooms first for a freshen up?' She glanced significantly at Val as she said this, making the younger woman shake her head.

'Oh no, we feel as fresh as daisies, don't we, Arbie?'

'Arbie?' Sybil repeated.

'Er, short for Arbuthnot,' Arbie mumbled, trying to find someplace to put his eyes that didn't include either his hostess or Val. He settled on a somewhat moth-eaten battle standard that looked as if it might have been carried by some distant Cherville or other when one of the Henrys had still been on the throne.

'Oh how delightful,' Sybil purred. 'I hope you don't mind if I call you Arbie too?'

'Oh no, rather! I mean, I'd be honoured and all that. . .' He corrected himself hastily and took his eyes off the tatty textile long enough to catch the disapproving glint in Val's eye, and his voice trailed off miserably.

Luckily, Sir Bayard began leading them towards the drawing room, which turned out to be a pleasant room full of natural light thanks to the large sash windows lining one wall. A soothing blend of greys, lavender and silver, it boasted a piano, several settees and a number of other people, who all looked up at the new arrivals with interest.

The only man in the assembly rose gallantly to his feet as the ladies approached. Tall, handsome, fair, he exuded athletic vitality and his quick, searching eyes didn't take long to alight on Val. 'Ah, Bill old chap, meet our famous author, Mr Swift, and his charming literary assistant, Miss Coulton-James. Bill Endicott,' Sir Bayard said, making the introductions. 'He and his valet motored down yesterday. And I don't know if you know Roger and Daphne?'

'No, I don't believe so,' Bill said, shaking hands with Roger rather perfunctorily Arbie noticed, before reaching for Val's hand last – and holding on to it somewhat forgetfully. Val glanced at Arbie to see if he'd noticed this, but Arbie was already looking towards the two women sitting beside each other on the sofa.

They were so alike that they could only be mother and daughter. 'Elizabeth and Bernadette Rowe.' Lady Sybil stepped forward to complete the necessary introductions. 'Dear Betty is my oldest friend – we've known each other since we suffered in boarding school together.'

'How do you do,' the two women spoke together, but it was Bernadette who took up the baton. 'I say, Mr Swift, I read that marvellous book of yours last year – the first one out, and thought it was a real hoot. But Lady Sybil's just informed us that you've had another one out this year? I shall have to look out for it. Mummy and I were wondering where to go on our holidays this year, and I expect you'll have recommended some wonderful places.'

As Arbie began to self-effacingly respond to this charming bit of flattery, the tea arrived. Val was shown to a second settee by Bill, who then promptly sat down beside her, whilst Arbie and the Potts-Gibbons retired to various chairs surrounding a low table. Lady Sybil poured the tea and handed around near-translucent Spode plates containing a mixture of mouth-watering biscuits, some still warm from the oven. Val accepted a shortbread and let her eyes dart about the room curiously.

She was sure that she could detect a definite 'atmosphere' in the room and was studiously trying to place it. Arbie – whom she credited (very erroneously as it happened) with all the sensitivity of a buffalo – had typically noticed nothing amiss. But she, always curious and interested in her fellow human beings, let her gaze wander from the mother-and-daughter duo to Sir Bayard before she caught Daphne's slightly concerned expression, and realised that she was not the only one attuned to some hidden tension within their company.

'So, what does a literary assistant do exactly?' Bill asked her, interrupting her speculations.

'Oh, you know, the usual. Research, note-taking, typing, all that sort of thing,' Val remarked casually, turning her attention his way. She took a sip of the excellent Indian tea and set her cup aside. 'Have you known the Chervilles long?' she asked, determined to find the cause of the undercurrent in the room.

'Oh, not so long as all that. I know her more than him, mind,' he admitted casually. 'We met in London at some dreary gallery exhibition or other and got on like a house on fire. I try to get down to town as often as I can. And you? Where do you hail from?'

'Oxfordshire,' Val said, and thought she detected some slight but instinctive movement in her peripheral vision. She traced it to the two Rowes, who, by the time she'd turned her head to look at them, were both biting into a garibaldi biscuit each and pretending to listen to Arbie waffling on about some haunted cricket pavilion or other.

When she turned back to Bill, she thought he looked a trifle paler than before, but then instantly doubted herself, as he responded to her answer as smoothly as ever. 'Ah, I know it well – I was "up" there, for my sins, alas, many moons ago now. Teddy Hall,' he added, using the name all those who studied there gave to St Edmund Hall College.

'What did you read?'

'History. Why, I haven't the faintest idea,' he added with a laugh. 'It's hardly of much use, is it?'

It was at this point that they were joined by a woman who entered the room as a little mouse might, skirting along one wall and sort of shuffling surreptitiously to a spare high-backed winged chair that was set just a little behind Lady Sybil. Dressed in one of those black tea-gown affairs that were now hopelessly out of date, she wore an equally outmoded hat and 'sensible' shoes. Aged anywhere between forty and sixty, she regarded the world through a pair of worried-looking hazel eyes. In accordance with her black dress, she wore expensive-looking long black gloves that fitted her small hands somewhat loosely.

'Oh, so sorry if I'm late,' this uninspired vision said. 'Dear Lady Sybil, you must think me atrociously rude.'

'Oh Agnes, as if anybody could.' Lady Sybil smiled lightly. 'Agnes Warren, you know Daphne, of course? Her father was an archbishop who gave the most wonderful sermons. . .' It turned out Daphne and Agnes were indeed acquainted. Sybil cantered through the round of introductions in a rather perfunctory manner, with Agnes twittering how-do-you-dos and nervous smiles throughout. Looking very relieved once the gauntlet had been run, she sank back into the wingback chair's upholstery, where she remained almost mute for the remainder of the tea-drinking ritual.

*

An hour later, Val surveyed her sumptuous room with far more appreciation than her father would have liked, had he known of it. But when a woman is shown to a room dripping in colourful Eastern silks, and containing a fabulous four-poster bed, charming French furniture and even a painting by a minor but respected Impressionist hanging above the dressing table mirror, what can she do but catch her breath in delight?

Fresh-cut flowers from the gardens added to the ambiance of

decadence, so much so that when a maid knocked on the door and asked if she wanted help with her unpacking, Val hastily declined. Alas, as one of many children of a not particularly wealthy country vicar, she knew that her meagre hand-me-down wardrobe would not meet with the approval of a woman who daily dressed the likes of their tres chic hostess, Lady Sybil.

With a sigh she hung up her best frocks in the wardrobe, distributed her unmentionables to a Chippendale set of drawers and consigned her collection of mediocre beads and bangles to the top of the dressing table. As she did so, there came a quick tap on her door. 'Hello, old girl, are you decent?' Arbie's muffled voice inquired from without.

Val walked to the door and threw it open. 'Come in, Arbie,' she said, a trifle wearily.

'What-oh, old bean, grand digs, ain't they?' he greeted her cheerfully, glancing around. 'Mine are just across the way, and remarkably similar. I think you'll find any number of geese had to donate a fair few of their feathers in the making of our mattresses,' he added, breezing along towards her window, where he gazed out with appreciation over the view.

'I'm sure they were delighted to make the sacrifice,' Val responded dryly. 'I see you've already spruced yourself up. For Lady Sybil's benefit, is it?'

'Eh?' Arbie warbled feebly.

Val scrutinised his nervous eyes (which rather reminded her of a dozy pony she'd once adored as an infant) and decided it simply wasn't worth her while sparring with him. He was already a broken reed. 'So, what do you make of everyone then? Bit of luck Daphne Potts-Gibbon and her husband turning up, isn't it? Such a lovely couple. And the Rowes seem very nice too. Did you notice Bernie's beaded bag?'

Arbie, who always noticed lady's accessories, nevertheless felt more than usually nonplussed by the question. 'Bernie?'

'Bernadette. Bernadette Rowe – she asked me to call her Bernie. And so I'm Val, of course. We both agreed that calling each other Miss Rowe and Miss Coulton-James and all that rot was just too exhausting. Well, we'll call each other Bernie and Val when nobody else is around to hear us,' she was forced to concede, for she was nothing if not honest.

It was one of her many traits that Arbie particularly deplored.

'Righty-oh. I thought you two were getting chummy over the crumpets,' he said, reaching out to pilfer one of her cut flowers and purloining it for his buttonhole.

'As were you and Bill Endicott,' she shot back. 'Didn't I hear you setting up plans to play billiards all night long?'

'Oh, er, we might have mentioned having a game or two,' Arbie muttered, and under her gimlet and knowing eye, began tugging at his tie, which had begun to feel as if it had taken on some of the more unrefined characteristics of a boa constrictor.

'Well, don't think you're going to get out of playing some bridge as well,' Val advised him succinctly. 'Daphne's a keen player, and so is Miss Warren.'

At this, Arbie looked a trifle blank (a far from unknown occurrence), and Val regarded him severely. 'Don't tell me you've forgotten her already? The lady who was last to arrive to tea?'

'Oh, the dowdy hen,' Arbie said cheerfully. 'There's always one, isn't there, at every party. Have you ever noticed? Come to think of it, at bashes like this you nearly always get a giddy socialite too, an awful dowager, a Casanova and a sportsman who can bore for England. You know the sort I mean – one of those coves who will insist on going up the Amazon in a wicker basket or some such receptacle or climbing a mountain in winter or something equally pointless, and then tells you all about it in eye-watering detail. Oh yes, and a vicar. Or a scholar. Either one or the other, but never both together oddly enough. It must be an unspoken rule or something about weekend parties.'

Val, only listening with half an ear to this waffle, took out a small compact and dabbed some powder onto her nose, then regarded her reflection in the tiny mirror thoughtfully. 'Well, as far as I can tell, there's no vicar or scholar here. And Daphne doesn't count, as it's her father who was the archbishop.'

'Well, I'm the scholar, obviously,' Arbie pointed out, his feelings slightly hurt that this should need saying. His indignation ratcheted up a notch or two as his companion burst into spontaneous laughter. 'I'll have you know, I'm a recognised man of letters,' Arbie added uncertainly, which only sent Val off into another paroxysm of laughter.

When she had recovered somewhat, she returned her attention to her nose-dabbing. 'Well, Lady Sybil certainly qualifies as the giddy socialite. The poor dear must be very giddy indeed if she regards you as flirting material.'

Arbie pretended not to know what on earth she was on about. 'Bill's the sportsman, although, luckily, he's not boring. Well, he hasn't been so far anyway. He rowed for his college at Oxford – must have been a few years before I was up myself. Or was he a reserve? Or it might have been cricket. Wasn't really listening at the time,' he admitted without compunction.

'Too busy eyeing the charms of the delightful Lady Sybil, were you?' Val put in archly. 'You'd better watch your step there, old bean. I can tell by the way her husband watches her that Sir Bayard is the jealous type.'

As Arbie began to sputter at this outlandish slander, she swept on pedantically. 'That still leaves us minus a Casanova and an awful dowager.'

'Well, I think we can both agree that we can well do without the dowager,' Arbie said, genuinely grateful. 'And as for a Casanova, we still don't know Roger Potts-Gibbon's true colours yet.'

'I'm sure he's a perfect lamb,' Val said staunchly. 'Daphne is far too sensible to have married a roue.' And with this firm pronouncement, she shut her compact with a snap and put it into her (alas) bead-less bag. 'I suppose we'd better head down. Dinner won't be for hours yet, but the evening is still but a babe.'

Arbie held the door open for her and was just following her out onto the landing beyond, when a few doors down, Elizabeth Rowe stepped out of another room. Behind her, a large bathtub was clearly visible. Arbie, no stranger to weekend parties, made a mental note to remember the location of this, his nearest bathroom, and to be sure to get to it in the mornings before any long queues could be formed and all the hot water ran out.

Elizabeth was holding something in her hand and regarding it with a slightly puzzled look. Sensing the presence of others, she looked up and gave a little start. 'Oh, hello. I've just found this in the cabinet.' She displayed a small bottle that bore the name of the Bayers Company. 'Someone must have accidentally left it behind. It's not yours, I suppose?' she asked diffidently.

Val shook her head. 'I haven't been in there yet. Is there no name on it?'

Elizabeth squinted at the small bottle, then looked a little shame-faced. 'Oh dear, I really must remember to bring my reading glasses with me wherever I go. I can only make out that it's Veronal.' She named the popular market brand for barbital, or barbitone, commonly used as a sleeping aid.

'Here, let me,' Val said, ever helpful, and reached for it just as Lady Sybil appeared around the corner that led to the main staircase.

'What's this?' she asked, having caught the tail end of the conversation. 'What have you got there, Betty?'

'Someone's sleeping medicine I think.'

'Oh, that's almost certainly Agnes's,' Sybil said with an impatient smile. 'That woman's always leaving her belongings scattered around the place. The maids are always finding that wretched book of hers in the salon, or her scarf in the morning room, or her knitting needles in the orangery. Was it in the bathroom?'

'Yes.'

She retrieved the bottle from her friend, read the label and nodded. 'There's no name on it, but I bet it's hers, even so,' was her only comment, and walking into the bathroom, opened the door of the cabinet situated over the sink and put it inside. 'I might as well leave it here. If she's forgotten where she put it and has to ask after it, it might remind her not to leave her things lying around so much. But I doubt it.'

'Now Sybil, have a little charity,' Elizabeth reprimanded her friend gently. 'As we get a little older, we can all expect to have these small lapses in memory.'

Sybil laughed lightly. 'Dear Betty – ever the "head girl". But you're right of course,' she admitted, pretending to acknowledge a chastisement that she certainly didn't feel. 'It's just that dear Agnes can be the limit. Has she regaled you with that dratted book of hers yet? No?' she added, after receiving only negative shakes of the head. 'Well, she will, believe me. It's her latest craze – how to live in harmony with your fellow man and achieve a higher plane of self-knowledge, or some such nonsense. It was without doubt written by a charlatan simply to make money out of the gullible. Now, is everyone going back downstairs?'

They all admitted that they were.

'Splendid.' Sybil took the arm of her old friend to lead the way. 'We're all meeting in the library. It gets the setting sun.'

*

In that pleasant book-lined room, which smelled of leather, old books and cigar smoke, they found Sybil's husband standing at a shockingly new-looking Art Deco cocktail bar, dispensing his efforts to Bill Endicott, Roger, Daphne and Elizabeth's daughter.

'Ah, more customers? Splendid!' Sir Bayard called to them. 'I know it's a little early, but the sun must be over the yardarm somewhere, eh?' He gave a guffaw. 'We like to keep things informal here, at the Hall. Drinks whenever, and all that. Change for dinner whenever you like, don't worry about sticking to a timetable here. Not in the army now, eh? Mr Swift, what's your poison?'

Arbie asked for an old-fashioned, whilst Val, daringly for her, opted for a Singapore sling. Lady Sybil requested a bellini, whilst Elizabeth, surprising Arbie a little, asked for a Manhattan.

'So, sir,' Arbie began, only to be interrupted at once by his host.

'Oh, call me Bayard. None of this "sir" business. Doesn't do when we're all amongst friends, eh?'

'Oh, righty-oh,' Arbie began again, a shade uncertainly. He'd discovered, from bitter experience, that people who said they couldn't stand social etiquette quite often got the goat the quickest when a chap duly ignored it. 'I was rather hoping to get to the village tomorrow and start sounding out the locals about your ghost. Is it far? The village, I mean, not the ghost,' he clarified hastily.

'Oh, not so much – a tramp of a mile or so. But dear chap, you mustn't think of walking. We've got a collection of old bangers in the sheds and whatnot. I'm sure our chauffeur can loan you something decent. An Austin, or Morris, or some such thing.'

Their host, clearly, was not a car man – not that Arbie minded. 'Oh, I say, that'd be rather super if he can,' he agreed enthusiastically. 'I shall have to take a run along the road that follows the railway tracks for some miles, I should think, and that'll certainly save me some time – not to mention the wear and tear on the old shoe-leather. As I understand it, your beastly signalman is very ambulatory, as far as his kind go. Most ghosts have the decency to haunt a single place, but your specimen, so I've been reliably informed, can be spotted anywhere along the line hereabouts, waving his lamp from here to Timbuctoo in either direction.'

At this, everyone laughed. 'Downright unsporting of him, if you ask me, old chap,' Bill commiserated.

'Yes, you'd think those in the hereafter would have more consideration,' Bernadette put in with a charming little gurgle, sidling up to stand beside Val. 'But *you* won't be going out after dark in search of this spook, will you, Val? I mean, Miss Coulton-James?'

'Oh yes,' Val said, with a great show of nonchalance. 'Part of the job, and all that.'

'Oh, I say, Val, you *are* daring,' Bernie said, aghast and admiring in equal measure. 'I'm not sure I could do it.'

'Oh, I don't know. I can't say as I find this particular ghost all that frightening,' Bill disagreed. 'I mean, he goes about waving his lamp to warn train drivers of danger, doesn't he? Sounds to me like the fellow's doing a public service. Hardly the sort of chap to put the wind up one, is he?'

'Ah, except when you see his lamp nowadays, it's supposed to mean you or someone you love hasn't got long to live,' Sir Bayard corrected him with some relish. 'Have to say, I'm glad I've never clapped eyes on him. Him or his "devil train" either.'

'Devil train?' Daphne repeated, into the startled silence that followed his last words. 'Did you say *devil* train, Sir Bayard?'

Their host looked at the archbishop's daughter and coughed a little over his straight whisky and soda. 'I'm afraid so,' he said apologetically. 'Oh, it's nothing to do with us, I assure you,' he added hastily, anxious to make the disclaimer. 'I mean with the Chervilles and Cleeves Lea Manor, or anything. It's just that, recently – during the last couple of years or so – some of the villagers have claimed to see it.'

'This is the stuff all right,' Arbie said, rubbing his hands together enthusiastically. 'Tell me more.'

'All grist for the mill, old chap?' Bill grinned at him.

'Absolutely. Bound to thrill my readers and editor alike. So, tell me, er, Sir Bayard,' – Arbie couldn't quite bring himself to drop the 'sir' – 'just what makes this train so devilish?'

'Oh a few things,' his host said modestly. 'It's said to come from nowhere and vanish equally mysteriously. That is, nobody can find out where it originates or where it goes. Certainly, the next town down the line never sees hide nor hair of it. And none of the farmers around here have found its lair. It just vanishes, one supposes, in a puff of sulphurous smoke.'

'Sounds like a magic trick to me,' Bill said dismissively. 'Sorry, Arbie my old China, but it all sounds like a bit of a dead duck.'

'Ah, but that's not its main party trick,' Sir Bayard said, a definite chill in his tone now as he cast the younger man a challenging stare, as if taking Bill's lack of awe personally. 'They say everyone knows when the devil train is coming past the village as they can see it for miles off.'

'How so?' It was Roger who spoke, looking more as if he simply wanted to contribute to the conversation than out of any burning desire to know.

'Ah, well, it's said in the village that they can see the fire in the sky as it approaches. We never see it here because the fold of the hill between us and them keeps it hidden from sight,' Sir Bayard explained.

And suddenly, the room fell preternaturally silent, and Val wasn't the only one who felt a frisson chill the skin on her bare arms.

'Fire in the sky?' Arbie asked, looking confused.

'Yes. Hasn't your research got that far?' their host asked curiously.

'Oh, only the ghostly signalman gets a mention in the local history books,' Arbie replied, defending himself and beginning to feel a shade uneasy. 'Poor Jethro Hoskins has been on the scene since the Old Queen was on the throne. But this train of yours, by your own admission, sounds as if it's a bit of a newcomer to the Middle Stratton ghost-stakes, what?'

'Ah, yes, I see your problem,' Sir Bayard acknowledged generously. 'An author's lot, eh? Well, you see, it's like this,' he swirled his cut-glass tumbler a little and watched his drink swish obligingly around at the bottom, 'when our unwanted visitor deigns to put in an appearance, it comes rattling through the valley at midnight belching out not smoke or steam from its stack, as you might expect, but apparently . . . well . . . hellfire itself.'

CHAPTER THREE

Well, that was a bit of a conversation stopper and no mistake, Arbie thought to himself a little while later, as he changed into formal evening clothes in his room. He was currently contemplating the highlights of the day so far, and his host's attention-grabbing discourse was, without doubt, the cat's pyjamas.

Despite Val's raptures about how it would make a gripping highlight for his chapter on Yorkshire's holiday destinations, he couldn't say that he was particularly mad keen on encountering Old Nick's personal locomotive, per se. Luckily, he was reasonably sure that the tales of a demonic train were just the local villagers egging each other on. Tall tales had a way of spreading and growing and had probably originated with some old-timer wandering home alone after having had one over the eight at the local pub, and then lying up in a comfortable ditch somewhere, whence he'd proceeded to have a no doubt vivid, but drink-induced, nightmare.

As he adjusted his bow tie in the mirror for the final time, he heard a discreet tap on his door and went to open it. 'Oh, hello, old thing,' he said casually to Val, already turning away from her. 'Want to come in for a jiffy? I just need to find my cufflinks.'

Val walked in and carefully twirled around so that her 'new' frock of pearl-grey silk swished becomingly around her shins.

Of course, it wasn't exactly new (being a hand-me-down from one of her mother's friends' more fashionable daughters) and was sadly so last season, but it was new to *her*, in that she'd never worn it before, and felt like the height of luxury. It came with a hip-bow and a velvet-lined collar that dipped almost to her waist. With it she'd worn multicoloured beaded necklaces that likewise fell nearly to her waist. She had put her hair up, secured with another hand-me-down (from the same source) of an egret feather and turquoise headband.

Arbie managed to get his cufflinks in place and glanced around his dressing table but could think of nothing he'd forgotten. His cigarette case was already secured in his inside pocket, as was his nifty little lighter. He turned to Val and found her eyeing him grimly. It was a look he instantly recognised. But what, he wondered, could he have possibly done wrong in the twenty seconds or so since she'd walked into the room?

'Err, what-oh, old bean, ready for the nosh then?' he temporised, trying to feel his way.

Val turned, letting her finery display itself once more, and tossed her head. 'You might say I look nice or something,' she said, vexed. 'It *is* the kind of thing that gentlemen do, you know.'

Arbie instantly brightened as the puzzle was solved. 'Oh, got you, old bean. And you do. Er, look absolutely smashing I mean. Top hole and all that,' he said. And seeing that the ice wasn't exactly melting just yet, was forced into more treacherous territory. 'New, er, dress? Hair! That headband thingy is positively the bee's knees.' Frantically he cast around for anything else he might have missed but could only think of shoes. 'Pretty slippers those,' he added hopefully. 'Sort of sparkly. . .' he trailed off with a hopeful smile.

Val's shoulders slumped a little.

'Cheer up, old thing,' Arbie, who felt he'd done his duty,

admonished. 'I met up with an old cove from my club who's been to one of Sir Bayard's previous bashes, and he tells me the nosh he serves up is top hole.'

'Well, that's all right then, isn't it?' Val said tartly and swept out of the room.

They made their way in silence down the stairs, then headed for the sound of voices coming from the library. Here they found the drinks party was still going on, although much depleted as half of the others were now absent, presumably also changing for dinner. Only their host, Roger and Agnes had made it back down before them.

Sir Bayard hailed them heartily and asked if they wanted sherry or another cocktail. Arbie, sitting with his back to his host on one of the sofas positioned opposite a large Adam fireplace, said he'd hold his fire, guessing that the wines served with dinner would be of a good vintage. Val again surprised Arbie by agreeing to partake of a glass of sherry.

Above the fireplace was a large mirror, one of those monstrosities with an ornate gilt frame rampant with cherubs and bunches of grapes and the odd satyr or two (who were usually up to no good), and a movement within its glass caught his eye. It took him only a moment to realise that the slight tilt of the mirror reflected back to him the bar area, and he was seeing his host reach for a decanter of pale liquid that looked to him suspiciously like an amontillado fino. Arbie, who had a talent for judging liquor just by its appearance, wondered if his host might just stretch to a Croft Port as well?

As he watched Sir Bayard's reflected image pour out a measure into a sherry glass, he decided he'd make sure and ask him for a glass of the amontillado tomorrow night.

Just as Sir Bayard was handing Val her glass, his wife swept past behind him in an eau-de-Nil number that instantly made Val feel dowdy in comparison. In place of beads, Lady Sybil wore emeralds, and the luxuriant feather in her headband made Val's own look positively moth-eaten.

'How lovely, I'm just in time – a glass of the same, darling, please,' she said, moving to Arbie's sofa and draping herself over the other end of it with the feline liquidity of a panther. Arbie tried not to gape. And failed.

Seated demurely in a Queen Anne chair opposite them, Val took a large swallow of her sherry, and Arbie watched her uneasily. It wasn't like Val to drink much, let alone quaff a fine sherry as if it was lemonade. He hoped that she wouldn't become squiffy. The thought of trying to handle a squiffy Valentina Coulton-James brought him out in a very cold sweat indeed.

'Ah, there you go, m'dear,' Sir Bayard said, handing his wife her drink. 'Oh, by the way, I've invited a chap I know over for dinner tomorrow. You'll like him – he's an amusing sort. Got a store of good stories, and he happens to be a demon bridge player,' he added hastily, as his wife opened her mouth with chastisement clearly on her mind.

'Oh, well, in that case, I suppose it'll be all right,' she subsided slightly. 'But honestly, Bay, I do wish you wouldn't keep springing surprises on me like this. It was bad enough . . . oh never mind. I've given up trying to house-train you, dearest.'

'Well, I'm sure Daphers will be glad of someone worth her mettle anyway,' Roger put in at that point, sensing that the marital teasing between his host and hostess hid genuine discord, and doing his best to smooth it over. 'As you know, she's something of a bridge fiend.'

'Oh dear, now you've quite alarmed me, Mr Potts-Gibbon,' Agnes piped up from the depths of a wingback chair in which she was currently engulfed. 'I was hoping for a rubber or two of bridge myself, but now I'm afraid I wouldn't meet your wife's exacting standards. I've been playing for years, and friends do say I'm fairly good, but I do get flustered sometimes.'

'In that case, Miss Warren, you must partner me,' Roger said, falling on his sword gallantly. 'I know how to put it across her, you see, if she steps out of line, and will come instantly to your aid.'

Agnes gave a pleased twitter and held out her white-gloved hand in a little coy gesture. 'Oh, thank you. I can tell you don't mean it, of course. I never saw a more happily married couple than you and dear Daphne. You must have read Dr Schuber's marvellous book?'

Roger rolled his eyes in Arbie and Lady Sybil's direction. 'Dr Schuber? Er . . .'

'Oh, but you must read it! It's marvellous – it's called *The Art of Harmonious Living* and it's simply changed my life. It's taught me to seize chances and not to let cautious behaviour rob me of living life to my best potential, and – oh, all sorts of marvellous things like that. I'm sure you'll find it helpful for you too. I've brought it with me, so I can lend it to you if you like?'

'I'm sure Roger didn't come here this weekend to read, Agnes dear.' Sybil, ever the gracious hostess, came adroitly to his rescue, earning her a grateful look in return.

'No. Of course he didn't. Oh my, I simply didn't think! Yes, that was very silly of me,' Agnes said, looking as woebegone as a starving sparrow that had just had its last breadcrumb pinched off it by an avaricious magpie. 'You've all come to relax and have fun. Please, forget I said anything,' she begged and did her best to dissolve into the upholstery.

Val, seeing her flush in mortification, leaned forward in her chair and patted her hand. 'I think that was a splendid idea, Miss Warren, especially as Arbie *hasn't* come to relax. In fact, just the opposite. He's here to work and find material for his own book.

And as a fellow author himself, I'm sure he'd be fascinated to read Dr Schuber's theories.'

Here she looked across at Arbie and shot him a sweet smile. 'Isn't that right, Arbie?'

He, neatly caught, tried to sit up a little straighter on the sofa and made a manful effort to keep his eyes from straying to Sybil's slender ankles, dangerously close to his thigh. 'Oh, yes indeed. I'd be utterly delighted,' he lied fervently.

Agnes perked up instantly. 'Oh? Really? I'm sure you'll find it ever so useful. I'll just go up and get it for you now, shall I?' she asked, ever helpful.

And before Arbie could get his brain into gear sufficiently fast enough to come up with an excuse to prevent such a catastrophe, Val very neatly scuppered him. 'Yes, why don't you do that, Miss Warren? That will give him plenty of time to read it over the weekend and get it back to you.'

As Agnes left at a happy near-trot to retrieve her precious book, Sir Bayard grinned at the look on young Swift's face. Unless he was very much mistaken, he had somehow managed to put himself in the lovely Miss Coulton-James's bad books and was now reaping the whirlwind. Lucky fellow! He could still remember the cut and thrust of courtship when he was the writer's age, and would happily have given him a run for his money if he were only twenty years younger and not married . . .

His thoughts crashed to a sudden halt, and for an instant, his face turned ugly. Sybil caught the expression and froze with her sherry glass halfway to her lips. Then, in the next instant, her husband's face cleared, and he sauntered over casually towards Roger.

'So – are you up for a game of cards tomorrow, Roger? Not bridge, but a real man's game – perhaps a spot of poker? I think Mr Swift here and good old Bill will be happy to oblige us. A guinea a game – what say you?'

Roger's eyes gleamed. 'Now you're talking, sir,' he agreed heartily. And he'd be careful to lose a good number of hands to the old boy too, which would be bound to put his host in a good mood.

*

Upstairs, not all the missing guests were in their rooms and still changing for dinner.

Bernie Rowe glanced nervously over her shoulder before tapping timidly on Lady Sybil's bedroom door. She was confident that both the lady of the house and her husband were downstairs but wasn't about to take any chances.

After listening closely for any sound coming from within (and failing to hear any), she quickly opened the door, darted a look around to confirm that the room was indeed empty, then slipped noiselessly inside. Her heart was pounding so hard that she could hear its beat echoing in her ears, and even though her throat felt as dry as sawdust she was determined to continue her course of action.

She tried to comfort herself with the knowledge that since she'd seen Sybil head downstairs a little while ago, and her maid leave the bedroom barely a minute or two ago, neither one was likely to return and interrupt her; even so, her hands still felt cold with tension.

She slipped quickly across the room and paused in front of her hostess's dressing table. A quick inspection told her that it was cluttered with everything that she'd expect – a bottle of very expensive and even more exclusive perfume from Paris, a prettily enamelled trinket box, a mother-of-pearl and silver brush set, various lotions and potions and powder puff.

But none of those things were of any use to her. She tried not to think what her mother would say if she knew what she was doing, and thrust such considerations aside. In her heart, she knew her mother wouldn't condemn her totally. After all, what she was doing wasn't wrong – not really. Not morally. She was sure of that.

She pulled out the thin top drawer of the dresser, wincing a little at the slight squeak it made, and breathed a sigh of relief as she found exactly what she was looking for. Several long, flat jewellery boxes lay inside, and she opened the first one only to scowl down at its contents, dissatisfied. Diamonds were too much. The second, by contrast, was a string of amber beads, which were too little. Like a larcenous Goldilocks, she was seeking the one that was just right. Unlike the heroine of the fairy tale, however, the third box wasn't quite right either, but by the time she'd opened the fourth box, casting frantic little glances behind her at the door as she did so, she finally found just what she was looking for.

She hastily thrust the contents of this box into her bag, being careful to put all the boxes back in the order in which she'd found them, and then shut the drawer, wincing again as it gave a little tell-tale squeak.

Next, she tiptoed back to the door, all the time quite convinced that it would open before she reached it, and either Sybil's maid would be there looking puzzled and suspicious, or it would be the grand lady herself. In which case, she'd just *die!*

But the door didn't open and when Bernie inched it open, tiny bit by tiny bit, and checked both ways down the corridor beyond, it was mercifully empty.

She quickly rushed out and shut the door behind her, literally running away from the scene of her crime. Not that it had been a *crime* exactly, she told herself as she ran. Not really. She wasn't intending to take anything away from Cleeves Lea Manor that didn't belong to her, after all. Even so, she still felt a little sick as she negotiated her way some length down the corridor, before slowing her pace, then finally pausing outside yet another door that was not her own.

This time, however, she felt no sense of guilt. She paused, took a deep breath, and then for the second time in just a few minutes, tapped quietly on a door and listened intently.

*

In her bedroom, Daphne attached a hundred-year-old pair of small garnet earrings in place, then reached for her dark-red silk stole. She was wearing the latest fashion, naturally, but it was of an understated and modest variety, a style for which both her birth and her nature had equipped her well.

As she reached for a dark-red lipstick and applied it very sparingly, she met her own troubled gaze in the mirror.

She did so hope that Roger wasn't going to do anything silly this weekend. Her husband, like most husbands across the land, fondly believed that his wife was in total ignorance of most of what went on right under her nose. And of course, like most wives across the land, she was no such thing. Which meant that she'd been well aware, last year, of just how livid her husband had become over some missed business opportunity or other.

At first, she had wondered if the dear old sausage had all but lost his shirt and had been too afraid to tell her, but that fear quickly passed when she realised that he wasn't trying to tighten his belt without her knowing. Nevertheless, he'd been very much put out by *something*, and being the intelligent woman that she was, it hadn't taken her that long to find out what that something was.

And she was not so unworldly that she didn't share his chagrin after she did. Losing out on a business transaction that would have almost doubled their wealth within six months or so was enough to make even the most placid of individuals hopping mad. But she, unlike her husband, had quickly become philosophical about it. As an archbishop's daughter it wouldn't have been the done thing for her to be so obsessed with Mammon anyway. Besides, her own view of life was far more equitable than that of a businessman, like Roger, whose sole raison d'etre was to accumulate as much money as possible.

Still, it was very vexing indeed to unexpectedly find oneself having to share a roof with the very person responsible for snatching so much of the filthy lucre clean out of your hands. But, whilst she didn't begrudge her spouse the ill-will she knew he was feeling towards one of their fellow guests, it worried her significantly, for she knew that Roger was not the forgiving sort.

She could only hope that he wouldn't . . . well . . . do anything rash.

Wiping away much of the meagre lipstick that she'd just taken the trouble to apply, Daphne met her apprehensive gaze in the mirror and let out a little sigh.

She would just have to keep a watchful eye on things for the next few days, that was all. How tiresome it all was. . .

*

Bill Endicott met Agnes Warren on her way back downstairs. She was clutching a book to her scrawny bosom and when she saw him, her eyes glittered. He was so handsome!

'Hello, dear Miss Warren,' he said cordially, his eye on the butler, who was just crossing the hall below them. 'I hope you're having a wonderful time?'

Agnes blushed. 'Oh yes, thank you, Mr Endicott. It's all so lovely here, isn't it?' she said coyly.

'Ah yes, our host makes sure of that,' he agreed, and as they reached the bottom of the stairs, he crooked his elbow in her direction and placed her hand, which was adorned with her best silk and lace glove, on his forearm. 'May I escort the loveliest lady here into the cocktail lounge?'

Agnes blushed again and twittered with pleasure. 'Oh, please don't let dear Sir Bayard hear you say things like that. I'm sure he's never been in a cocktail lounge in his life. Nor have I!' she added hastily, lest he misunderstand her.

As the butler passed into his pantry, his last view of the mismatched pair was of Bill inclining his head towards the lady, the better to hear her as she made some remark or other.

As he picked up a silver epergne and started to polish it vigorously, Jardine decided that he didn't like Mr William Endicott much. That young man was far too charming for his liking, and he could tell that the man's valet didn't rate him highly either. And that said a lot about a man who was supposed to be a gentleman.

As the butler energetically buffed away, he was unaware that he was frowning. But it was not, perhaps, surprising, that none of his random thoughts were particularly pleasant ones. He was sure that his lord and ladyship had had a disagreement of some kind, which was nothing new, but still, it hardly made for a nice atmosphere with guests in the house. And he wasn't too sure about this writer of ghost stories. To his mind, subjects like that were rather common. At least Daphne Potts-Gibbon was pure class, although her husband, to his mind, was not quite . . . well . . . quite the ticket. A self-made man was all well and good, but still. . .

There was just something about this weekend party that didn't sit well with him. He couldn't quite put his finger on it, but there was a definite sense of unease somewhere. The faithful retainer shook his head, sighed, and continued to vigorously polish his silver.

He would be glad when it was all over.

In the library, Bill was escorting a flushed-looking Agnes back to her chair and seemed about to take a seat near one of the occasional tables, when he quickly veered off. Val, who had been watching him, wondered what had put him off.

But there was only Elizabeth Rowe sitting there, demurely sipping from a glass of sherry. She looked up with a smile when her daughter hurried into the room and joined her. Val saw Bernie glance quickly at the clock on the mantelpiece to see if she was unfashionably late.

She wasn't.

'Ah, just waiting for Daphne then,' Sir Bayard said absently, but even as he spoke, the lady in question walked sedately into the room. Evidently the butler had seen her arrival, for a moment later he appeared, as if by magic, in the doorway.

'Dinner is served, m'lord,' Jardine said mellifluously, and turned to lead the way.

Arbie rose and smiled at Bernie Rowe. 'Miss Rowe, may I escort you in to dinner?' he offered gallantly. Val tossed her head at this and met Bill's eye firmly. Bill, happy to follow suit, promptly offered her his own elbow. Sir Bayard did his duty and asked Agnes to accompany him, and Sybil promptly snaffled Roger's arm. Daphne – left man-less by the uneven numbers, but totally unfazed by this breech of etiquette amongst friends old and new – walked into the dining room arm in arm with the equally unfussed Elizabeth Rowe.

*

'At which point I turned to him and said, Bunce, my good man, if you can't learn to shoot better than that, you'd better take up archery – and preferably, somewhere in the antipodes.'

Sir Bayard's slightly slurred anecdote ended with a round of appreciative laughter.

Arbie accepted a refill of his wine glass from one of the silent footmen who served at the table, whilst across the way, Bill Endicott reached across to lift the fruit bowl and present it to Agnes Warren, who had been attempting, without much success, to snaffle a peach for her dessert plate.

'Oh, thank you, I do so love fresh fruit,' Agnes simpered. 'And Sir Bayard's heated greenhouses are such a wonder for soft fruit especially.'

'No need to demur, my dear Miss Warren. A peach is worthy of another peach,' Bill said gallantly, making Agnes duck her head in pleased confusion.

Roger watched this little bit of by-play with a cynical and curious eye, then started a little as he caught Elizabeth's gaze on him. She raised a slight eyebrow at him, as if acknowledging that she too had noted the odd little incident, and then turned to talk to Sybil, who was seated opposite her.

Bill turned smoothly from Agnes to Arbie. 'What say you to a spot of a hundred-up in the billiards room later. Five pounds on it?'

'You're on,' Arbie said at once. He'd had some time now to take the measure of his fellow diners and he was pretty sure that the handsome Bill Endicott fancied himself as a bit of a gamesman, and probably wasn't above taking money off unwary casual acquaintances to supplement his wallet. Arbie had learned all about his sort in the common rooms of Oxford and his London clubs. But what poor old Bill didn't know was that he, Arbie, was anyone's match on the baize!

Over on his left, he could hear Val talking to Sir Bayard about sheep, of all things, but when his hostess caught his eye, he hastily looked away again and took a gulp of wine. He had the feeling that a chap could get in deep waters, very quickly, with the likes of Lady Sybil.

Val listened with only half an ear to the perils of late snow during the lambing season, but went out of her way to keep a close watch on their hostess, and hadn't failed to note that although she talked to everyone during dinner, as a good hostess should, she spoke least of all to Bill. This surprised her slightly, for she'd have thought that the golden-haired, handsome Bill would have been a particular favourite of hers.

Or perhaps she was imagining things, for as she ate and chatted and watched, she realised that neither of the Rowes talked to Bill much either. Perhaps the poor man, despite his Adonis-like looks, was a bit of a flop with the ladies? She had noticed this curious phenomenon once or twice amongst some of her father's more comely curates. But in their case, the poor dears had either been much too shy to woo the ladies, or had not yet had the chance to cultivate a charming manner.

Neither fault, she was sure, could be applied to Mr Endicott, who, right now, was topping up Miss Warren's wine glass and utterly ignoring that poor lady's protestations that she 'only liked the barest little drop'. For two pins, if she could have reached him, she'd have kicked his shin underneath the table in reprimand. For it was one thing to harmlessly charm the wallflower of the party, but sometimes handsome and vain young men didn't realise the hurt they could inadvertently cause. Susceptible Miss Warren was already beginning to shoot starry-eyed glances in his direction. And no doubt, when the weekend party was over and he went on his merry little way, the poor old dear would be heart-sore for weeks to come.

Men!

After the cheeseboard had been dispatched, Lady Sybil caught the eye of Elizabeth and gave the little murmur that meant it was time for the ladies to retire to the lounge, whilst the men enjoyed their brandies and cigars in the library. All the men rose as the ladies left and then settled back at the table for a spell of gossip.

Sybil led the way to the lounge, where the maids were already setting down coffee trays on various tables. Val and Bernie sat down together to set about discovering if they had any friends in common, for Bernie's Oxfordshire town of Woodstock wasn't that far away from Val's home in the Cotswolds near the Gloucestershire border.

Elizabeth and Sybil talked of their schooldays, but Elizabeth was kind enough to keep drawing Agnes and Daphne into their discussion, and after three-quarters of an hour or so, the men wandered in to join them, and a game of bridge was quickly set up.

Val watched as Bill and Arbie hastily left for their game of billiards, then joined Daphne, with a little trepidation, at the card table. She knew how to play bridge quite well, of course, for it was an accomplishment that young ladies of her class were always taught, along with needlepoint and how to play piano, but she had the feeling that Daphne would be a ferocious player, and wasn't surprised to be proven right in very short order.

As she called a tentative trump and hoped that Daphne was in a forgiving mood, she noticed that, over by one of the windows, Elizabeth and Roger (who were sitting this game out) were deep in earnest conversation, their heads bent close together over the intervening coffee table. It struck her as slightly odd, as she didn't think, from what she'd observed of her fellow guests that the two people had met before tonight, and wondered, absently, what they could have found to talk about so soon that was so fascinating.

Then her partner, Miss Warren, took a wild punt on spades, and Daphne pounced, and it was all Val could do to keep track of her own cards and the play she must make. Bernie, who was partnered with the terrifying Daphne, snuck her friend a sympathetic glance but didn't dare make any sort of play that could help her defend Agnes's foolhardy call.

Eventually the bridge game broke up, with Daphne the acknowledged queen of the table, and Agnes approached Val diffidently and offered her a book. It was a hardbacked book, with a green leather cover and a heavily embossed title. 'Oh, Miss Coulton-James, I wonder if you could perhaps pass this on to Mr Swift? I meant to give it to him before, but somehow never did, and I wouldn't want to intrude on his game-playing with dear William.'

Val took it with a smile, promising to deliver it before the night ended. Indeed, she assured Miss Warren, it would give her the greatest of pleasure.

Agnes turned away, a glance at the clock telling her that it was well past her bedtime. But as her eyes sought out Lady Sybil, that she might bid her goodnight, she found Roger Potts-Gibbon beside her.

'Ah, Miss Warren, I was hoping to have a little chat with you before you retire. May I?' he asked, indicating a cosy corner where two chairs were set close together beside a little occasional table. Although his tone was light, there was a seriousness in his eyes that made Miss Warren feel just a bit nervous. Whenever clever men of business wanted to talk to her, she did worry so that she wouldn't understand what they were saying. . .

Elizabeth Rowe watched Roger and Agnes for a moment, then wandered over to the window, where she stared out thoughtfully at the night beyond.

Outside, it was now fully dark and a tawny owl, sitting in an elm tree overlooking the front of the house, watched the golden light that often marked out the habitations of the strange two-legged animals with wide nocturnal eyes.

He hooted, listening for – but not hearing – the answering call of his mate.

He hooted again.

Now, the annuls of literature have always regarded the call of almost any nocturnal creature as a sign of ill-omen. Unfortunately for the residents of Cleeves Lea Manor that night, however, none of them heard the tawny owl's cry, and so went about their business in blissful ignorance of any warning.

Yet afficionados of ghost stories, legends, ancient poetry or folk tales rife with the chronicles of doomed lovers might have felt vindicated to know that, before dawn arrived, one of the people in that big country house would not live to see its welcome light.

CHAPTER FOUR

Saturday morning arrived with a slight mist that quickly gave way to hazy sunlight. Arbie, mindful of his promise to himself yesterday to arise at a decent hour and get to the bathroom before the others, duly indulged in a deliciously hot bath and then shaved leisurely.

He had bought no man-servant with him, for he had been raised by his uncle, who didn't believe in them. Uncle also probably didn't want prying eyes around their house for reasons of his own, but Arbie hastily stopped himself from pursuing that line of thought. As far as his uncle was concerned, Arbie preferred to maintain the self-delusion that his beloved relative was merely a slightly eccentric gentleman who was – by and large – perfectly harmless.

Arbie was so seldom 'up with the lark' that after he'd waltzed happily down the stairs he was a little disconcerted to see that the servants had yet to open up all the downstairs rooms, and though there was the heartening scent of cooking bacon emanating from somewhere, his experience at such social occasions told him that breakfast was still many minutes from being served.

With his mouth watering at the thought of the kidneys, bacon, eggs, sausages, kippers and kedgeree which would no doubt await him presently at the help-yourself-buffet that was the norm at such do's, Arbie felt at a bit of a loss. Somewhat belatedly, it occurred to him that early-morning risers must be quite a nuisance to the servants, who couldn't be expected to rejoice in having them skulking about underfoot whilst they were so busy. He hesitated for a moment in the hall, wondering if he should take a morning stroll and remove himself from the scene altogether.

But to do so on an empty stomach was surely folly!

Then he had it; Sir Bayard had promised him the run of his library day or night, for his more literary-minded ancestors had, in their time, managed to accumulate all sorts of wordy curiosities, including a fair share of local history. With a bit of luck, it wouldn't take him long to give the old shelves a quick look-see and hoick out some volumes that needed to be winnowed for anything of interest. (They'd be certain to keep Val busy for most of the day, thus leaving him free to do a spot of fishing.) And presenting them to her would also prove once and for all that he wasn't quite the work-shy chap that she thought he was!

With this happy thought rattling around in his brainbox, he made his way to the library and stepped inside. It was a little gloomy, for the curtains here were still drawn, marking it as one of the rooms that the between maid had yet to reach. And whilst it wasn't the done thing to go about opening curtains oneself all willy-nilly (maids and homeowners could be a bit territorial about such things), he had no other choice if he wanted to see what he was doing.

Once the long velvet curtains had been drawn back, allowing the weak morning sunshine to filter in and highlight a shower of dancing dust-motes, he turned around and was heading for the wall of shelves nearest to him, when he was brought up sharply.

For a moment, his heart did a little jump in his chest, for

there was someone sitting in one of the armchairs! He could clearly see the top of a head peeking up over the one facing the sofa.

'Oh, hello there,' Arbie said cheerfully, the nasty jolt at suddenly finding himself not alone quickly passing. 'I thought I was the only one up. Hope you don't mind me opening the curtains and whatnot? Bit of a cheek I know. Awfully sorry if you wanted to have a bit of peace and quiet in a darkened room and all that. I dare say it was the port, was it?' he swept on sympathetically. 'I must say, Sir Bayard's cellar, whilst very fine, can lure one into taking a drop too much. Beastly things, aren't they, hangovers?'

As he was talking, he was also walking around the sofa and the table in front of it, and saw, without too much surprise, that the sufferer of an early morning 'head' was Bill Endicott. He was sitting somewhat slumped in the chair and appeared to be gazing gloomily down at his feet. No doubt he was silently bewailing his excesses of the night before and trying to nerve himself up to move some random body part. A big toe maybe. Best not to rush the process, as Arbie knew from bitter experience himself.

'A spot of tomato juice and a healthy dollop of Worcestershire sauce is what you need, my lad,' he advised briskly. But now his voice was less cheerful and more uncertain. Bill, he could now see, was still dressed in his evening suit, which meant he hadn't gone to bed at all, so the poor blighter must have been well and truly soused. Might he still be a bit blotto even now? If so, he might turn belligerent and noisy if aroused, which might well become very awkward indeed. What if one of the ladies heard and came down to investigate the ruckus?

'I say, Bill old chap, buck up. We've got to get you on your feet and up the wooden hill and into a cold bath before. . .'

Once again Arbie's voice weakened and then ceased

altogether. Unwillingly, he moved towards Bill's chair then crouched down and sat back on his heels, the better to get a good look at the other man. And Arbie didn't like what he saw one little bit.

His billiard partner of the night before looked very pale. And was very still. So still, in fact, that Arbie couldn't see him breathing.

'Bill,' Arbie said miserably, and put a tentative hand on the other man's cheek, hoping against hope that the unexpected touch would set Bill upright in his seat, snorting and demanding to know what the deuce he thought he was playing at.

But Bill didn't move. And Bill's face was distinctly chilly.

Arbie none-too-elegantly got back up onto his feet. His legs felt as if all their muscles and sinews had been transplanted with jelly, and walked, in a not-altogether straight line, back to the door. There he stepped outside, closed it, and came face to face with the disconcerted butler.

'I'm so sorry, sir, I had no idea any of the guests were up yet,' Jardine said, recovering his sangfroid almost instantaneously. 'Can I offer you tea or coffee in the morning room? Breakfast will be served very shortly.'

'Er, thank you, no, er, Jardine,' Arbie managed to get out in a creditably calm voice. 'Er, is Sir Bayard up yet, do you know?'

'No, sir, I don't believe either he or her ladyship are available just yet. It's her ladyship's habit to rise considerably later.'

Even in such ghastly circumstances, Arbie was aware of the slight censure in the butler's tone and felt himself shrink a little. To be a guest in a chap's home and not cut the mustard with the chap's butler was a calamity that would horrify many a man, and the thought that he'd have to add yet more black marks against the quality of his character made him quail a little inside. But, damn it, he had no other option.

'Ah, yes, that's a little awkward,' Arbie said and half-glanced over his shoulder. 'You see, one of Sir Bayard's guests is . . . er . . . a little under the weather. Do you have a local doctor in the village by any chance?'

Enlightenment dawned, and Jardine thawed a few degrees. 'Yes, sir, Doctor Pinchcliffe, sir.'

'Right. Yes. Good-oh. You have a telephone in the house, I take it?'

The butler inclined a regal head.

'Yes, right. Well, perhaps you might give the medical gentleman a little tinkle on the old horn and ask him if he might just pop over? Pretty sharpish if he can make it. Oh, and I think it might be as well if you ask Sir Bayard if he can come down here to the library at his earliest convenience.'

Jardine, very stiff-backed now, and with none of the growing alarm that he felt showing on his face, gave a slight bow and set off on the tasks he'd been given.

Arbie, after a moment's hesitation, slipped reluctantly back inside the room. Now that he was forewarned of its contents, his stomach didn't lurch about quite so much, and some sense of strength had returned to his knees. Carefully, he approached the silent man in the seat, and stood for a moment or two, simply feeling wretched.

It must be his heart, he mused unhappily. Fit, healthy chaps like Bill sometimes did surprise one by simply conking out. Perhaps he'd had a faulty ticker all his life and never knew it? He'd heard such tales before. Bit of a facer for the man's doctor, not picking up on it though. . .

His eyes dropped to the table and the solitary fluted glass resting there, with a small measure of pale wine or spirit left in the bottom of it. For some reason, his mind jumped to the word 'Champagne' but he couldn't have said why. But looking over at the bar, he did indeed see an opened bottle of Bollinger, which was now probably as flat as a pancake, residing in a silver ice bucket.

He associated Champagne with a celebration of some kind, but there was only one glass on the table. So, poor old Bill must have been drinking alone? A bad sign that. Perhaps it wasn't his heart but his liver that had given up the good fight?

Then he noticed a piece of paper, neatly folded, and lying on the tabletop a little away from the glass. It looked to him like a page torn out of a notebook, for he could see faintly ruled, pale blue horizontal lines on it, with an equally faint margin in red ink. It was the sort of notebook half the world probably carried around in their jacket pocket or handbag. Arbie frowned at it for a moment, wondering just why it seemed to him to be so incongruous, then reached down and picked it up.

If he'd been asked, he couldn't have said why he did it. Instinct maybe, or perhaps lingering shock had simply affected his usual habit of leaving things well enough alone. Because leaving things well enough alone, Arbuthnot Lancelot Swift had come to believe, was by far the cleverest thing a chap could do.

Yet, in that moment, he couldn't have let that little piece of paper remain unread if someone had bet him a thousand guineas that he could!

Not without a little trepidation, he unfolded it, read it and then abruptly sat down. (It was lucky for him that the sofa was directly behind his knees, otherwise he'd have ended up parked on the floor.)

What he had read, in a well-schooled, masculine hand, was nothing less than a suicide note. The sad missive had indeed been written on a page torn out from a notebook. It had no date written on it, nor was there any salutation, but its meaning was clear enough.

I have gambling debts that are getting me down a bit. I've always liked to take chances in life, and in the end, I always seem to come out ahead somehow, but right now, things are feeling a bit more heavy than usual on that front.

Then six months ago, poor old Pongo Smythe bought it in that awful train smash just outside of Marylebone. I'd known him since we were in short trousers, and it turns a chap up to have one of his oldest pals just pop off without so much as a cheerio, or a promise that you can have his stash of marbles.

To make matters worse still, I lost my last job over some dashed silly argument or other. And it's not as if Nick Bright isn't a decent soul, for he is, but somehow, I just can't seem to stick to a routine. I don't blame him for giving me the elbow, but it does make a chap question whether he's any good or not, doesn't it?

Mother died last year. Bit of a facer, that.

And what else? Oh, I could list a whole lot of things that aren't much in themselves, but add them all together and . . . well, there you are. One pretty miserable chap.

It wasn't signed. There was no formal apology for the coroner for putting him to all this trouble, or any last words of comfort for his loved ones. None, in fact, of the usual offices one would expect of a well-bred cove about to shuffle off the mortal coil.

But then perhaps Bill hadn't cared a fig for the niceties. When a chap was so down that he felt the only way out was self-annihilation, perhaps . . . Arbie shook his head.

Feeling guilty for reading the last private thoughts of a dead man, he re-folded the note and put it back where he'd found it. It would be a job for the coroner now. And the police would have to be brought in. There was no way of avoiding it. Poor Sir Bayard and Lady Sybil would weather the storm, of course, for although there'd be the usual furore, there would be no actual scandal attached to *them*.

Though it would be dashed hard on them for all that, Arbie thought, looking at the dead man with a slowly rising anger. 'Damn it all, why couldn't you have done the decent thing and just thrown yourself off London Bridge like everyone else, Bill old boy? It's a bit rum bringing all your woes to someone else's door like this,' he chastised.

When, as if in a direct response to this plaintive query, there came a distinct tapping on the door behind him, Arbie almost leapt out of his skin before common sense told him that it was no ghostly manifestation, but probably only the returning butler. But for a moment there. . .

Shaking his head at the woeful state of his nerves, Arbie walked to the door and opened it just wide enough to slip outside before closing the door firmly behind him. The same sense of decorum that had prevented the curious butler from simply walking into the library unannounced now prevented him from commenting on this latest example of the famous author's somewhat unusual behaviour.

'I have informed Dr Pinchcliffe, sir, who is on his way. Sir Bayard is dressing and will be down shortly. Is there anything else you require?'

Arbie shook his head. 'No. Er . . . not at the moment,' he said. He would leave it to Sir Bayard to send for the police.

'Very good, sir,' the butler said and withdrew. Once out of the hall, he made straight for the kitchen, where the cook was busy with the porridge, but she stopped stirring the massive cooking pot instantly when she saw the look on his face.

'Here, I say, Mr Jardine, you do look a bit peaky. Whatever's the matter?'

The butler sighed. 'There are doings,' he said darkly, 'in the library. You mark my words.'

At this, the tweeny, busy ironing napkins, looked up, her eyes round with excitement. Noticing her curiosity, the butler simply shook his head at the questioning face of the cook and departed to his pantry.

*

Sir Bayard descended the stairs into the hall, and glancing left and right, finally spotted Arbie Swift lurking outside the library door. Although the Lord of the Manor had not seen combat in the Great War, he'd been in uniform, the same as nearly every man of the right age, and there was something about the author's stance that brought to mind someone standing guard.

'What's all this I hear from Jardine, Mr Swift? Someone's been taken ill? Probably had one over the eight I expect. Please tell me it's not Roger!' he said with a slight note of unseemly glee in his voice. 'What would his father-in-law the archbishop have said?'

'No, sir. It's not Mr Potts-Gibbon. And I'm afraid it's a bit more serious than that,' Arbie said forlornly.

Sir Bayard's smile instantly fled. 'Well, all right, let the dog see the rabbit then,' he said gruffly. 'A man can't tell what's needed to be done until he's assessed the situation for himself, can he?'

'No, sir,' Arbie agreed, opening the door and letting the older man pass him by. Sir Bayard took several steps into the room, then stopped dead. Arbie, following on his heels, did the same, then watched nervously as the Lord of the Manor took in the form of the silent and unmoving man in the chair.

Sir Bayard's jaw clenched a little, then he seemed to abruptly relax. 'That's Bill Endicott,' he said flatly, but with just a faint hint of disbelief in his voice. As if he couldn't quite believe it.

'Yes, sir,' Arbie agreed quietly.

'He looks dead as a doornail.'

'Yes, sir, I'm afraid that he is. Jardine has sent for the doctor.'

As he watched Sir Bayard, he saw how pale he became, but that was hardly surprising, for his host was not a young man, and he'd just received a very nasty shock. And then his expression, which had previously been blank, slowly morphed into something else. Puzzlement? He certainly looked a little nonplussed, Arbie thought. And then – unmistakably, a small upwards pull of his lips told Arbie that the sight of the dead man *pleased* him in some way.

Instinctively, Arbie took a step back and blinked. Surely, he must have been mistaken in thinking he'd seen that smile.

And then Sir Bayard's face abruptly settled back into its usual resting expression.

'Extraordinary,' he said. 'Simply extraordinary.'

'Er, yes, sir,' Arbie agreed quietly.

'Must have been his heart, I suppose,' Sir Bayard went on, but when Arbie gave a slight cough, he shot him a swift, penetrating gaze. 'Well, out with it. What's bothering you, young fellah?'

Arbie pointed at the table. 'There appears to be a suicide note, sir,' he said helplessly.

'Well, I'll be. . .' Sir Bayard then said something in plain, old-fashioned Anglo-Saxon that would most definitely have shocked Daphne's father, had he been present to hear it. It didn't shock Arbie, it had to be said, mostly because the man had just expressed his own thoughts in a nutshell.

*

A few minutes later, Sir Bayard crossed the hall, intent on telephoning for the police. It wasn't something he relished doing, and in fact, had argued briefly against it, but the writer fellow had been annoyingly insistent. He himself had been all for burning that self-pitying little missive and tossing the ashes into the fire, thus saving Endicott's kith and kin the unpleasantness of having a suicide in the family, but Arbuthnot Swift had been surprisingly persistent that nothing on the table was to be touched.

This display of backbone had surprised Sir Bayard rather, for his own assessment of the great man of letters had left him with the distinct impression that, whilst the man might have brains, he was far too lazy to use them, and on the whole, had the air of a wastrel who wanted nothing more from life than to float through it with the least amount of inconvenience whilst happily skipping from one pleasurable enterprise to another.

Nevertheless, he had firmly stated that if Sir Bayard didn't telephone for the local constable, then he would. And after a moment's reflection, the peer supposed, grudgingly, that his guest had a point. It would almost certainly turn out to be a coroner's case, and if it could be proved that he, Sir Bayard and local magistrate, had interfered with evidence, then things could get very sticky indeed.

Yes. He supposed it was better to do things by the book. But he'd have to be damned careful of what he said and did from now on, by Jove! One slip-up could spell disaster.

As Sir Bayard swept his unhappy way towards the telephone booth, behind him, Val was coming downstairs and was just in time to see his back as he disappeared. She was wearing a white-and-blue sprigged muslin dress that suited her lithe frame and pale colouring perfectly. With her hair arranged in an intricate French pleat, artfully threaded through with a silvery-blue ribbon (Lady Sybil's lady's maid had pounced on her before Val could stop her) she looked as pretty as a picture, Arbie had to admit.

Then she turned, spotted him standing outside the library door, and her lovely blue eyes instantly narrowed in suspicion. 'Arbie? What on earth are you doing up this early?' she demanded. 'You don't usually get out of bed for hours yet.'

At this unwarranted (if accurate) attack, Arbie felt his blood pressure begin to boil. Was this all the thanks a chap got for finding a dead body and organising things with aplomb? Next time, he'd jolly well stay in bed until noon and let some other poor muffin go about finding any dead bodies that happened to be scattered about.

'And why are you standing there like a stuffed bear? I'd have thought you'd be in the morning room, guzzling rashers of bacon by now.'

Arbie gazed at her, speechless. The sheer calumny of it!

At the mention of bacon, though, his tummy rumbled audibly.

'Arbie,' Val said, her voice going quiet and uncertain now as she drew level with him, and she could see him better. 'What's wrong? Why *are* you standing there like that?' Her blue eyes were wide open now and beginning to look alarmed. She put a comforting hand on his arm. 'Here, old bean, steady on. You look like a gaffed fish. What's up?'

At the sound of her suddenly soft voice and the feel of her gentle touch, Arbie's shoulders slumped. 'Oh, I say, Val, something rather rotten has happened,' he confessed.

'Rotten? What? Where? In the library?' She looked behind her. 'Who? Is it serious?'

Arbie, reeling under the barrage of questions, could only look at her helplessly.

'Oh, don't give me that lost-puppy-dog look,' Val said, now seriously rattled. For all that she ragged him, she knew that he was made of the right stuff really. And for him to look so sombre, things must be dire. 'Just tell me what's going on. Who is it?'

At the trepidation in her voice, Arbie stood up straighter and pulled himself together. 'I'm afraid it's Bill, old bean. I know you were rather taken with him, and all that, and I'm really sorr—'

'He's been taken ill?'

Arbie swallowed hard. 'Worse, Val old thing. I'm afraid he's. . .'

Val swallowed hard. 'Dead?'

'As a dodo, old thing.'

Val walked to the nearest hall chair and dropped into it. She was still sitting there, deep in gloom, when the doorbell clanged, and Jardine passed her on the way to open the door. 'Ah, doctor, thank you for coming so quickly, sir,' they heard him say.

*

The doctor and Sir Bayard passed into the library together, both ignoring Val and also Arbie, who was still standing in self-imposed guard duty at the door.

Val turned her gaze away from him as she heard footsteps on the stairs above her, and then turned her face quickly away again as she spotted Agnes Warren's dowdy form sweeping around the curve. She just didn't think she could cope with that lady's fussing ways right now. Luckily, Agnes didn't spot Val, who was sitting very still indeed, and headed instead away from them and towards the morning room, whence breakfast was now no doubt being served.

Arbie found himself suddenly ravenously hungry, but a quick glance at Val confirmed that, should he suggest that they follow her into brekkers, she would have something scathing to say about it. No two ways about it, he was probably stuck there for the duration of whatever consultations would have to go on. He only hoped the others had the decency to leave him the odd kipper or two. Perhaps a sausage. A few morsels of scrambled eggs. . .

Hard on Agnes's heels came the Potts-Gibbons, who were talking quietly between themselves, and, like Agnes, failed to spot the silent Arbie and Val further down the hallway. A few minutes later, Elizabeth and her daughter came down, and although Bernie spotted Val, Val quickly shook her head at her, and the other girl, after a slight frown of puzzlement, carried on walking beside her mother.

Once again, it fell silent.

Then, after what felt like an age, but almost certainly wasn't, the library door opened again, and the doctor and Sir Bayard stepped out into the hall.

Doctor Pinchcliffe, a dapper, dark-haired little man who could have been any age between thirty and fifty, was talking smoothly. 'So it's best if I stay until the authorities arrive. No chance of signing a death certificate, as I've explained, but it seems at first sight clear enough. And finding that bottle of Veronal in his pocket only . . . oh. Sorry.' He broke off abruptly as he spotted Val, who was now rising slowly to her feet.

The doctor bowed to her and then glanced at Sir Bayard. 'I think it's best if we keep this door locked until,' he glanced again at Val, a pale and lovely young lady who shouldn't be burdened with the harsher facts of life, and lowered his voice theatrically, 'the police arrive.'

Arbie, catching his host's eye and interpreting his silent look without any trouble at all, nodded gravely, then turned to Val and forced a smile onto his face. 'Come on then, Val old bean, let's go and join the others. I think we could both do with a strong cup of tea, what?'

CHAPTER FIVE

In the morning room, with the table laid out for breakfast, Arbie noticed that everyone else was now present, including Lady Sybil, who must have come down another staircase rather than the one in the main hall. Or else she'd come downstairs one of the two times Arbie had been inside the library, and so he had missed her descent.

'Ah, here come the slug-a-beds,' Roger greeted their entrance jovially. 'Looks like a lovely morning. If it lasts all day, I might just take a rod out this afternoon. There's a private fishing reserve here on the estate, with a good salmon run. I know they don't usually get here until around May, but the weather's been so good, who knows? And there's bound to be plenty of other fish to be had. Fancy joining me, oh man of letters?'

Arbie could have fallen on his neck and kissed him. He'd had experiences before – two in fact – of what happened when you had police and a dead body in the same house, and he was not overly keen to repeat the exercise. And now this wonderful fellow had just offered him an escape from what was to come – at least for a couple of hours. 'Rather!' he said enthusiastically. 'Just lead me to 'em. I packed my favourite lures too, just on the off chance,' he admitted.

He then took up a warmed plate and began to explore the covered silver dishes on the sideboard, delighted to find good helpings of everything still left. Although he didn't have quite the same appetite as he might have had if poor old Bill hadn't finished his innings so precipitously, still, a fellow had to keep his strength up, didn't he?

Accordingly, he rationed himself to bacon and eggs but eyed a full toast rack with approval.

Val, he noticed, was desultorily sipping away at a cup of tea, and studiously avoiding watching the others eat. He wondered if she would agree to going back home early now, but if his previous experiences of Val and murder victims were anything to go by, he knew there was no chance of that. What's more, this time he was determined he wouldn't let her drag him into trying to find the culprit themselves or. . .

He brought himself up abruptly. Now just why was he thinking along the lines of murder? True, they had been mixed up in two murders before, but in this case, it certainly looked like suicide. Tragic yes, but mysterious? No.

No need to get the collywobbles, old man, he warned himself. And yet there was something niggling him. . . Mentally he shook himself like a wet dog and thrust all bad thoughts away. He was not going to get tangled in things, and that was that!

Sitting in the spare seat between Miss Warren and Lady Sybil (now there was a combination to make a chap's head spin), Arbie sensibly (cowardly?) turned to the spinster, who like Val, was limiting herself to a cup of tea only.

'Did you sleep well, Miss Warren?' he asked politely.

'Oh yes, thank you. The Chervilles have such wonderful beds, have you noticed? There was a lovely mattress on mine, and I slept the night quite through, which is unusual for me. I often wake up several times during the night, but not last night. Why, I was quite surprised when I woke up and it was already light. It must be all this lovely fresh country air. . .'

The lady waffled on in the same vein for some time, whilst

Arbie listened with barely one ear and tackled his breakfast. Once or twice, he caught Val's anguished eye on him but refused to say anything to the others about what they knew. Breaking the news of Bill Endicott's departure to his guests, Arbie decided firmly, was strictly a job for the man of the house.

And as if thinking of him had summoned him, at that moment Sir Bayard entered the room. Daphne, who was in the act of reaching for a piece of toast, commented idly, 'Is Bill still not up? I thought athletic types liked to be up and doing bright and early.'

Sir Bayard cleared his throat uncomfortably. 'Yes, er, speaking of Bill. . . I'm afraid I have some rather bad and shocking news on that front.'

The sombre tone of his voice brought a sudden stillness and silence to the room as all eyes turned to him.

It was Lady Sybil who broke it. 'News? What news, Bay? You do look rather frightful, my dear. Is something wrong?' Her voice, whilst striving to be resilient, had a certain reediness in it that made all the women in the room look at her quickly, and then just as quickly away again.

'I'm afraid something is, old girl. You'll have to brace up, I'm afraid,' her husband said, staring at her rather forcefully before adding quickly, 'I mean to say, we all will. There's no easy way to put this, but I'm afraid poor Bill is . . . well . . . gone.' He shrugged his well-padded shoulders helplessly.

'Gone?' Sybil repeated, her face going extremely pale under her make-up. 'You mean he's left the house? Without saying goodbye?'

'In a manner of speaking,' Sir Bayard said gruffly. 'He's left not just the house, but, well, the world as well.'

Val saw Bernadette Rowe reach out and clasp her mother's hand tightly. Agnes Warren gave a little gasp and sagged in her chair. Roger glanced at his wife, a question in his eyes, and Daphne, not noticing it, simply frowned.

'I'm sorry but are you saying Mr Endicott is dead?' Daphne asked, her soft, cultured voice robbing the words of some of their starkness, whilst at the same time succeeding in settling everyone's nerves just a little. It was as if, when women like Daphne were around, nothing truly bad could happen. Nothing that could not be handled in the right and proper manner, anyway.

The archbishop's daughter continued to look at Sir Bayard steadily, and he reluctantly nodded.

At this, Miss Warren gave a little muffled sob and buried her face in her napkin. Lady Sybil's hands clenched into white-knuckled fists. Roger sat up a little straighter. The Rowes remained utterly silent and still, as if afraid to move. Arbie's eyes flickered briefly over them all, before returning to his host.

'He must have been suddenly taken ill then, I take it?' Daphne said calmly. 'How awful. Do you know what happened? Was it his heart?'

'No, er, not his heart. And he wasn't taken ill either,' Sir Bayard mumbled unhappily.

Again, Daphne frowned, a genteel frown that didn't disrupt her outward features much, but both Val and Arbie had the feeling that behind her eyes, a quick and lively intelligence was diligently at work.

'He's had an accident of some sort then?' she offered next, her gaze still fixed levelly on their host.

Sir Bayard shuffled his feet and looked a little shame-faced, as if he felt the need to apologise for having to disappoint her. 'No – not an accident either, I'm sorry to say. Oh – dash it,' he finally exploded, 'the thing is, it rather looks as if the poor chap decided to cash his chips in early.'

At this, Miss Warren predictably gave another little muffled moan into her napkin whilst Lady Sybil opened her mouth then abruptly closed it again, biting off whatever it was she'd been about to say with a snap of her teeth that was audible. Elizabeth Rowe closed her eyes tight, whilst, in contrast, the eyes of her daughter widened significantly, making Arbie think (inconsequently to be sure) that the Rowes didn't mimic each other in all things after all.

Daphne's gaze flickered at the import of Sir Bayard's word, and she seemed to draw back into herself a little, perhaps in the instinctive reaction of an archbishop's daughter to the thought of suicide. Her husband moved his chair closer to her and put a reassuring hand on her back.

Val watched them all, feeling cold and a little sick, but also a shade defiant. She hadn't known Bill long – in fact, barely at all – but there had been nothing about him that led her to believe that he'd do something so drastic as to kill himself. He was too full of himself and of life for one thing. He'd radiated such a devil-may-care attitude that she was confident that he was one of those men who breezed through life taking it all in his stride. The sort of man to duck and dive, and probably sail a bit close to the wind every now and then, and maybe not care much about the consequences of his actions on others. And whilst that might be rather reprehensible, men like that weren't the sort to let themselves get bogged down by despair.

She could no more believe that Bill had taken his own life than she could believe that Arbie would ever do so!

'But, Bay, that's . . . that's . . . *impossible*,' Lady Sybil spluttered. 'I simply don't believe it.'

So I'm not the only one, Val thought mutinously.

For a moment, the Lord of the Manor merely regarded his wife with a grim little smile. 'I can't see why else he'd leave a suicide note, my dear,' he said flatly.

Val, shocked, glanced quickly at Arbie, who caught her look and gave a brief, confirming nod.

'Oh dear!' Miss Warren wailed.

'That's terrible,' Elizabeth said flatly.

'Have you called the police?' Daphne demanded.

'Oh – yes. Well, I had to,' Sir Bayard admitted, rather like a little boy admitting to having scrumped the best plums from the tree. 'It'll mean an inquest, you see, so there was no alternative. The authorities *had* to be called in. Although it'll mean all sorts of damned impertinent questions being asked of us, I daresay. And not just us, but the servants as well. *They* won't like it, I can tell you that,' he added darkly. 'Dare say half of 'em will hand in their notices.'

'Bay!' his wife chided, and he flushed like a reprimanded schoolboy.

'Well, my dear, they won't like it,' he muttered obstinately. 'It'll mean all kinds of fuss and unpleasantness in the house. And I must apologise to you all,' he added, looking around the table at his silent, shaken guests. 'I know you must all want to pack up and leave at once, and I don't blame you, but I think the authorities might prefer you to stay for a little while yet.'

'Yes, of course we must stay,' Daphne said flatly, speaking for them all, and it spoke volumes for the lady that not one of them thought of gainsaying her.

*

Inspector Felix Battle unfolded himself awkwardly out of the back of the local police station's only car and stood on the gravel, uneasily observing the splendid old house. He was forty-one years old, six feet six inches tall, and as gangly as a heron. He was already going grey and was dressed in a grey suit, which only further enhanced his comparison to that water bird. And a large beak-like nose served to add an unfortunate cherry on top of the cake, as it were.

For all that, his wife and his family loved him well enough, as did his superiors, for the Inspector was a man who liked to work. And although none of his colleagues suspected him of having an unduly high intelligence (which was a distinct drawback anyway in most chief constables' opinions) he tended to get things done in an unspectacular but comfortably predictable manner.

He was a Yorkshire man born and bred, and in fact, his father's family had owned and farmed land in the neighbouring valley since William the Conqueror had come over with his fancy French ways. And whilst Mr Battle senior was not quite 'landed gentry', he was a mason and a councillor of the parish, and had raised his family to be good Presbyterians. Perhaps that made it inevitable that when Sir Bayard Cheville had reported the death of one of his weekend guests, everyone had agreed (with a mutual sigh of relief) that the Inspector was just the man to send around and sort it all out to everyone's satisfaction.

After all, a reliable and solid pair of hands, who could be counted on not to frighten any aristocratic horses, was an asset not to be sniffed at.

Beside him, his sergeant, Paul Jellicoe glanced around the beautiful setting and tried not to be envious. A proud Welshman, his thoughts couldn't help but go immediately to the potential that such good sheep pasture offered his lordship, and he was busy trying to mentally tally up the probable size and lineage of Sir Bayard's flocks, when his attention was dragged back to the real work at hand by his boss.

'Let's hope this turns out to be as clear cut as the Superintendent made it sound,' Battle said, from his usual lofty height.

Jellicoe, nearly a decade younger and possessed of the dark hair and eyes of his ancestors, was used to glancing upwards whenever he had to address his immediate superior, and he did so now, smiling briefly. 'From your lips to the Almighty's ears, sir,' he agreed.

He had lodgings in the nearest town, and was hoping he wouldn't have to spend too much time away from his landlady's superb cooking and her equally superb daughter, who was finally consenting to 'walk out' with him on a regular basis.

The two policemen approached the front door which opened as if by magic at their approach. Jardine, who had heard their car arrive, greeted them cordially. He would have preferred it if they had arrived at the tradesmen's entrance, but things since the Great War had never been the same.

'Inspector Battle, Sergeant Jellicoe,' Battle introduced them briefly. 'I believe Sir Bayard Cherville is expecting us?'

'Yes, sir. This way please,' Jardine said. He led them quietly and without fuss to the locked door of the library. 'I'll tell the master you're here.'

The two policemen had only to wait in silent patience for just a minute or so, before the Lord of the Manor himself appeared.

'Ah, yes, thank you for coming,' Sir Bayard said, reaching into his pocket for a key. 'I thought it best to, er. . .' He waved the key in the air, then cleared his throat, and somewhat clumsily unlocked the door and stepped inside. 'We called the local doctor, naturally, a good man, by the name of Pinchcliffe. He's waiting in the lounge in case you want to talk to him.'

'Thank you, sir. We'll certainly want to do that a little later,' Battle agreed blandly.

Both men looked around them for a moment, taking time to assess the room before moving over to the silent man in the armchair. Sir Bayard couldn't help but notice that the Inspector did indeed have huge, flat feet (as all policemen were said to possess), and for a moment felt an insidious desire to burst out laughing. Naturally, he fought to quell it ruthlessly. He couldn't be seen giggling like a hysterical schoolgirl, after all. That wouldn't do at all.

Unaware of Sir Bayard's dilemma, Jellicoe got out his notebook.

'Name, sir?' he said, pencil poised.

'Sir Bayard Cherville.'

The Inspector's lips twitched a little, and he quickly put up a hand to cover it.

Jellicoe bit back a small, long-suffering sigh. 'I meant the deceased, sir.'

'Oh – quite; so sorry,' Sir Bayard said, going red about the ears. 'That's Bill Endicott. William Endicott, I should say.'

'I understand he was a guest of yours?'

'Yes. He's one of a party I invited down for the weekend. Have to show hospitality, and all that. It's expected of one.'

Battle gave the other man a quick look. The fellow was a bag of nerves, he mused silently to himself. Well, there wasn't necessarily anything in that, he thought placidly. It was bound to shake a man up, having one of your guests depart to the hereafter whilst under your roof.

'If you can give me a list of the other guests, sir, and their addresses, I'd be much obliged,' the Sergeant said. And as they conferred on producing this, the Inspector bent down to look at the dead man more closely.

He was a good-looking and well-set-up sort of chap, he supposed. Fair, dressed well and looked as if he wouldn't have too much trouble attracting the ladies. No wedding ring. His gaze moved down to the single glass containing what looked like the remains of a white wine.

And then he saw the piece of paper. With his handkerchief he picked it up and read it, one eyebrow rising slightly as he did so.

'Has anyone touched this, do you know?' the Inspector asked, interrupting his sergeant in the middle of writing down an address in Woodstock, Oxfordshire.

'I didn't,' Sir Bayard said quickly. 'But I think the chap who found him might have. Blast if I can remember now. You'd have to ask him,' he added. 'He's an author chappie, so he might not have been able to resist it. You know, it would be his sort of bag, wouldn't it? A letter. Writing and all that sort of . . .' He trailed off as the Inspector straightened up to his full, startling height and regarded him sharply.

'An author did you say?' Battle said, a shade ominously.

'Name, sir?' Jellicoe asked automatically. 'The author's name, that is,' he added helpfully.

'Swift. A. L. Swift. He writes this *Gentleman's Guide to Ghosts* and whatnot,' Sir Bayard informed them brusquely.

At the mention of this name, both the Inspector and the Sergeant drew in their breath sharply.

'Do you know, er, know of him then?' Sir Bayard asked weakly, disconcerted by their reactions.

'Oh yes, sir,' Battle said heavily. 'We know all about Mr Arbuthnot Lancelot Swift. Don't we, Paul?'

'Yes, sir,' his sergeant agreed without enthusiasm.

For it was true that their fellow police colleagues on both the south coast and in the Cotswolds had been most vocal about the author's 'helpful' presence during their respective murder cases. And now it looked as if it was the turn of the Yorkshire constabulary to have the dubious honour of making that gentleman's acquaintance.

Truly, Felix Battle thought bitterly, his cup of joy runneth over.

*

The doctor was sent for, and the Inspector met the dapper little man with a smile and a polite handshake.

'Well, this is a rum business,' Dr Pinchcliffe said, looking down at the dead man glumly. 'You'll be wanting your own man brought in of course,' he added, 'but whilst I'm here, might I be of some use?'

'Thank you, doctor. I'll just bother you for a few details if you don't mind,' Battle agreed. 'You were called here about an hour or so ago now, Sir Bayard informs me?'

The doctor agreed that this was so. 'And you found Mr Endicott just like this?'

'Yes. He didn't appear to have been moved, if that's what you mean,' the doctor said, anxious to be helpful. 'I also found this in the dead man's pocket.' And so saying, he withdrew a small bottle from inside his own jacket pocket and handed it over.

The Inspector looked at it and sighed a little. 'It would have been better if you'd left it where it was, doctor,' he said mildly, using his handkerchief to retrieve it, and then wrapped it up in the linen square as tenderly as he would swaddle a baby.

The little man flushed slightly, and then held up his hands, which were still in very fine gloves. 'I nearly always wear these when making an examination, so I haven't smudged any fingerprint evidence as you can see,' he explained stolidly. 'And I thought it best to remove it and keep it safe. As you can see, it's Veronal – a common sleeping aid – readily available I'm afraid, but it can be deadly if you take too much. The recommended dose is 0.6 to 1 grain, as is clearly marked on the label.' He swept on, rather more coolly than before, 'Anything 3.5 to 4.4 grains can be fatal. I couldn't help but notice the glass with the remains of spirits in it and thought, under the circumstances, it would be best to remove the bottle and keep it safe.'

'Indeed,' Battle said expressionlessly.

The little doctor, who hadn't taken at all to having to crane his neck to look so far up, found himself heartily disliking the policeman. 'I also noticed that there were no signs around the man's mouth – no bruising or reddening of the skin on the face, to indicate that he might have been forced to drink from the glass.'

'Yes, I noticed that too,' the Inspector said blandly. 'And in your opinion, is Mr Endicott's, er, state consistent with a man who has taken too much of this Veronal stuff?' Battle enquired next.

'That's impossible to say with any certainty, naturally, without the proper tests being run,' the doctor said cautiously, 'but there's nothing outwardly to suggest that death *couldn't* have been caused by the ingestion of an overdose. And if it turns out that there are traces of the drug in the glass. . .' He nodded down at the elegant fluted glass, and shrugged.

'You found no other signs of violence on the body?'

'I only did a very cursory check, but nothing stood out, Inspector. No bruises on his hands or wrists, and none on his neck or throat. But, again, once the chap's been laid out on the mortuary table, your medical man will have the opportunity to give him a proper examination.'

'And can you give me an idea of the time the poor gentleman, er, expired?'

Here the doctor launched into a lecture about how difficult that was, how ambient temperature could affect things and whether a substantial meal had been consumed by the deceased and when, not to mention the tricky calculations needed surrounding the science of rigor mortis, but eventually he wound down and, somewhat reluctantly, concluded that his best estimate was not much before midnight, and no later than four o'clock in the morning. But the Inspector was not to hold him to that.

'Of course, the Veronal might well be the gentleman's own prescription,' Pinchcliffe mused, but without much conviction, 'so I'd advise you to consult with his doctor on that. But I have to say, it's unusual for as fit a young man as this chap appears to be, to be prescribed it. Usually, it's not the young and healthy who have trouble sleeping. Then again, he may well have an underlying condition we know nothing about.'

The Inspector nodded. 'Very well. Well, thank you, doctor, you've been most helpful.'

The little man nodded, a bit stiffly, and silently took his leave. Jellicoe watched him go with a wry smile. 'I think you ruffled his feathers a bit, sir.'

Battle shook his head and growled something under his breath about people who couldn't leave things well enough alone. 'And speaking of meddlers,' he finished with a grimace, 'I'll have to have a chat with the finder of the body, and then briefly interview the others. Better get someone to come and take Mr Endicott away, Sergeant, then you can start interviewing the servants. I especially want to know if this young man's bed was slept in, who locked up and when, and who was the last to see Mr Endicott alive, and in what circumstances.'

Jellicoe nodded, then hesitated. 'Was that a suicide note you found, sir?' he asked.

'It appeared to be. We'll have to get a sample of this chap's handwriting and get an expert to check it, just in case. But so far, it appears to be all fairly cut and dried.'

'Well, that'll please the powers that be,' the Welshman said cheerfully, and left to do his boss's bidding.

Battle stepped back out into the hall and followed the sound of voices, which immediately stopped the moment he appeared in the doorway of the breakfast room. The scent of bacon made his tummy rumble, reminding him that he'd had to make do with only toast and tea himself, so as he glanced around, his unprepossessing face looked much more intimidating than his actual state of mood warranted.

To those seated at the table, the appearance of a scowling six-foot-six giant came as a distinct shock.

'Mr Arbuthnot Swift,' this apparition said, in a deep, resonating voice that instantly struck fear into man and beast.

Or at least, it struck plenty of fear into one Mr Arbuthnot Swift.

The Inspector's eyes, sweeping across the scene, took them all in in an instant. Sir Bayard he knew, of course, and the two dark-haired ladies had to be mother and daughter, they looked so alike. A very pretty, blonde young lady might possibly be a relation, whilst Daphne Potts-Gibbon he recognised from the papers, where photographs regularly appeared of her attending charity occasions and performing good deeds. The man who was sitting close to her was probably the husband. A middle-aged woman was sitting sniffling into her napkin, but for some reason the Inspector was sure that she could not be Lady Cherville. Which left a very striking ash-blonde woman with turquoise eyes who looked much too young to be Lady Cherville, and a rather lethargic-looking young man with too much dark hair, who was dressed in Oxford bags, white shirt and tweed jacket, and some kind of fancy tie.

'Er, yes,' this young man squeaked, half-heartedly holding up a hand. 'That would be me.'

'Inspector Battle,' the formidable visitor responded. 'I want a word with you.' And he crooked an imperiously beckoning finger.

Arbie gulped audibly, reluctantly got to his feet and made his way around the table. He was very much aware of everyone staring at him. It made a fellow feel dashed uncomfortable! Worse, he himself felt as if he was about to be arrested for something, which was hardly conducive to good digestion.

So, when he moved past her and Val pushed her chair back and got up to follow him out, he felt quite ridiculously glad of her support. It wasn't until they were back outside in the hall that Battle noticed her.

'And you are, miss?' he demanded.

'Valentina Coulton-James, Mr Swift's literary assistant,'

the poised young blonde said coolly. Her chin was up, and she looked ready to bite his ankles if he should try to send her away. The Inspector – who hadn't reached his rank without having learned a great deal about protective females – merely sighed a little and gave a brief nod.

'Pleased to meet you, miss,' he intoned, clearly not meaning it. 'Is there anywhere private we can go to talk?' He turned to the young man beside him. 'I shall need to talk to everyone in due course and get their statements.'

'I think the lounge is free,' Arbie said diffidently. He led the way to the lounge and watched the stork-like Inspector glance around and then pick the largest, most sturdy-looking chair in which to sit down. Arbie sank onto another chair, whilst Val, after a slight hesitation, chose one of the small sofas.

'I understand it was you who found Mr Endicott's body?' Battle asked bluntly, casting a quick glance from under his bushy grey eyebrows the lady's way, anxious to check on her reaction. As far as he was concerned, if she would insist on being present, then she would jolly well have to cope with the consequences; but he was relieved (and not particularly surprised) to note that, apart from a brief tightening of her lips, she remained composed.

'Er, yes, I did, that's right. Poor old Bill,' Arbie muttered.

'May I ask what you were doing in the library so early in the morning, sir?'

'Yes, of course. I went there to look up some reference books. Sir Bayard has given me the run of his collection, you see,' Arbie said. 'We're here researching the ghostly signalman and the ghost train that are said to haunt the railway line hereabouts, and I wanted to get background information on the area in general. Local myths and legends and any sights to see, all that sort of thing, you know.'

Battle regarded the young man dispassionately. 'Yes, I heard you wrote books,' he said flatly. 'Was the door open or shut?' he suddenly shot out.

'Shut,' Arbie said just as promptly. And, when the Inspector raised an eyebrow at him, he shuffled uncomfortably in his chair. 'I just notice things, that's all. Always have, ever since I was in short trousers.' He spoke apologetically, as if admitting to a fault.

'Were the curtains drawn or closed?'

'Closed.'

'They were open when we were called in.'

'I opened them.'

'Not the maid?'

'No.'

'Not the butler?'

'No.'

The rapid question and answers had Val turning her head to regard the two men like a spectator at a tennis match.

'I see.'

Arbie flushed. 'I opened the curtains so that I could see the titles on the spines of the books, don'tcha know? I don't think the maid or Jardine had got around to opening the room up yet.'

'You were up *that* early, sir?' he said. Arbie would have found his incredulity rather insulting if he'd stopped to think about it. 'Is that your usual habit?'

'Oh yes,' Arbie lied smoothly. Not for the world would he try to explain to this intimidating man that he'd only been up so that he could hog all the hot water. The policeman looked the type who probably took freezing cold dips in lakes in the middle of winter or hiked about the dales for miles in blizzards just for fun.

Naturally, Val's eyes widened a bit at his blatant fib, but she remained loyally quiet.

'What did you do when you saw Mr Endicott? Please be

specific,' the policeman said, reaching into his inside coat pocket and withdrawing a notebook and pencil. He usually relied on either his sergeant making notes or his own prodigious memory, but he wasn't above jotting down his thoughts as an aide memoire.

Arbie swallowed hard at this sign of officialdom. His uncle had a deep distrust of authority when it took it into its head to start recording a man's words for posterity (or a court appearance), and he'd imparted this caution to his young charge at an early age.

Manfully overcoming his inbuilt inhibitions, Arbie proceeded to give Battle a coherent, concise and comprehensive account of his actions, but his inner thoughts and feelings he kept firmly to himself. When he'd finished, there was a brief, thoughtful silence.

Then – 'You say you picked up the piece of paper on the table and read it?' Battle said heavily.

'Yes.'

'Just curious were you, sir?' the policeman asked dryly at this further evidence that people just couldn't leave things well enough alone.

Arbie flushed. 'I don't know. I'm not sure what I was thinking as a matter of fact. I was feeling a bit off-kilter I suppose. It shakes a chap up finding another fellow dead like that. Dash it all, I'd been drinking and joking and playing billiards with him just last night. I saw it and picked it up and read it without knowing why. Rather wished I hadn't, if it's any consolation to you,' he added. 'It was rather beastly.'

'Suicide notes usually are,' the Inspector agreed dryly. Then, in that abrupt way of his, he shot out another question. 'Known him long?'

'Only met him when I arrived here yesterday.'

'Know any of the other guests.'

'Not a one of 'em.'

'And you, miss?'

At this, Val jumped slightly, and automatically sat up straighter on the sofa. Now that it was her turn, the Inspector reminded her of a rather alarming geography master at her old school, who had a similar habit of shooting questions at your unprepared head.

'Er, no, I don't know any of them. Although I have met Mrs Potts-Gibbon once before, a long time ago. It was at an ecclesiastical conference. My father is the vicar of Maybury-in-the-Marsh,' she added, by way of clarification.

At this, Battle looked glummer than ever. 'I see. And what did you make of Mr Endicott?'

Val and Arbie instantly glanced at one another, each wondering which one of them the man was addressing now.

'Er, he seemed like a decent enough sort of fellow,' Arbie ventured tentatively. 'I found out we were both Oxford chaps, but not the same college, and he was a few years older than me, so our paths never crossed there. He did a bit of rowing, I understand. Told me he now lived in York. That's about it, I'm afraid.'

'And you, miss?'

'Oh, like Arbie, I only met him last night as well. I got the feeling that he was . . . well . . . he was very handsome of course, and very charming.' Here she shot a look at the young man who was, presumably, her employer, but Mr Swift merely looked blandly back at her.

'I see. A lady's man, you would say then?' Battle nudged her.

'Yes, that's the impression I got. Not that *I* was particularly taken in by him, naturally,' she added primly.

'Naturally,' Battle hastened to echo. 'When was the last time either of you saw Mr Endicott last night?'

'It was just before we went to bed, I think,' Arbie told him.

'Did anything about his behaviour give you cause for

concern? Was he unduly taciturn, perhaps, or did he appear depressed in any way?'

'Neither of those things,' Val said firmly.

'Had he had a lot to drink?' This was directed at Arbie, who shrugged.

'Only what we all had, Inspector. A cocktail or two before dinner. Wine with the meal. Nothing too excessive,' Arbie said. 'He wasn't drunk or maudlin, if that's what you're getting at.'

'I see. And at what time did you retire?'

'About half past eleven I think,' Arbie said, glancing across for confirmation from Val, who nodded. 'We'd travelled up by train that day and we were feeling a bit tired.'

'I see. And were you the first to retire?'

'Yes,' said Arbie.

'No,' said Val, at the same time. Then added, 'Miss Warren went up about an hour before us. You wouldn't have known that, Arbie, you were still playing billiards with Bill.'

'Miss Warren? Would that be the old maid . . . er, I mean the poor lady who seemed so upset at the breakfast table just now,' the Inspector asked.

'Yes, that's Miss Warren,' Val said primly.

'Was she a particular friend of Mr Endicott's?'

'Oh no, I don't think so,' Val said at once. 'Nobody ever mentioned that they'd met before, and they appeared to be strangers to me. I think Miss Warren would have been dreadfully upset no matter who . . . I mean, she's a very dear soul, but perhaps not very. . . That is, she's a bit fluttery . . . oh dear. Let's just say she's, oh, how can I put it . . .'

'She's an old hen, Inspector,' Arbie put in helpfully.

'Arbie! That's rather unkind,' Val reprimanded him. 'I was going to say that she's somewhat of a sensitive soul, Inspector.'

Battle nodded. 'I see. So, as far as you know, was Mr Endicott acquainted with *anyone* else in the party?'

The Inspector saw both the younger people glance at each other, as if in silent consultation, before Arbie spoke. 'I think he only knew our host and hostess, Inspector.'

'All right. I take it that neither of you woke during the night? There was no disturbance of any kind?'

'No, slept like a log,' Arbie said with satisfaction.

Val merely shook her head.

'All right, well, I think that's all. Can you ask Mr and Mrs Potts-Gibbon to come in next? Oh, and Mr Swift,' he added sternly, as the other man made to rise. 'I know all about your, er, little forays, into police investigations in the past, and whilst that might have been tolerated *down south*' – he said the last two words in the same tone as he might have said 'outer Mongolia' – 'it won't be tolerated *here*. Understood?'

'Oh, clear as crystal, Inspector,' Arbie said happily. 'You can take my word for it, our noses will be restricted absolutely to our own business. Isn't that right, Val?' he said, giving her a telling look.

Val smiled sweetly at them both. 'Of course, Inspector. We wouldn't *dream* of interfering.'

CHAPTER SIX

'Well?' Battle said to his sergeant, an hour or so later, as the two men met back in the library. The mortuary van had just removed Bill Endicott's body to the local hospital, where the police surgeon was waiting for him, and the Welshman was quickly scanning his notes.

'Right, sir. It seems the butler does his rounds when the last guest has gone up to bed, checking that the doors and windows are all locked and such. He also checks each room to make sure any fires are banked down, and the fireguards are in place and whatnot, and he says all the lights were out, and the library door shut at a quarter past midnight.'

'Last ones to go up?'

'The Chervilles, sir, as you might expect. The maid who sees to Mr Endicott's room said the bed definitely hadn't been slept in. The butler confirms that Mr Endicott retired a few minutes after midnight.'

'That tallies with what Sir Bayard said. According to him, Endicott and the Potts-Gibbons couple all went up the stairs together at around about the same time. Any of the servants have anything to say about the dead man?'

'Nothing out of the ordinary, sir. The maids all liked him, but I got the impression that the butler was less impressed.'

'Yes, I thought that might be the case,' Battle said with a

brief, humourless smile. 'Any of them admit to seeing him any time after they'd all gone to their own rooms? Nobody heard a strange sound and went to investigate, that sort of thing?'

'No, sir. The man's valet said his master rang for him at just gone midnight, and he went in and turned down the bed and laid out his nightclothes and whatnot. He asked if Mr Endicott wanted a night cap, but was told no, and was dismissed. That's the last time he saw him.'

'All right.' Battle nodded. 'So, what it amounts to is this. The dead man comes here for a weekend party, knowing none of the other guests. He dines, seems normal in his manner, eats a good dinner, and retires to his bedroom. He doesn't undress though and at some point in the early hours, goes downstairs with a bottle of Veronal to the library, where he pours himself a drink and adds a lethal dose – drinks it and dies. Leaving behind a suicide note.'

The two men stood in silence for a moment.

'It all seems straight-forward enough, but why didn't he do it at home, sir? That's what I'm wondering,' the Sergeant said, a shade plaintively.

Battle grunted. 'Curious, isn't it,' he agreed. 'It's almost as if the chap had a grudge against his hosts. Or else he didn't want to die alone at home, with just that valet of his. Although, if that was the problem, why not surround himself with his proper friends? You'd have thought a good-looking and popular chap as he appears to have been would have a whole bunch of 'em.'

Then he shook his head and sighed. 'Well, there's nothing more we can do here for now. We'd best get off to York and start making enquiries there. See if anyone noticed that Endicott was down in the doldrums recently. Start up the car – I'll go and take our leave of the Lord of the Manor. I'm going to have to ask him to ensure that all his guests stay here until after the inquest –

which probably won't be until Monday. The coroner's away in Leeds at the moment, and that's the earliest he can make it back, apparently.'

'They won't like that much, I bet,' the Sergeant predicted cheerfully.

*

From his bedroom window, Arbie watched the police car leave with a sense of relief. A quick glance at his watch told him that it was not yet noon, and he very much wanted to get out of the house for a while. He supposed that the fishing expedition with Potts-Gibbon wasn't really the done thing. It would seem too callous. But there had to be something he could do instead.

Apart from wanting to escape the gloomy atmosphere, he had a nasty feeling that Val would expect him to do some work, or something even more dire, if he let her corner him.

He headed downstairs and as the fates would have it, the first person he bumped into was Val herself. She was coming out of the lounge with their hosts, and he just caught the tail end of their conversation.

'Of course we'll do as the Inspector wants,' Val was saying, 'but we couldn't trespass on your hospitality to do it. We'll find somewhere in the village to stay and—'

'You'll do no such thing,' Sir Bayard interrupted her staunchly. 'Wouldn't dream of it! There's only the village inn, and I wouldn't trust the blaggard running it as far as I can throw him!'

'Of course you must stay with us,' Lady Sybil cut in smoothly, eyeing her husband's reddening face with amusement. 'Really, Bay, you should watch your blood pressure!'

'Well, I don't like the chap,' her spouse grumbled. 'He *says* he was in the merchant navy, but if you ask me, the man was probably little better than a pirate. Sly, that's what he is – very sly.'

'Really, Bay!' Lady Sybil gave a tinkling laugh, then turned back to Val. 'But I agree that the Job's Rest isn't somewhere that a lady should stay. Amos Fairley doesn't have a wife, and I suspect the rooms there are somewhat less sanitary than you might like. So, of course you and Mr Swift must stay here as long as you like.'

'What-ho, do I hear my name being taken in vain?' Arbie asked, skipping lightly down the last of the stairs and joining them in the hall. 'I take it the good Inspector has been making demands?'

'We have to stay for the inquest on Monday, Arbie,' Val informed him. 'Especially you – I expect they'll want your account of, er, things.'

Arbie nodded glumly. 'Right you are.' Then, seeing that there was no getting out of it with Val standing right beside him, he turned to his host and forced a look of enthusiasm onto his face. 'I say, sir, I hope you won't think me a rat deserting a sinking ship and all that, but I really must get on with my research. I was hoping the offer of some old jalopy still stands? I was thinking about going into the village and getting some personal accounts of our ghostly signalman. I take it there are a few who claimed to have come across the unfortunate Mr Hoskins and his ghastly signalman's lamp in person, so to speak?'

'Oh yes – I daresay,' Sir Bayard said, waving a vague hand. 'Just head out to the stables. Postlethwaite will set you up with something. Good huntin'!' he added with a guffaw.

Thanking him, Arbie and Val set off.

Val, naturally, had her notebook and pen already stashed in her bag and ready for action.

*

The chauffeur was indeed able to supply them with a car, a Crossley that was used for the household's more mundane outings when the Rolls would have been considered unsuitable. It was somewhat prone to rust, and the pale primrose-yellow wheels had turned more of a sickly shade of beige over the passing years, but it had all the appearance of being (more or less) weather-proof. The springs weren't exactly new, however, and Arbie found the ride to be rather a trial on one's posterior, but luckily the village of Middle Stratton was only a mile or so from the manor. A signpost informed him helpfully that they were just over five miles from the sea.

'If this lovely weather holds, we must take a trip out to the coast,' Arbie mused, braking to let a young leveret survive its mad dash across the road with its big ears intact.

'That would be nice,' Val agreed, then felt obliged to add sternly, 'but only once we've done all the research that we need for the book. Who knows – if we hunt around a bit, we might come across a quaint little fishing village nobody's discovered yet that you can recommend for the guide.'

Arbie, who'd had a lazy day spent on some deserted beach in mind (with a full picnic hamper, of course), sighed heavily.

Middle Stratton was a standard specimen of its kind, boasting a church, a pub, a village shop and a village green, with the usual straggle of various cottages and houses disappearing around bendy, narrow lanes. He pulled up beside the village green, where a grocer's cart stood nearby, the horse grazing contentedly on the grass on offer. Out here in the wilder parts of the countryside you still saw more of this mode of transport than you did of automobiles and vans.

That the Crossley was recognised immediately as belonging

to the manor was obvious from the way the villagers began to twitter amongst themselves when Arbie and Val stepped out of it. When you expected Postlethwaite and got strangers instead, it was indeed a red flag day.

'Where do we start?' Val asked, looking around curiously. She was dressed in a navy-blue dress with a long velvet collar of a lighter blue that matched her eyes perfectly. Her long blonde hair had been transformed into a fetching chignon by the enthusiastic lady's maid who took more delight in Val's locks than she did herself, and every male eye in the vicinity had turned to look at her.

These male eyes consisted of the grocer's boy, who was returning to his cart after making his deliveries to the shop, an old man sitting on the wall surrounding the churchyard who, judging by the disreputable state of his trousers and tatty jumper had probably been a shepherd all his working life, and two farmhands who were walking past carrying mattocks.

'The shop,' Arbie said firmly. Had he been alone, he'd have headed straight for the inn, the hotbed of gossip in any village, but after hearing Sir Bayard's opinion on the landlord, there was no way he was going to take Val in there.

The customers in the shop instantly fell silent as the little bell set over the door stopped jingling and all eyes had turned to find two young toffs entering the premises. An old man, stooped by some problem with his back, respectfully tugged at his cap. Val gave him a charming smile that pleased him enormously.

Arbie, looking around at the goods on offer, decided that he didn't need a tin of cocoa powder, nor any bootlaces, and most definitely wanted nothing to do with the rather vicious home-made toffee that had stuck to the inside of a vast glass jar. Instead, he played it safe.

'A copy of the local paper please, a packet of matches and some stamps. Oh, and a tin of tobacco.' He named the brand he'd seen lying on one of the tables back at the manor, hoping that it was the squire's choice. Had to keep your host happy, what?

The owner of the shop, a middle-aged stick-thin woman with sharp eyes, a sharp nose and an even sharper chin, set about gathering the purchases together, whilst the rest of her customers, mostly well-padded women in well-worn coats and hats, huddled together like nervous sheep and watched him as if he were a stray collie entering their fold.

'Lovely day, isn't it?' Arbie offered up hopefully. 'Jolly warm for April and all that.'

'Yes, we've been lucky with the spring this year.' It was the shop owner who spoke, but her eyes were riveted on Val's hair. Clearly, she'd never seen anything quite like it.

'We're here about the ghost,' Val said flatly. Unlike Arbie, she had no misconceptions about their chances of wheedling their way into any of the villager's good books and had decided to get straight down to business. 'Mr Swift writes books,' she continued in the same no-nonsense vein, and Arbie abruptly flushed as all eyes turned censoriously on him.

'Oh. Well. Somebody has to, I suppose,' one of the women muttered, probably trying to be kind.

'We've been told the ghost of a signalman is sometimes seen in these parts?' Val said, turning – obviously – to the stooped old gentlemen and giving him another smile. 'I was hoping you might know something about it?'

'Oh, ah, that'll be 'yon Jethro Hoskins,' the man obliged, his voice as thin and piping as a flute. 'Fifty 'nor more a year ago it were, now, I reckon, when t' goods train heading to Leeds crossed the bridge over the gully and it collapsed under 'em. Killed the driver and the fireman, o' course.'

There was a little murmur of pity from the rest of the listeners, but no one interrupted the speaker. Clearly the stooped old boy was a man who commanded some respect. 'There had been a fierce bad storm t' night afore, or so they do say, and they reckon ol' Jethro had gone to check t' state of t' bridge. When he did, he didn't like the look o' it, so when he heard the train a-comin', he ran across the bridge swinging his lantern like to warn the driver, but he were too late.'

A collective sigh went around the room.

'They reckon he tried to jump to one side to avoid the engine, like, but t' bridge were too narrow, see, and he got crushed. Then the bridge went and collapsed as well, and he went down with the train, kit and caboodle. Well, they sent some young men down to recover the bodies o' the fireman and the driver from the engine, and they were buried decent enough, like in their own villages, but they never did find poor ol' Jethro. They reckon, 'cause he wasn't in the actual train, the water carried him off. The river 'twere that high, see, on account of the storm and all the rain and run-off from t' hills, and he was washed clean out to sea. Poor blighter. Us villagers had a whip round for him and the stone mason made a memorial for him. It's set in the churchyard yonder, under the ol' yew tree.' He tried to point out of the window towards the churchyard wall, but his stooped shoulders left him unable to raise his arm fair enough, and he ended up pointing at a stack of corned beef tins instead.

Again, another murmur, this time of civic pride, rippled through the listening women.

'Now, they do say, those that work on t' railway, that sometimes the engineers and drivers still see a ghostly red signal light when they approach that bridge. Yes, 'um do, so they do!' He nodded at this so emphatically that Arbie was afraid the old boy might fall over. As it was, he had to take a firm grip on his walking stick to remain upright. 'Course, t' bridge was rebuilt whilst the ol' Queen was still on t' throne, God Bless Her, better 'n before they reckon, so it's safe as houses now, but it do give the drivers and engineers a turn when they see a red light a-shinin' when t'aint nobody there.' At this, he ran abruptly out of breath and stood there sucking in air.

Arbie gulped in a bit himself. 'I imagine it does,' he agreed faintly.

'And what about the devil train?' Val asked pleasantly, and there fell a deadly, hostile silence.

Even the stooped old man seemed to withdraw into himself, like a tortoise pulling his head back into his shell.

'Sorry, young miss, don't know what you're a-talking about there,' the old man said apologetically, and then waving his stick in a gesture of goodbye in the general direction of the shop owner, he turned and toddled off.

Val turned her energies back to the proprietress, eyes glinting with the light of battle. 'We have it on very good authority' – she stretched the truth a bit without batting an eye – 'that a ghost train can be seen coming through the valley sometimes. Shooting flames from its stack. Apparently, its glow can be seen for miles around.'

The woman behind the counter sniffed through her sharp nose and tried to put a smile on her face. Arbie really wished she wouldn't. The effect was quite hideous.

'Somebody's been telling you tall tales, I reckon, young miss. T'ain't no such thing as a ghost train.' Here she tried a nonchalant laugh, which came off about as well as her attempt at a friendly smile. 'Stands to reason, don't it?' she pushed on gamely. 'Jethro, bless him, was flesh and blood, and if his restless spirit still roams about, feeling guilty for failing to stop the train, well, then, that's one thing, and all right and proper, I'm sure. Makes sense, don't it? But how can a machine become a ghost? A great hulking piece of metal can't have a soul, can it? Which means it can't rightly become a spirit, can it? That's just plain daft, that is, ain't it? That's what I say. Ain't that right, ladies?' she appealed to the others.

There was a general mumble of agreement at this, and the shopkeeper nodded in gratification. 'Now then, was you wanting anything more?' she asked briskly, holding out her hand emphatically.

Arbie, galvanised into digging into his pockets for coins to pay his bill, quickly stepped forward to receive his goods. The tobacco, matches and stamps he allocated to his various pockets, and the newspaper he tucked neatly under his arm.

Val, not at all intimidated by the silent audience, moved up to stand beside him. 'Has anyone here in the village seen Mr Hoskins? With their own eyes, I mean. If so, we really would like to talk to them. Although I suppose a second-hand account from someone else will do at a push.'

'For the book, is it?' a timid voice piped up from amongst the small herd of shoppers behind them.

'Yes, that's right,' Val said, turning away from the gimlet eye of the owner. 'Anyone who's seen the signalman's lamp might get a mention too. Isn't that right, Mr Swift?'

'Eh? Oh, yes, certainly, if they don't mind seeing their name in print,' Arbie agreed. 'Mind you, some of the people I talk to like to remain anonymous, of course.'

'I reckon ol' Andy Batty won't care about the fame so much, just so long as you oblige him by pouring a good quantity of liquor down his throat, the rascal,' a particularly portly woman with fierce red hair muttered.

'The old soak,' someone else whispered.

There was a nervous tittering at this.

'I take it this Mr Batty's been up close and personal with Jethro then?' Arbie asked amiably.

'So he *says*,' the woman with the red hair felt emboldened enough to snort. 'He's been happy enough telling all and sundry the tale of how he ran into the signalman for nigh on these thirty years or more. Don't suppose he'll have any trouble telling it one more time.'

'Splendid! And where might I find this excellent witness?' Arbie asked, already having a good idea, and not much liking it.

'In the Job's Rest, where else?' It was the shop owner who spoke.

Arbie's heart sank. 'Yes, I thought you might say that.' He sighed.

*

The Job's Rest was situated where quite a lot of village pubs are, right next to the church. Some said this was so that the parson, after giving his Sunday sermon railing against the 'demon drink', didn't have far to go to slake his thirst after thundering on about so much hellfire. More charitable souls said that it was so that the mourners at funerals didn't have far to go for a reviving restorative.

This particular example of the village pub was one of those long, low buildings with windows set high into the eaves. Half of it was thatched, but an extension put on a hundred years or so ago was tiled. It was built of good, weathered York stone but had a mishmash of windows, acquired over the centuries, giving it a raffish, cobbled-together air.

The sign, swinging on noisy hinges from one crooked gable, depicted an Old Testament prophet type approaching a welcoming light in a far off-building, but Arbie, looking at the inn's disintegrating thatch and warped front door, decided that if he'd been Job, he'd have kept right on walking.

Luckily, there was a beer garden to be seen set at one side, and leading Val firmly into the somewhat overgrown shrubbery, he brushed off a lichen-covered ancient wooden bench set under an equally lichened beer table and looked around nervously. A passing robin gave him a beady eye back.

'Don't worry – nobody will notice me here. And even if they did, they couldn't possibly know Daddy,' Val told him. 'So it's not going to get back to his ears that you brought me here. Oh Arbie, do stop looking like a nervous donkey and go and bring me a lemonade,' she said crossly. 'I promise not to step foot inside the beastly place,' she promised, nodding towards the seedy inn.

Arbie wilted in relief. 'Thanks, old bean. You're a sport, Val. I always said so.'

Val brushed away the compliment, but her cheeks became a little pink. Then she straightened her tennis-honed shoulder muscles and said sternly, 'You just be sure to come back out here with this Andrew person in tow so that I can hear what he has to say as well. You need me to take the notes,' she pointed out, inarguably. 'No gossiping at the bar and then coming back to me sozzled with some half-hearted second-hand account of things.'

'Val! I'm never sozzled,' Arbie said, hurt. Then, shifting a little from foot to foot under her level blue gaze, qualified reluctantly, 'Well, never in the middle of the day, anyway.'

With that, he turned smartly on his heels and disappeared inside.

She could only have been sitting there in pensive silence for less than a minute or so, however, when a voice cried out unexpectedly from the direction of a holly bush, making her nearly jump out of her skin.

'Valentina Coulton-James! As I live and breathe – fancy meeting you here of all places!'

Aghast, Val half-turned on the bench and watched a young man step into the garden from the lane and walk towards her across the unmown, weedy grass. Around five feet seven inches or so and sporting a mop of sandy hair, his light grey eyes were lit up with pleasure. She knew that he was twenty-seven years old and was the eldest son of a wealthy solicitor, worked as a junior in his father's firm, and that he lived in Stow-on-the-Wold, a market town not far from her Cotswolds village of Maybury-in-the-Marsh.

'Geraint!' she said accusingly. 'What on earth are *you* doing here?'

*

'I say, Val, that's not the sort of greeting a chap wants to hear when he spots the love of his life sitting all alone and abandoned in some out-of-the-way backwater,' Geraint complained, sitting down on the bench opposite her. 'I say, you do look smashing!'

Val felt herself flush in anger. 'Oh, forget about all that soft soap and such guff. You should know by now that it doesn't work on me,' she said, watching his face fall and feeling like she'd just kicked a puppy that had been bounding joyfully about her feet. 'Geraint, I mean it! What are you *doing* here? And don't you dare try to give me some flannel about how you just happened to be in the area or some such waffle. *Nobody* would just happen to be in this area. I mean, just look at it.' She waved a hand to indicate the unremarkable surrounding hills and dales.

'Oh, well, you know, I just fancied a bit of a holiday,' the young man mumbled, pulling his collar (which suddenly felt rather too tight) a little away from his neck.

Val folded her arms mutinously across her chest and glared at him. 'You followed me, didn't you?' she accused bitterly. 'When I forbade you to do any such thing!'

'Oh, now, don't be like that,' he began miserably.

'Did Daddy put you up to this?'

'No, I swear he didn't. I swear it – he knows nothing about it. It was all my own idea.' And then, meeting her flashing blue gaze with a sudden stiffening of his backbone, the young man set his jaw firmly. 'Dash it all, Valentina, a chap can't just let a lovely young girl like you rush about in wildest Yorkshire chasing ghosts and who knows what, with a cad like Arbuthnot Swift!'

CHAPTER SEVEN

It was rather unfortunate that just as Geraint's angry statement rang out in the beer garden, Arbie, laden with two drinks and followed by a gangling gentleman with a newly pulled pint of his own, reached the bench and table.

'Here!' Arbie yelped, cut to the quick. 'Who are you calling a cad?'

Behind him, the grey-haired man with a weather-beaten face took a large quaff of his ale and watched the proceedings with interest. It had been a while since he'd seen two gentlemen of the upper ranks indulge in some fisticuffs. And, if he remembered rightly, very entertaining it had been too.

At this cry from a wounded heart, Geraint shot up and looked around. On spotting Arbie, who was taller, bigger and more handsome than himself, he immediately puffed out his – rather unfortunately inadequate – chest. 'If you're Arbuthnot Swift, then you!' he cried passionately.

Arbie gaped at him, truly baffled.

Now, Arbie had only three times in his life before been called a cad – whether justly or not, he staunchly believed, was still up for debate. But one thing these instances had in common was that he knew his accuser, and he had at least a fair inkling of why he'd been accused. (Except for the second incident, when he and Dingo Dodge had got totally pie-eyed at an undergraduate party, after which he had no recollection the next morning of whether he had, or had not, actively participated in dyeing the dean's cat bright green, with the inventive use of harmless food colouring.)

But this chap, he could have sworn, he'd never met in his life before. Nor could he, for the life of him, imagine what he'd done (lately) to bring about this performance of braggadocio.

'Arbie, this is Geraint Kirkwood,' Val said, introducing them, ice in her voice. 'Geraint, apologise at once.'

At this Geraint blinked, but understandably baulked. Not only was he now toe-to-toe with his perceived rival, but there was an onlooker in the mix as well, and no chap could back down in such circumstances. 'I most definitely will not,' he huffed predictably.

The man who could only be Andrew Batty glanced from man to man, then let his eyes rest appreciatively and approvingly on the young lady. It was clear by the look on his face that it didn't do lads any harm to fight over a beautiful lady now and then, and this one was certainly worth getting a black eye for!

'Look here,' Arbie began uncertainly. 'I don't believe I know you from Adam, do I?'

'No – though we've lived in the same area for a while, somehow we've never run into each other,' Geraint said, managing to sound insultingly pleased by this fact.

'In that case, what exactly am I supposed to have done that's burned your biscuits, old bean?' he demanded.

Geraint began to look as uncertain as Arbie, but he kept his chest puffed out, like a prize pouter pigeon about to be awarded first prize in a pouter pigeon competition. 'You're trying to poach my girl, that's what!'

Now, whatever Arbie had been expecting his accuser to spout, it certainly wasn't *that*. And it really didn't help that for one dizzying moment his brain misinterpreted this accusation and provided him with a mental image of Val in a big cooking pot, holding a stick of celery in one hand and a carrot in another, being passively poached. And even when that absurd image quickly blinked out and he realised the true nature of the man's grievance, his brain only boggled all the more.

Was it possible – could it be – that this poor sausage truly believed he had nefarious designs on Val? On *Val* of all people?

'What? Eh? Me?' Arbie finally managed to stutter. 'I never poached someone's girl in my life!' he yelped self-righteously, his voice ringing with anguish at being so traduced. Then, he added a little less self-righteously, 'Er, which girl is this we're talking about, specifically?' Because, even now, he simply couldn't believe that anyone, not even this absurd idiot, could seriously suppose that he and Val could ever tie the knot.

At this very unfortunate remark, Andrew Batty took a giant gulp of his ale and took a precautionary step backwards, no doubt anticipating a roundhouse of a left or right hook to be administered by the pouter pigeon.

But in fact, Geraint was so flabbergasted that he could only open his mouth, close it, open it again, then close it, reminding Arbie of nothing so much as a winded guppy.

'H-h-how dare you,' Geraint finally managed to get out. 'I'm talking about my fiancée, Miss Valentina Coulton-James.'

'*You're engaged to Val?*' Arbie said, rearing back like a startled horse. 'Well, you've been keeping that quiet, old thing,' he said faintly.

At the same moment, Val shot to her feet and decried, 'We are *not* engaged!'

Andrew Batty nodded, eyes gleaming. This was entertainment all right.

Arbie shot an unfathomable look at Val, who was too busy glowering at Geraint to notice. For his part, Geraint straightened his shoulders, refrained from glowering at Arbie and held out a pacifying hand to his beloved.

'Oh, but Val, you know we are really. I gave you my grandmother's ring.'

'You offered it,' Val corrected him icily. 'I didn't accept it.'

'I asked your father for your hand, and he was delighted,' Geraint persisted.

At this Val slumped back down onto the bench. 'Oh, sit down both of you,' she said crossly, and like well-trained spaniels the two men sat obediently. 'Geraint, we'll discuss our personal business, *in private*, later,' she added ominously through gritted teeth. She looked so irate that Arbie wouldn't have been at all surprised to see actual steam coming out of her ears.

Val speared the lanky newcomer with a ferocious glare as well. 'You too, Mr Batty,' she said severely.

Mr Batty (no fool he, and a quick learner besides) sat down quickly.

'I'm so sorry you should be subjected to such a scene, Mr Batty, especially when you've so kindly consented to help us,' she said sweetly, switching tactics without batting an eyelid. 'Geraint, Mr Batty here actually witnessed seeing the ghost we've come to research. Isn't that right, Mr Batty?'

'Ar,' the man agreed cautiously, taking another sip of ale.

Geraint gave a disbelieving snort at this and continued to glower across the rustic wooden table at Arbie.

Val made a great show of taking out her notebook and pencil, all the time shooting venomous looks at her (alleged) betrothed. She was feeling guilty about not mentioning Geraint to Arbie and feeling even more annoyed that she felt so guilty. After all, it was no business of his who was wooing her, was it? As she turned to a new page, she fixed both men with one final glare that, had they been butterflies, would instantly have pinned them fatally into a specimen board.

'I'm Mr Swift's *literary assistant*,' she stressed heavily, 'and will be taking down your statement. This will then be included in the next edition of *The Gentleman's Guide to Ghost-Hunting* if Mr Swift deems it worthy of inclusion. Is all that clear?'

Although she was nominally talking to Andrew Batty, it said much for her tone, that all three men nodded wordlessly.

Geraint flushed, but still looked stubborn. Arbie, not yet sure which way was up and which way was down, merely looked blank. Andrew Batty, sensible man, continued to drink his ale.

'Right then,' Val said hardily. 'Mr Batty, perhaps you can tell us about the time you saw the ghost?'

Andrew Batty shot a look at Arbie out of the corner of his eye and saw the author give a small nod. Thus encouraged, he straightened up a little and took a fortifying quaff of ale.

'Right then – let's see. T'were nigh on twenty-five years ago now, I reckon. At any rate, I was twenty-two, and coming back over the fields from ol' man Pready's farm. I were his cowman,' he added in explanation. 'And I was on my way 'ome to my ma's for tea.'

'What time was this?' Val interrupted, all business, writing steadily.

'Must'a been getting on for half-four, I reckon,' the cowman said, scratching his stubbly chin with an audible rasp. 'Mind, this were middle o' t'winter, so 'twas already nigh on dark, like. What's more, there was a storm a-coming. I'd seen it heading our way over on the far hills a'fore setting off, so I was a'hurrying home to avoid getting a drenching, like. Now, ol' man Pready's farm lies t'other side from my ma's cottage, which meant I had to cross t'track, just on over by Syke's Style. And that's when I saw it.'

Here he paused and took another quaff of his now nearly depleted ale. 'And a'fore you ask, I was as sober as a judge,' he added solemnly, giving Arbie a strong suspicion that he'd had to make this assertion many times before. 'Stands to reason, don't it?' he carried on defensively. 'Ol' man Pready, he weren't the sort to put up with a man being in his cups when he's supposed to be working and earning his wages, I can tell you. Ask any of 'un around here he remembers him. A right tartar he were,' he added admiringly.

'Yes, I'll make a note of that,' Val promised him with a brief smile, and wrote ostentatiously in her book. She repeated, '"Sober as a judge". Right, got that. So, what happened next?'

At this, the cowman's face became genuinely sombre. 'Well, t'were like this,' he began, and then shifted a little on his seat. 'Now mind this – I ain't going to make more of it than t'were, like, as some folks do who like to make themselves look big.' He scowled ferociously at them, as if he suspected them of thinking him to be one of these braggarts. 'I'm just going to keep it plain an' simple, and say what I saw and nothin' more. And if that ain't exciting enough for your book, mister, then fair enough, you just leave me out of it,' he said, looking square at Arbie.

Arbie, now sufficiently recovered in his wits to the point where he could string his sentences together, nodded. 'That's splendid – that's exactly what we want, in fact. No embellishments, don't you know, no bells and whistles. Just a straight-forward account of what happened. That's the ticket, eh Val?' he encouraged.

'Indeed, Mr Swift,' Val said primly, again shooting a fulminating look at Geraint, who at this display of secretarial wizardry, was beginning to look less like a pouter pigeon and more like an uncertain duck.

'All right then, now that's settled,' the Yorkshire man said, putting down his empty pint pot and falling quiet for a moment as he gathered his thoughts. Then he began. 'Like I said, t'were dark, but not midnight dark, but winter afternoon dark. I could make out hedges and such like and could still pick out the gap where Syke's Style was. Well, I'd clambered over that all right, and was just heading up the embankment to cross the railway tracks, when summat caught my eye. I wasn't thinking nothing of ghouls or ghosts, you understand, just thinking about Ma and me tea, and hoping it was crumpets. Or cheese on toast. So my mind were on me belly, but you know how 'tis, when summat moving brings you out of yourself and you suddenly take notice of what's going on around you?'

All three of them assured the man that they did.

'Ar. Well, so it were like that then.' Mr Batty nodded sagely. 'I was just about to put one of my boots on the iron bar of the first track on t' railway, when I see it, way off down the line to my left. A red light.'

He reached for his pint, remembered it was empty and gave a little sad sigh. 'Yerse, a red light,' he repeated thoughtfully. 'Well, I were a little surprised, cause I couldn't figure out what it were. I knew there were no houses down there, so it couldn't ha' been an oil lamp shining through some red curtains like, in some old biddy's window, or nothin' like that.'

He shook his head in remembered puzzlement. 'Well, I kept on crossing the tracks. I was still thinking about the coming rain and wanting to get home a'fore it arrived, see? I was steppin' out sharpish and had got to the other side of the tracks, and headed onwards up the path between the little stand o' trees that stood between me and 'ome. And I'd just passed this big ol' sycamore which marked the beginning of the trees proper, when I looked behind me and down a bit, where the railway tracks were, and blowed if I didn't see it again. A red light.'

'Can you describe it for us, Mr Batty?' Val asked eagerly, forgetting to remain on her high horse, so much had she been drawn into the man's simple but strangely compelling tale.

'Yes – was it very bright for instance?' Arbie asked.

'Oh no, sir, not bright,' the cowman said at once. 'Not proper bright like – and not big neither. It was a red glow – a spot in the darkness. But as I stood by that tree and watched it, I could see it was *moving*.' On the last word, his voice lowered a little.

And all three of his listeners became aware of a coolness on the back of their necks.

'Well, I can tell 'ee, it began to put the wind up me a bit then, see. Because I'd 'eard tales o' Jethro Hoskins ever since I was a nipper, see? As a kid I loved hearing about him – he was the local hero, an' all that – trying to save them men on the train and dying along with them and all. But, well, after you grow up, you don't believe in no such tales about the bogeyman or ghosts or barguests, do you? So, to begin with, like, when I first saw t'light, I didn't really think much on 't. But stood by that tree, all alone, with t'wind beginning to pick up – and seeing that little red glow bobbing up and down and getting slowly closer. . .' He shrugged.

'You say it was getting closer,' Arbie put in, leaning forward in excitement and putting his elbows on the table, fixing Andrew Batty with interested eyes. 'What gave you that impression?'

At this, the cowman scratched his head, and then gave a huffing sort of a laugh. 'Don't rightly know, really. Except to say that it started off just a red pin-prick o' light, like, and now it was more of a glow the size of an egg. And t'way it moved . . . sort of see-sawing from side to side, like. It took me a little while to understand what t'movement reminded me of – and when it did . . . well, I took to my heels,' he added, looking and sounding a little shame-faced now. 'And never did I look back, I can tell 'ee! Now then.' And he nodded emphatically.

'But what did it remind you of, man?' It was Geraint who was first to get out the question that they'd all intended to ask.

'Well, it looked like a lamp would move if someone was walking along the tracks with it hanging down from one hand,' Andrew said, as if the answer was obvious. 'You know, how it moved a little with each step someone was takin'.'

'And you say this red light was moving parallel with the railway tracks?' Arbie asked.

'Oh ar, no question o' *that*!' Andrew said flatly.

'But did you see who was carrying it?' Val asked, with some effort managing to keep her tone steady and professional.

'Nah – as I said, I didn't hang around long enough to check,' Andrew said, looking down mournfully into his empty tankard. 'I weren't standing more'n twenty-five yards from t'track by then, and like I said, it were getting nearer and nearer to me. I took off running for 'ome. And I reckon any 'un in my shoes would'a done the same, now then.'

Here the man scratched his unshaven cheek again and gave another snuffling sort of laugh. 'I ran into our kitchen just as the rain hit, so I never did get wet,' he recalled. 'Ma took one look at me, and o' course, knew summat was up. I told her to leave off, but you know what mothers are like. She nagged and nagged at me until I told her what I'd seen.'

'And what did she say?' Val asked, fascinated.

'She told me not to say anything to my pa, or he'd box me ears for being so daft,' Andrew said, with a wry grin. 'And he would'a too!'

'That's it?' Geraint said, leaning back in his chair and looking put out. 'There's nothing more?'

'Nah, that's yer lot,' Andrew said sadly. 'I told 'un before I started, I weren't going to make up any tall tales like.'

'But it was probably someone just walking home, like you were,' Geraint said, sounding disappointed.

'Oh ar?' Andrew challenged. 'Why'd he 'ave a red glass lamp then, eh, clever clogs, tell me that? A man who walks in the dark wants a white light so he can see where he's going. Stands t' reason, don't it?'

'Well, clearly it was someone who worked on the railway,' Geraint said.

'Oh ar? And what would he be doing on that stretch o' line, at that time o' night? There weren't a train due until the seven eighteen. And it's a straight stretch o' line for miles just past Sykes's Style. And why would anyone have any reason to stop a train there? Ain't nothing for miles – no stations, nothing.'

Andrew shook his head. 'Anyways, next day I asked young Billy Joiner, who worked as fireman on the Leeds flyer, if there'd been any works or doings on that stretch the previous night, and he said there were nothing doing. Even t'storm that came through were little more than a quick blast o' rain, nothing that could'a washed out the gravel from under t'tracks or had t'big wallahs worryin' and sending out people to check on 't.'

'Now *that's* interesting,' Arbie said quietly, then, seeing Val looking at him, added, 'that there had been a storm coming, I mean. It was a storm that damaged the bridge just before Jethro and the train met their joint end, remember? So now I'm wondering if there's any correlation between the ghostly sightings and the weather? Specifically, storms?'

'Oh Arbie, that's marvellous!' Val said, clapping her hands as she caught on. 'If we can get enough accurate dates for enough sightings, I can check and see. It shouldn't be too hard – ever since the Air Ministry put out weather reports for our brave airmen in the Great War, they've been sending out weather reports to all newspapers. The *Yorkshire Evening Times* will be bound to have published them, I just need to check out the back issues in the library!'

'Hmm, pity they'll only go back so far,' Arbie said. 'Our

ghostly signalman has been wandering about since Victorian times. What we really need is to see if we can get our hands on some amateur meteorologist's records, going back the past fifty years or more. And since those Victorian gentlemen scientists tended to make detailed records of everything from moth numbers to rainfall, I can't see why we shouldn't strike lucky. We'll have to advertise. That's the ticket.'

'I'm sure we'll find someone willing to share their grandfather's weather journals,' Val said, thinking positively. 'Oh, just imagine if we can link every sighting of Jethro Hoskins with a storm event! Our readers will love it! We can even recommend that they head up this way during the off-season, when storms are more likely to occur. It'll please the hotel owners ever so if we can give their off-season bookings a boost.'

At this perspicacious bit of reasoning, Geraint was now beginning to look from Val to Arbie and back again with troubled eyes.

When Val's father had first told him that his daughter had gone off to Yorkshire hunting ghosts with the writer chappie that she'd hooked up with in the last couple of years, he'd taken the impetuous decision to hare off after her, but he hadn't expected to encounter this! He had no more believed that Val could be serious when she'd said she wanted to have a paying job – and with a mountebank who professed to believe in ghosts, of all things – any more than he'd believed that the said mountebank could be anything other than a cad of the first order.

Who else would take advantage of a young, sweet girl's innocence in this way?

But now he was seeing with his own eyes and hearing with his own ears evidence that seemed to suggest that he might have got things a little bit wrong. Maybe this was a professional arrangement after all? Or was he just being taken for a fool?

'Now look here,' Geraint began stiffly.

At the same time, Andrew said, 'I need another pint,' and got to his feet.

'Val, type up Mr Batty's account at once please, and then get on to that weather research, would you?' Arbie said.

'Now look here,' Geraint said again.

'Right you are, old bean,' Val said happily, shutting her notebook with a veritable snap and swivelling around on the seat. 'I wonder if there's a train to the nearest town? They're bound to have a newspaper archive I can look at.'

'Now look here,' Geraint tried again. 'I can drive you to the station, Val. . .'

But Val was already off, without so much as a backward look his way, leaving just Arbie and Geraint eyeing each other uncertainly across the wooden table.

'Now look here,' Geraint began yet again, and then, when he found he wasn't interrupted, had to take a moment to sort out just what it was he wanted the other man to 'look here' about. Then, remembering, he said flatly, 'Have you really given Val a job? I mean, a proper job, all this writing lark and whatnot? With proper wages and such?'

'Yes, I suppose I must have,' Arbie admitted, still not quite sure how it had happened. And then a realisation crossed his mind that was so horrific and riddled with hideous pitfalls that he went quite pale. Because it suddenly came to him that, at some point, he was going to have to try and figure out how much he was supposed to *pay* her. Somehow, they'd never got around to such specifics before. And the thought of having to negotiate with Val what her new position was worth in cold, hard pounds, shillings and pence sent the shivers up and down his cowardly spine.

So much so, that, typically, he thrust the thought away to be dealt with another time.

Instead, he regarded Geraint thoughtfully. 'I say, old bean, is it really true that you've asked Val to marry you?' he asked. For he hadn't thought the fellow had been born who would take on such an endeavour.

Geraint bridled, and once more stuck out his chest like a pouter pigeon. 'I most certainly have,' he stated proudly. And then was instantly bamboozled as a wide, wondering smile lit up the other man's face.

'Oh I say,' Arbie said, overcome with emotion, and thrust out his hand to be shaken. 'Well done, old man! I wish you all the best.' And he shook Geraint's hand so heartily that the slender young man almost bounced on his seat. 'I can't tell you how pleased I am to hear it.'

'You can't?' Geraint said faintly.

'No indeed,' Arbie assured him joyously. 'Oh, I say, this calls for a drink. Let me buy you the best whisky in the house. Or would you prefer brandy? Cognac? What am I saying, a drink! Let me buy you a whole bottle!'

*

A jubilant Arbie and a somewhat discombobulated Geraint Kirkwood drank a little more than they should have, and were just making their way from the beer garden and back to the village lane, when a man emerged from the front door of the pub. The entrance to the Job's Rest wasn't the biggest, and it was set well back and under a low-hung thatched porch, so Arbie didn't see him until he'd hailed them.

'Hello there – is one of you the man who's writing this here book that everyone's been yattering on about?'

Arbie and his companion stopped and glanced behind them.

Arbie saw a man who was around five feet ten or so inches, very thickset, and with greying hair going thin on top and deep-set dark-brown eyes set rather close together. He had a not-very-clean towel casually tossed over one meaty shoulder and a tattoo of an anchor on his forearm, which instantly proclaimed him to be the landlord.

'That would be me,' Arbie admitted warily.

'Ah. I be Amos Fairley,' the man introduced himself, walking forward along the uneven paving stones towards them and pausing momentarily to peer into a bucket that had been left on the path. He didn't seem to approve of its contents much but didn't let it detain him, and carried on until he was standing next to them.

Arbie got the distinct impression that the publican was regarding him with something less than favour and began to feel a mite uneasy.

'I can't make head nor tails of it,' the man said shortly. 'Some 'un said it was a travel guide, and would be good for business, bringing in tourists and the like. But old Batty says you was here to write about ghosts. So, which is it, mister?'

Looking into the man's dark and unfriendly eyes, Arbie found himself instantly sharing Sir Bayard's opinion of the village innkeeper. But nothing of his thoughts showed on his face as he launched into a bright and breezy description of *The Gentleman's Guide*.

When he'd finished, the other man grunted. 'What folks *will* spend their money on,' he said insultingly, then shook his head and smiled. The smile didn't reach his eyes though, and his lips didn't seem to think much of it either. 'I dare say that dolt Andy Batty has been giving you all sorts of ideas, am I right? You shouldn't take much notice of him, if I were you. The man probably sees leprechauns too, when he's been at the cider. And unicorns, I wouldn't be surprised, grazing under the jubilee oak too, on the stroke o' midnight.'

Arbie smiled affably. 'Actually, I've been hearing about

something much less delightful than reports of unicorns in the moonlight. I've been reliably informed there's a devil's train to be seen hereabouts, belching sulphur and fire and whatnot. You ever seen or heard it, landlord?'

Amos Fairley threw back his head and laughed heartily. At least, that's what Arbie assumed the humourless gargling was supposed to signify. 'Don't tell me that old chestnut is still doing the rounds? Let me tell you something, young fellah-me-lad! That started years ago when we got the northern lights up here, and some new incomer from down south, who was drunk as a lord and never havin' seen such a sight, got confused, like. He were weaving his way across the tracks after having a kip in the ditch, and nearly got clipped by the Bingford milk train, which couldn't a'helped. It put the frighteners on him so much that when he noticed the fire in the sky he reckoned he'd seen Old Nick's personal caboose!'

'How distressing for the poor chap,' Arbie mused mildly, not believing a word of it. 'Don't happen to know where I could find him, do you? Tales like that are meat and drink to my readers, don't you know.'

'Oh, he upped sticks and moved back down south yonks ago,' Amos said. 'I heard he died in some boarding house in Bognor.' His tone seemed to imply that if you would go off and live in some boarding house in Bognor, what else could you expect?

'Pity,' Arbie said, then shrugged. 'Oh well, best be getting off. . .'

The landlord nodded. 'If you'll take some good advice, you keep away from the valley at night. There are poachers in the woods, and I ain't talkin' about the likes of Jonas Sorrel and his rabbit snares neither. I'm talking about lads who come down from the towns and sell meat to the markets. Rough lot, those are, and they don't take kindly to people poking their noses about in their business. Just a word to the wise, eh?' he said, tapping the side of his nose. 'Wouldn't want a fine gentleman like you having to deal with roughs like we get around here, know what I mean?'

Arbie did, indeed, know what he meant, and with a suddenly racing heart, he forced a smile onto his face, thanked the landlord kindly and sauntered off with a frowning Geraint in tow.

They were both careful to keep quiet until they'd turned a bend in the lane and the pub was out of sight, then Geraint began angrily. 'Here, I say, I didn't like that fellow's attitude! It was tantamount to warning you off! The cheek of it. I'd bet you ten shillings he's buying illegal venison off these poaching gangs. If I wasn't staying at his wretched little inn for the weekend, I'd give him a piece of my mind.'

Before Arbie could reply to this, however, they heard quick footsteps and looked up to see Val coming towards them, a look of chagrin on her face. 'Would you believe, I just missed the last train to town. Now I'll have to wait until Monday – hopefully I can do it either before or after the inquest. If not, we might have to stay an extra night. I wonder if Sir Bayard will mind, or should we book into a hotel in the nearest town, do you think?'

'I thought you were definitely leaving on Monday,' Geraint said, instantly suspicious again, and shooting Arbie a measured look. 'Least wise, that's what your father told me.'

'Oh yes, we were and it was all set, but – oh it's so horrible. One of Sir Bayard's guests committed suicide in the night, and so we have to stay and attend the inquest,' Val said, all in a rush. Then added, 'And don't you dare go scuttling back and telling tales to Daddy, or try getting me to leave right away either,' she added, 'or I'll never speak to you again. I mean it!'

Geraint turned angrily to Arbie. 'Is this true? Have you got her mixed up in something unsavoury again?' he demanded.

Arbie nodded glumly. ''Fraid so.'

'Well, what are you going to do about it?'

'Who? Me? What can *I* do about it?' Arbie asked reasonably, beginning to feel very hard done by.

'You can get Val well away from this place,' Geraint said hotly.

'The police have asked us to stay, and they won't take it kindly if we try and leave.' It was Val who spoke, her voice like steel. 'Not that it's any of your business, Mr Kirkwood,' she added for good measure.

'Oh Val! Don't be like that. I don't like this place – it's weird,' Geraint complained. 'We've got ghostly signalmen, demonic locomotives, an out-and-out villain of a pub landlord and now we've got chaps doing away with themselves in the night. . .'

'What's this about the pub's landlord?' Val asked.

Geraint gave a little snort. 'The fellow just practically warned us off venturing out at night, the cad! You ask me, we should all leave, right now.'

'He did what?' Val said, looking from one man to the other.

'He told us the ghost train was just the northern lights, or some such guff,' Arbie explained helpfully, 'then told us to keep out of the valley at night because of poachers. Apparently, they're a rough lot around here. Mind you,' he added with a thoughtful frown, 'I'm not sure I. . .'

It was then that Val put her hands on her hips and a grim little smile began to play on her lips. Arbie watched this happen with a feeling of utter dismay, for he knew exactly what this meant. And, sure enough, her next words sent his stomach dropping into his boots with foreboding.

'Of course, we're going to do no such thing! In fact, we'll go and do a ghost watch this very night. Midnight, isn't it, that this devil's train is said to rattle through? Well, we'll be there at the railway tracks waiting for it. Won't we, Arbie?'

'Eh?' Arbie said weakly. He had, obviously, intended to stay safely in his bed that night – and every other night that they stayed at Cleeves Lea for that matter.

'I forbid it!' Geraint yelped. 'It's too dangerous.'

'You can't forbid it,' Val told him coolly. 'This is our job, it's what we do. Track down thrilling stories for the book.'

'In that case, I'm coming too!' her lovesick swain said passionately.

'Oh, good show, old man, that's the spirit!' Arbie cried happily, reaching out and once more pumping Geraint's hand with heartfelt fervour. 'The more the merrier, I say.'

CHAPTER EIGHT

Back at Cleeves Lea Manor, Bernadette Rowe was feeling a distinct sense of déjà vu. For, once again she was walking quietly along the upstairs landing, and once again was listening out for the approach of a maid, her heart pounding sickeningly in her chest.

When she reached Bill Endicott's room, she cast a final look around, opened the door and slipped inside. She wasn't aware that she had been holding her breath until she heard herself expel the air in her lungs in a long hiss.

Quickly she approached the burr walnut wardrobe and opened it. She knew little about police inquiries and had been wondering all morning if the police had searched Bill's room yet. She had been hoping against hope that, in such a case of obvious suicide, they'd have felt no reason to be overly officious and might have confined their investigations to a brief and cursory check. But if she was wrong, and they had in fact made a thorough job of it. . .

Her mouth and throat went dry.

Bending down, her hands shaking, she reached inside and pulled out Bill's sports bag. She already knew it contained his tennis things, and she rooted around frantically until her hand found a tin of foot powder. As an athlete, Bill had known the importance of keeping his feet dry and free of infections, and the tin of powder had been more than half full.

Now, opening it, she breathed a massive sigh of relief to see that the level of powder was exactly how she'd left it. Holding it over the open canvas bag, so that if any grains should be disturbed, they would fall into the bag and not onto the carpet – or far worse, her clothes – she very carefully dipped her forefinger and thumb into the middle of the white talcum and slowly brought out a string of dust-covered pearls.

Even after having been so mistreated, the white orbs still glowed with the pride of natural pearls – their nacre-like glow striving to radiate beauty even though coated in the masking white powder. They were a very fine set of graduated pearls and had to be worth a small fortune. But then, when had Sybil ever demanded anything but the best, Bernadette mused wryly.

Carefully, she wrapped them up in her handkerchief and thrust them into her bag. Putting the lid back on the tin of powder, she returned it the sports bag, rearranged the tennis paraphernalia around it and returned it to the floor of the wardrobe.

Shutting the wardrobe door quietly, she tiptoed to the bedroom door and opened it a crack. The landing was deserted. Slipping out, she walked quickly back to her own room, where she all but collapsed onto her bed.

Disaster had been averted!

*

Back in the lane, Arbie listened to Val and Geraint arguing about whether Geraint should be allowed to attend the ghost hunt at midnight. Val was determined he should not come, but Geraint, bless his misguided little heart, was equally determined to come and play Sir Galahad to her very reluctant damsel in distress.

Arbie, wearying of the back and forth, had walked on a few yards to give the lovebirds time to coo (or screech) their way to some sort of compromise, when he spotted Sir Bayard Cherville doing something very peculiar indeed.

Instead of striding down the middle of the lane, for all the world like the master of all he surveyed (for he did, indeed, own most of the houses in the village), the Lord of the Manor was, instead, hugging a large hawthorn hedge that bordered the inn and looking as if he very much desired to become one with the shadows and greenery. What's more, he kept glancing around as if checking to see if he was being observed, and this furtiveness had Arbie instinctively stepping back out of his host's line of sight and hugging the greenery himself.

Apparently satisfied that the only two people now visible in the lane – Val and her paramour – were far too occupied with themselves to notice him, Sir Bayard ducked and wriggled his way through a vague gap in the hedge. This alone astonished Arbie, for the man must have snagged his clothes good and proper.

Unable to resist the lure of intrigue (when it posed no direct danger to his own skin, naturally), Arbie hot-footed it to the gap and very carefully peered through it. He was just in time to see Sir Bayard slip into the rear entrance of the inn. The presence of a compost heap in proximity to what was obviously an outside privy told him that this unsavoury entrance could only be used by tradesmen and the drunken sots who were tossed out on their ear come closing time. And was most definitely not the natural environs of a peer of the realm.

Arbie straightened up and frowned. He didn't understand this at all. Cleeves Lea Manor was stocked to the gunnels with the finest of spirits, beer, wine and liqueurs. Of course, a man might want to venture into the village to get out from under a wife's eye and the servants' feet every now and then. But why not just saunter in the front door, like everyone else?

Could it be that – contrary to what he'd told Arbie earlier – he and the alarming landlord might have some common business to discuss? But try as he might, Arbie just couldn't imagine it. The two men were poles apart.

Aware that a silence had now fallen, Arbie turned quickly and found Val and Geraint watching him curiously. Instantly, Arbie felt guilty, then angry because he had nothing to feel guilty about. Then he realised that a chap really had no call to go sticking his nose into another chap's business – especially that of his host, which rather smacked of biting the hand that fed him, and he felt instantly guilty again.

Remembering his uncle's long-standing advice on what to do if you were ever caught out doing something you shouldn't, Arbie casually thrust both hands into the pockets of his Oxford bags and sauntered back towards them, whistling an airy little tune, looking the picture of innocence. 'What-ho, chaps, is it all sorted then? Is Geraint coming or not?'

'Geraint is,' Geraint said defiantly.

'Well done, old sport!' Arbie slapped him on the back, causing that smaller gentleman to have to take a quick step forward to maintain his balance. 'We'll meet up after dinner then. We need to be out of the manor by ten-thirty at the latest. Be sure to wear dark clothes and bring a warm coat and a torch if you have it.'

'Oh. Right-ho,' Geraint said, slightly taken aback, as he'd expected to have yet another argument, this time with his rival. He was still half-convinced that these so-called ghost hunts were just the author's dastardly plot to have his girl all alone with him in the dark and he was feeling rather put out by Arbie Swift's seemingly genuine compliance.

'In the meantime, why don't you show Val the sights?' Arbie suggested, further confounding him.

'What a fabulous id—' Geraint began.

'I need to write up my notes,' Val said at the same time. 'Arbie, do you have your typewriter with you?'

'Oh, er, yes, I'm sure to have packed it,' Arbie said vaguely, for he hadn't so much as looked for it yet. As a successful author, he tended to loathe the thing.

Val sighed. 'All right. I'll walk back to the manor then, since it's such a nice day,' she said, hoisting her bag firmly over her shoulder.

'And I'll see you safely back,' Geraint said hastily, offering her his arm.

Val sighed and took it.

The moment they were out of sight, Arbie hot-footed back to the thin portion of the hedge, bent slightly at the waist and peered inside. A customer, who looked as if he'd had more than a pint or two, staggered outside and weaved his way to the privy. And as he did so, Arbie heard muffled voices coming from somewhere above the garden.

He lifted his eyes up to the bedroom windows of the inn and saw that one of them was slightly open. And through it, he could hear his host's distinctive voice. Although he couldn't make out individual words, the rumble sounded angry.

He now knew that Geraint was putting up at the Job's Rest but it was hardly the high season for visitors, and besides the inn looked as if it might have only one or two guest rooms to offer. Which led him to conclude that, as he'd suspected, his host didn't have business so much with Amos Fairley as with the rather dandified cove who'd got off the train at the same time as himself and the Potts-Gibbons.

Of course, that man might not be staying at the inn but visiting relatives in the village. But for some reason, Arbie couldn't believe that such a one would opt to visit such rural surroundings without good reason. He looked the sort who frequented night clubs that were regularly raided, and private casinos. Besides, when he'd got off the train, he'd glanced around to get his bearings and had only set off towards the village when he'd seen the signposting pointing the way.

So where else could he put up but at the undesirable Job's Rest? Arbie thoughtfully sucked in air through his teeth, wondering what Sir Bayard and the odd customer from the train could have to discuss. Curiouser and curiouser, as Alice in Wonderland would have put it.

Hearing a horse clip-clopping towards him, Arbie abruptly withdrew his head from the hedge and wandered towards the village green where he casually lounged on a wooden bench. A wood pigeon, sat in an elm tree opposite him, watched him without much interest.

Less than five minutes later, Sir Bayard popped out of the hedge, gave a swift look around and then set off back towards his manor, swinging his walking stick and looking casual.

Arbie admired his technique. His uncle would have been proud of him.

Arbie had just got up and was heading back towards the parked Crossley when he spotted the stranger from the platform stepping out onto the lane. He had obviously exited the inn via the front door, and glancing around, set off without much enthusiasm for a stroll.

Dressed ostentatiously in a black suit with silver accessories, he wore some sort of hat that wouldn't have looked out of place on a bullfighter or a Mexican bandit. He carried an ebony cane that he twirled constantly.

Now there's a wrong 'un if ever I saw one, Arbie could hear his uncle saying so clearly in his head that he actually answered him out loud.

'Too right, Uncle,' he muttered. And continued his journey back to the car. If he passed Val and Geraint on the way back, he'd give them a jaunty tootle on the horn and just breeze on by. The last thing he wanted to do was put a crimp in young Geraint's courting!

*

Dinner that night was an odd affair. Although nobody could be expected to be in high spirits exactly, it seemed to Arbie that everyone was more on edge, rather than feeling sad about the loss of one of their number.

Lady Sybil seemed to watch her husband whenever she thought he wasn't looking, whilst his host seemed in a worried, taciturn mood.

Arbie did his best to lift the atmosphere by relating some of his more comical 'ghost' stories, and Daphne Potts-Gibbon did her best to aid him by telling more genteel but witty tales of High Church, bishop's gaiters and the misfortunes of a stuttering curate.

Elizabeth Rowe was doing a good job of pretending not to observe Roger Potts-Gibbons, who, in turn, kept shooting nervous little glances at Agnes, of all people.

Arbie, seated opposite Agnes, couldn't help but notice that she was looking pale and as he observed her, she reached into her bag and took out a lace and linen handkerchief which she twisted nervously. Arbie noticed that, for the first time since he'd met her, her small hands were bare of any gloves, but it was the look on her face which held his attention the most. She looked – well, *frightened.* It gave him a bit of a start, for it was his contention that fluttery middle-aged women of her ilk were, in reality, as tough as old boots underneath, and when faced with an actual crisis, rather than little domestic upsets, could usually be relied upon to show the fortitude of a regimental sergeant major.

As the courses came and went, Arbie kept one eye on the clock. He was not looking forward to tonight's foray into the valley, but at least it would get him away from the odd, foreboding atmosphere of the dining table.

*

The ladies had retired to the lounge for coffee and Val was just wondering how best to make her excuses and leave. They'd explained to their distracted host over dinner that they'd be out until the early hours, but he'd merely said that Jardine would hear them when they rang the bell and admit them.

As Val drained her coffee, Agnes leaned across the coffee table separating her from her hostess and said uncertainly, 'Dear Lady Sybil, I hardly know how to ask for such a favour from you, especially at a time like this, when we're all at sixes and sevens, but would you mind awfully if I sent for my niece? Well, she's really my goddaughter, but we're as close as blood relatives.'

Lady Sybil smiled diffidently. 'Your goddaughter?' she echoed uncertainly.

'Yes, Samantha – Samantha Remington. Her mother was my best friend at school. Her father manages the Brightwell estate for the Earl.'

'Oh, we know the Earl,' Sybil said, looking relieved.

'It's just that I've never been to an inquest, you see,' Agnes began nervously, twisting her handkerchief restlessly between her fingers, 'and I know I won't be very good at it. I get so muddled and confused by new things, and I'm already feeling so frightfully upset, as we all are. This awful business with Mr Endicott has made me feel almost ill with worry. But Samantha is such a sensible, *competent* sort of girl. She left home to do a secretarial course you know, and then worked for a very well-known and established company in Oxford for a number of years, before returning to Yorkshire. I feel sure she'll be of great help to me, explaining how things work and just keeping my nerves steady. I know it's an indisposition, but I feel. . .'

Lady Sybil, sensing an even longer and more meandering plea was forthcoming, ignored the malapropism and cut in neatly.

'By all means, Agnes, dear, send for your Samantha. She sounds splendid! Just the sort of companion you need at awkward times like these.'

Agnes's wrinkled, worried face relaxed into a wavering smile. 'Oh, thank you so much. I'll telephone her at once then, if I may? She's bound to have a friend who can run her over tomorrow – she knows ever so many young people with cars and things.'

Sybil, who'd just retrieved a black onyx and silver cigarette holder from her purse, waved both hand and holder in a vaguely encouraging gesture, and turned immediately to Daphne who was seated on her left, barely noticing as Agnes gratefully scuttled away. Val took this opportunity to explain to her hostess that she and Arbie really should prepare themselves for that night's ghost-hunting, and then excused herself.

Upstairs she dressed in her darkest clothes and donned her sensible walking shoes, packed for just such an occasion. When she knocked on Arbie's door a few minutes later, she saw that he was dressed in dark clothes as well and was carrying a large lamp, as yet unlit.

'Don't worry, old bean,' he said cheerfully, holding the paraffin lamp aloft. 'This one's got clear glass – so it'll only produce a nice white light. We wouldn't want to get mistaken by any of the locals for old Jethro Hoskins, would we?'

*

As pre-arranged, they met up with a very sceptical Geraint Kirkwood outside the inn and, proceeding in the Crossley a mile or so out of the village, began to scout around for an advantageous viewpoint.

They wasted a lot of time as Arbie really wanted to find the stretch of railway where Andrew Batty had had his encounter all those years ago, but since none of them knew either the direction of the farm where he'd been cowman or his mother's cottage, they eventually had to admit defeat and drove farther away from the village.

Arbie was pleased to see that there was a nearly full moon, which was shining a lot of pale light on the landscape, but not so pleased by the gathering clouds that were more and more frequently blocking it. After driving for about five minutes, he said cheerfully, 'All right, chaps, by my reckoning, we've now come far enough to have got a fold in the hills between us and the manor.'

'And that's important, is it?' Geraint drawled sceptically from the back seat.

'Shush!' Val reprimanded him primly. 'Kindly remember you're here on sufferance, Geraint. You're only here to observe and be a witness to anything that we might see or hear,' she informed him loftily. Then, having assured herself that he was sufficiently subdued, she leaned across and whispered to Arbie, 'Er, why is it significant again, old bean?'

Arbie whispered back, 'Remember Sir Bayard saying that you can't see the devil's train from the manor, because the track where it's seen is hidden from Cleeves Lea by the hills?'

Val clutched his arm in excitement. 'Right. So now we must be somewhere in the right area at least. I can see the moonlight glinting on the tracks for a fair way in each direction now, so we'll be able to see anything coming in good time.'

Arbie nodded. 'I checked the timetable, and there's nothing due until the milk train at 3.52am. Yes. This is as good a spot as any I think,' he agreed and looked around for a place to pull over to the side of the narrow road.

Since it was almost impossible to take any photographs at night, or sound recordings in the open air where every sheep bleat or wind gust distorted everything, there was very little equipment to carry, for which Arbie was grateful, and within a few minutes, they were ready to set off. And since they already had a fair view of the valley anyway, they didn't need to walk too far down a sheep-nibbled field to find a good place to stop. After spotting a handy tree trunk that would make a comfortable seat for the next hour or so, Arbie declared himself satisfied.

Val, no novice now to ghost-hunting, very smartly went about finding the smoothest, flattest part of the large trunk on which to perch her bottom and settled down quickly. Arbie found the next best spot, leaving a rather baffled Geraint to make do with one of the rougher areas available to him.

'I say,' Geraint said, once he'd done this, and striving to sound thoroughly unconcerned, 'this ghost-train business *is* all a lot of bosh, isn't it? I mean, we're not taking it seriously?'

'It's a reported manifestation,' Val said flatly, 'which means we give it due consideration. We owe it to our readers to give them as accurate an account as we can, after all.'

Arbie, who was certain that all his readers really wanted from his books were new places to visit and amusing tales about local ghosts to spice it up a bit, wisely said nothing. Val was clearly intent on demonstrating to her erstwhile paramour that she and Arbie were all about business and nothing else, and in this endeavour, he was heartily happy to aid her. The sooner the dozy legal boffin stopped looking at him with so much suspicion and concentrated instead on getting Val to the altar (and thus out of his hair), the better.

'So, er, have either of you two actually seen anything . . . [*gulp*] . . . er, that might be described . . . [*gulp*] . . . as, er. . .'

Arbie, kind-hearted fellow that he was, was unable to listen to a fellow chap suffer for long and said reassuringly, 'Don't fret, Geraint old boy, I think the chances of us seeing an actual otherworldly train are rather miniscule.'

'Oh, right-oh!' came the relieved response.

There followed about ten minutes or so of silence. Then Geraint said diffidently, 'So we really do just sit here and wait then?'

'Yes, that's really what we do,' Arbie agreed amiably.

Five minutes passed. Then, 'And we're also looking for a red spot of light too, are we?'

'Yes, Geraint,' Val answered him, 'if it's the signalman who shows up.'

'Eh? I thought Arbie just said . . .'

'We're supposed to watch in silence,' Arbie pointed out wearily, without the least hope of attaining such a blessed state.

He did, however, get at least three more minutes of silence, before Geraint's voice once again interrupted the proceedings.

'Anybody know what time it is? I mean, does Old Nick's engineer run his train strictly according to the timetable?' His voice was jolly, but Arbie could detect the nervousness behind it and couldn't help but grin.

'Shush!' Val hissed.

'Sorry. It's just, if this ghost train only shows up at midnight, why did we set off so early? We could have stayed indoors, in the warm and with a stiff drink for at least . . .'

'Shush!' Val hissed, running out of patience.

'Sorry.'

In the darkness, Arbie smile widened. Amateurs, both of them! He could keep ghost-watches perfectly well on his own for hours and hours at a time in perfect silence. Well, apart from the occasional bout of snoring of course.

His ears were now fully attuned to the sounds of the night. He was aware of sheep all around him, occasionally shifting about, but mostly content to lie still in the grass. Occasionally something forced into flight clattered about the treetops. And there was the faintest of breezes, rustling the low-lying scrub.

'I say, did you hear that?' Geraint said.

Val heaved a sigh. 'What?'

'Sounded to me like a sort of . . . whine. Faint, but . . . a whine.'

Arbie too thought he'd heard the same thing, but was not about to say so.

'I think I hear it too now,' Val said tentatively. 'Arbie, is Jethro Hoskins supposed to whistle or something?'

'No – at least not that I know of,' Arbie said, slipping off the log and standing upright. He walked a few paces forward and looked away to his right. He was aware of first Val and then Geraint crowding around him.

'Look over there – to the right. Do you see it?' he asked softly.

'What? A man with a lamp?' Geraint asked, aghast.

'No – the sky. Look at the sky!' Arbie said. At the same time, the faint singing whine was getting louder. But it was now a sound that was perfectly familiar to him. In fact, he'd heard it many times before in his life, and he knew that Val and Geraint would have heard it too. It was the sound the railway lines made when a train was approaching.

'The sky's faintly red,' Geraint said, sounding puzzled. 'But we've long since had sunset, and sunrise isn't for . . . Oh, by Almighty Cringe,' he choked. *'Do you see it?'*

But of course, they could all see it now. It was impossible *not* to see it. Coming from the right at great speed and belching fire and an eerie orange smoke from its funnel, a monstrous, heavy black locomotive came hurtling through the night towards them.

CHAPTER NINE

'I thought you said we wouldn't see a train!' Geraint shouted accusingly in Arbie's direction, as if this was all his fault.

Arbie thought that was rather uncalled for.

He was then further confounded by Val flinging her arms around his waist and trying to burrow into him, like a squirrel trying to wriggle into a hole of a tree, and he thought he might even have heard a little scared sob, and his conscience immediately smote him. For, ever since his encounter with the ill-tempered landlord of the village inn, Arbie had begun to harbour suspicions of his own about the so-called Middle Stratton ghost – or devil's – train.

Automatically, he put a comforting arm around her shoulder and tried to tell her not to be afraid. But the train was now at the stretch of track closest to them, and he doubted she could have heard him above the tremendous noise.

He looked grimly ahead, but it was impossible to make out the face of either the driver or fireman. Trying to calm his companions, he yelled out cheerfully, 'Don't worry, it's not as if it can leave the tracks and chase us over the fields, is it? And it'll be gone in a moment.'

As he shouted, though, his mind was racing. He was no expert on trains, but he thought he recognised the engine itself as an old class locomotive, not long out of commission.

It hauled only one large, windowless carriage. But by far the most fascinating thing about it was that fire-spitting chimney. It was extraordinary, and he'd certainly never seen anything like it before. No wonder it put the wind up the locals! The first poor shepherd or farmer to have seen it must have got the wind up, good and proper.

As it rattled past them and continued up the line, the fiery show began to recede, and Arbie found himself sniffing the air, looking rather like a very unimpressed Pekinese. 'Ugh – the thing stinks,' he said plaintively.

Val, who could now hear him clearly and instantly took note of the total lack of panic in his voice, abruptly lifted her head to look at him. 'You're not frightened,' she said, amazed.

'Eh? Me? No, of course not,' Arbie said manfully, wondering why on earth she should have thought he would be.

Val, who knew him so well, was about to make a pithy comment on that, when she felt herself being yanked away from his side.

'Take your hands off her, Swift, you swine!' Geraint yelped. 'I knew it. The minute you get the chance, you take advantage of her.'

'Eh?' Arbie bleated.

'There's a moon, you know, I saw you, taking her in your arms like that, you. . . you . . . you . . . Casanova.'

'But she was the one. . .' Arbie began hotly, then somewhat belatedly broke off, realising that accusing a lady of throwing herself at you wasn't the sort of thing a chap could do.

'Will you two stop arguing?' Val said, all but stamping her foot in temper. 'Can't you see it's getting away? Shouldn't we do something?'

At this, both the men stopped glaring at each other and turned baffled eyes on the slim, silver-haired girl in the moonlight instead.

'Er, do what exactly, sweetheart?' Geraint murmured doubtfully.

'Well, get after it of course,' Val said crossly. 'Follow it. Quickly – before we lose it.'

'It's on railway tracks, Val old bean,' Arbie pointed out helpfully. 'We already know where it's going – it's going further down the line.'

Val drew in her breath impatiently. 'Yes, but *where* exactly? We need to follow it.'

'Bit hard to do in a car, wouldn't you say?' Arbie said breezily. 'The road only runs so far parallel to the line, then the railway line cuts off cross country.'

'What do we do then?' Val demanded.

'Well, we could always settle back on the log and see if Jethro Hoskins puts in an appearance,' he said diffidently, and then, perhaps taking stock of the prevailing mood, added meekly, 'or we could go back and call it a night.'

*

'Well, at least we know it's real,' Arbie said, some minutes later, after dropping off a still fuming Geraint at the inn.

The outline of Cleeves Lea Manor was now in sight, but Val, sitting beside him, was still inclined to be mutinous. 'What do you mean?'

'Well, I mean we know it's a real flesh-and-blood (so to speak) train,' Arbie pointed out. 'You saw it, heard and smelt it – that was no ethereal otherworldly machine.'

'Oh, yes, I suppose there's that,' Val said wearily. In truth, now that the excitement and (yes, she could admit it to herself) fright had passed, she was feeling tired and lethargic. All she wanted was to get off to bed with a hot, milky drink.

'Perhaps we should stick to the ghostly signalman from now

on, eh?' Arbie said hopefully and was relieved when he felt her nod in the darkness beside him.

Jardine, as promised, was indeed on hand to admit them to the manor, and after Arbie had watched Val's drooping figure climb the stairs, he told the butler that he needed to make a phone call, and asked if the exchange was open all night.

The butler informed him that it was, and after wishing the gentleman good night, retired gratefully to his own bed.

Arbie stepped into the telephone booth in the hall and set about placing his call. Most people, he knew, would be well abed at this time of night and would find a telephone call at this hour downright alarming. But he was not calling 'most people'.

His experiences tonight were enough to convince him that he had stumbled into something well over his head, and he needed a second opinion. And if his suspicions were right, there was only one man that he could rely on to help him. Well, *rely* was not perhaps the word that most instantly sprang to mind when he considered his . . .

'Uncle!' he said happily, as way down near the Gloucestershire border, the receiver was lifted and answered. 'Just the fellow I need. I say, Uncle . . .'

*

Sunday dawned slightly more cloudy and less bright than the previous days, but at least there was no sign of rain. Yet.

Arbie was up at a much later hour, so there was only the inevitably lukewarm bath to be had, before shaving, dressing and heading downstairs. There, all the others were already gathered and in various stages of breakfasting. Arbie joined Val and the two Rowes at one end of the table, after heaping his plate with good helpings of almost everything going.

'I can see ghost-hunting gives you an appetite, Mr Swift,' Roger remarked cheerfully from down the table. 'Have any luck with your ghost?'

'Oh no, 'fraid not,' Arbie said.

'But we did. . .' Val began eagerly, before Arbie gave her foot a soft, warning kick with his own under the table.

'But we did only watch one small part of the tracks,' Arbie chipped in to hastily prevent her from mentioning the train. He saw her look questioningly at him and shook his head slightly in warning. Later, he would ask her to keep all mention of the ghost train to herself, and to tell her swain to do the same. Instinct (and a natural regard for his own skin) told him that the less said about seeing that amazing locomotive the better.

'Ah, so you're not giving up then?' Sir Bayard said, not sure whether to sound encouraging or disparaging. 'That's the ticket!'

It was then that they heard the doorbell, and a few moments later, Jardine's steady tread as he walked the length of the hall to answer it. A low feminine murmur answered the butler's greeting, and a few moments later, Jardine appeared in the doorway.

'A Miss Samantha Remington.' He addressed the room in general, but it was Agnes who responded at once.

'Oh, how wonderful! I knew she'd come – didn't I tell you, Sybil? She's so reliable. Such a good girl.'

Lady Sybil gave a small sigh and forced a smile. 'Of course – Jardine, take her bags to her room, would you, and show her in? The poor girl is probably famished after her journey.'

Jardine bowed and returned with 'the poor girl' and all conversation abruptly halted.

From Agnes's descriptions of her worthy, clever, hard-working modern goddaughter, nearly all those present were expecting to see a modest young lady, perhaps bespectacled, wearing a Sunday-best hat and professionally dull clothes. What they got was something very different indeed, and Arbie was not the only man in the room to draw in his breath sharply. Most of the women also took a deep breath, but for vastly different reasons.

Into the amiable ambiance of the unremarkable breakfast room walked a woman in her mid-twenties. Around five feet ten inches or so, she was slender with large dark eyes and a flawless complexion. She was wearing a plain long skirt of emerald green and an almost mannish blouse in lustrous silver-grey silk with tiny pearl buttons. Over this she wore a sumptuous full-length coat that could only have come straight from a Parisian shop. She had high prominent cheekbones and a sharp pointed chin, giving her a fox-like appearance. But it was her waist-length, luxuriantly rich brown hair, shimmering like shot silk, that was her crowning glory. Held back with a simple white velvet ribbon, it slithered and moved around her like a living, rippling cloak.

Her make-up was perfect, her jewellery refined but eye-catching. She moved in a gentle aroma of perfume that was unmistakably the work of a famous French perfumier. On her head was perched a hat of such perfection that it made even Lady Sybil blink. Twice. It was held in place by an eye-catching, decorated silver hat pin that those who knew about such things immediately identified as a Chester Art Nouveau piece designed by no other than the great Charles Horner himself. Every woman in the room instantly coveted it.

'Hello, Aunt Agnes, dear, what have you got yourself into now?' this vision asked dryly. Her voice was deep and rich, and slightly arch.

Arbie, suddenly aware that his mouth was wide open, closed his jaws and hoped nobody had noticed. A quick glance around reassured him that everyone was still looking at the woman in the doorway, and he swallowed whatever it was he'd been masticating before he could choke on it.

'Samantha my dear, do come in and meet everyone,' Agnes was gushing, waving her small pale hand rather ineffectually at the assembly. 'Everyone, this is my goddaughter, but she calls me aunt because it's so much easier, isn't it? Samantha, this is Sir Bayard and Lady Cherville. . .' Agnes quickly did the rounds, and when it came to Arbie's turn, '. . . and this is our wonderful, famous author Mr A. L. Swift . . .' Arbie felt his face flush rather warmly.

When the introductions were finished, Samantha Remington moved towards the table, taking off her pair of soft, kid gloves and letting them rest between the handles of her alligator-skin handbag.

'Thank you so much for the invitation, Sir Bayard,' Samantha addressed her host smoothly and with a slight smile. But her eyes, Arbie noticed, which were a dark chocolate colour, were observing him keenly. Sir Bayard rose abruptly to his feet as she approached and took her proffered hand with a face that was kept carefully devoid of expression. No doubt, Arbie surmised with some inner amusement, he'd been well trained by his very beautiful wife to never knowingly acknowledge another striking woman.

'Not at all, my dear. Your poor, er, aunt has been so looking forward to your arrival. She, like the rest of us, has been sorely tried these past twenty-four hours or so,' he murmured politely.

'Yes.' Samantha's triangular-shaped face tightened. 'So, I understand. There's been quite a catastrophe I hear.'

Val, who was watching her with something approaching fascination, couldn't quite make up her mind whether the new arrival was stunningly beautiful or rather plain. She had one of those baffling faces that could seem to be both at the same time. But in many ways, her physical arrangements were almost irrelevant, for she was one of those women who had charisma by the bucket-load. There was also a sense of repressed energy about her that almost made your skin tingle in response, and Miss Remington was so obviously very content in her *own* skin that it was somehow almost obscene.

Daphne Potts-Gibbon was thinking much the same things, but she wasn't so much struck by the paradoxes of the woman, as taken up with the dark energy being given off by the newcomer. Although there was nothing in Samantha's voice or demeanour to show it, Daphne was convinced that this striking young woman was holding back an enormously strong emotion of some kind. Exactly which emotion she couldn't tell – but it made her sigh inwardly.

She rather feared that if poor Agnes expected this creature to soothe her nervous brow any time soon, she was in for a disappointment.

'Oh Samantha, dear, it's been dreadful,' Agnes began with a slight tremble in her voice. 'A young man . . . Oh dear, I can't bear to say it.'

Samantha regarded her godmother with a not particularly sympathetic eye. 'You'll have to tell me all about it in a minute or two, Aunty,' she told her coolly. 'Right now, I could do with a strong cup of coffee.'

At this, Lady Sybil remembered her duties as a hostess and implored her to help herself to the breakfast dishes. Roger pulled out a chair for her, and Elizabeth Rowe highly recommended the kedgeree.

'So, Aunty,' Samantha said, after accepting a cup of fresh coffee from Jardine, and refusing everything but a slice of toast. 'You were rather incoherent and unclear on the telephone yesterday. Perhaps you can explain what it's all about now more sensibly?' She took a sip and waited.

There was a tense moment of silence, before Agnes gave a little sigh. 'It's as I told you, dear, a young man, Bill Endicott, er . . . took some of my sleeping medicine . . . at least, I suppose it was mine . . . and, well, he died in the library,' she finished rather abruptly.

As a precis of the situation, it lacked a certain coherence but in essence Arbie supposed it conveyed the basic facts clearly enough.

Lady Sybil let out a slow breath. 'It's been ghastly for everyone as you can imagine.'

Samantha's generous mouth gave a sudden twist. 'I expect it was most ghastly for Bill,' she pointed out mildly. Her tone was so casual that it took a moment for the meaning of her words to sink in. When they did, there was a little ripple of a shockwave that swept around the table.

'Did you know Bill?' It was Sybil who recovered and spoke first, her voice sharp with suspicion.

'Oh yes – well, that is to say, as one knows people that you bump into regularly around town,' Samantha said, adding the tiniest of dollops of gooseberry jam to a small square of toast. 'And by town, I mean York, of course, not London. You know how it is when you move in the same broad circles. We'd cross paths in the same restaurants now and then, and then met up in a group for a show and a dance.' She shrugged one elegant, bony shoulder and popped the piece of toast into her mouth.

The sound of her crunching it seemed exaggeratedly loud in the silence of the room. She lifted her napkin and dabbed it to the corner of her mouth.

'I must say,' Samantha went on, 'the idea of Bill doing away with himself strikes me as very unlikely.' Her eyes met those of Lady Sybil over the rim of her coffee cup. 'Very unlikely indeed.' Then her eyes shifted to Elizabeth Rowe. She saw her daughter reach out and put her hand protectively over that of her mother's, and Samantha's lips twitched slightly. She might have been amused or disgusted, it was hard to tell.

Her eyes then flicked to Roger Potts-Gibbon, met, clashed and moved on from those of his wife, and finally fixed on Arbie.

Who gulped, audibly.

'I understand, at least from what I could garner from Aunty's rather rambling explanations over the telephone, that you were the one to find him, Mr Swift?'

'Yes,' Arbie squeaked, cleared his throat and tried again. 'Yes, I'm afraid that's so.'

'And did *you* know Bill before this weekend?' she asked. Val, who had very acute hearing, didn't miss the slight emphasis on the 'you' and felt Bernie, who was seated beside her, become tense.

'Oh, I'm afraid not,' Arbie said amiably. 'Never met the chap before in my life – but he seemed like a good cove to me. Gave me a splendid game of billiards.'

'He didn't seem depressed then?' Samantha said.

'Not to me,' Arbie agreed candidly, then added quietly, 'but the suicide note he left behind made it quite clear that he had his fair share of woes, which goes to show, one never can tell, doesn't it?'

'His what?' Samantha said sharply. The revelation of a note had clearly rocked her, and her sharply raised voice was the first indication of spontaneity in her performance so far. Underneath her make-up, she had gone quite pale, and she gripped her knife so tightly that her knuckles became stark and white also.

'Oh, Samantha dear, it's all quite dreadful,' Agnes said, her voice wavering on the edge of tears. 'What on earth could have made him act so?'

Samantha slowly put down her knife and took another sip of coffee. She made a visible effort to relax her tense shoulders, and even went so far as to give a slight shrug. 'Yes, Aunty. That *is* the question, isn't it? When you called me and asked me to come down, you weren't very specific about things. But then,

I expect that's what the inquest is for, isn't it? To examine the evidence and find out.'

At this harshly realistic statement, Agnes gave a little wail. 'And I shall have to testify because of the Veronal. Oh, how I wish I'd never brought the wretched stuff.'

'Yes, just how *did* Bill come to get his hands on it, does anybody know?' Samantha asked, pragmatic as ever.

'Oh dear, I've no idea, I'm sure,' Agnes said helplessly.

'Agnes, you left it in the bathroom for anyone to find,' Sybil reminded her flatly, which only made the older woman's eyes shimmer with more unshed tears. 'If you recall, Betty found it, and gave it to me, and I put it back where it was, but then asked you to keep it in your room?'

'Oh yes, so you did,' Agnes agreed. 'But I forgot to collect it. I had so much on my mind, what with Dr Schuber's wonderful book to read, and trying to practise my bridge playing, and. . .'

'Ah, that begins to explain some of it then,' Samantha cut across her flatly. 'Aunty, do buck up and drink some more tea, there's a dear. You know you always feel better after a good cup of tea. Later on, we'll sort through your wardrobe and pick out something suitable for you to wear tomorrow, and then I'll go over things with you – what you can expect, and that sort of thing. I asked a solicitor friend of mine about inquests, and he gave me a good run-down on all the usual procedures.'

'Oh, Samantha, how clever of you,' Agnes said, brightening visibly. 'I'm sure I won't feel half so frightened if I know what to expect.'

'The main thing to remember is answer all the questions clearly, don't waffle, and don't volunteer any information that isn't asked for,' she advised sternly. Then she looked at her godmother, who looked like nothing so much as a bewildered rabbit, and sighed. 'I'll give you some coaching,' she said more gently. 'I take it the police are requesting that everyone is present?'

She glanced around the table and there was a general agreement that this was so, and slowly, the general, polite conversation of the breakfast table was resumed, but all the previous friendly spontaneity that had existed in the room before Samantha Remington's advent was now gone.

*

'Well, I, for one, don't like her,' Lady Sybil said to her husband an hour later. They were back up in their bedroom, and Sybil was sitting in front of her vanity table re-applying her make-up. After the appearance of their unexpectedly chic visitor, she was also feeling the need to don one of her more expensive day dresses.

'No, I could see she was putting your back up,' Sir Bayard said dryly, watching her moodily from the window seat.

'And I wasn't the only one,' Lady Sybil defended herself quickly. 'Did you see the way she looked at poor Betty?'

'Hmm? Oh. Yes. Well, I suppose now that I know about what happened last year, that's understandable, isn't it?'

'What do you mean – "now that you know about what happened"?' Sybil shot back. 'I told you at the time all about poor Marcus drowning at the Henley regatta. You just forgot about it, as you always do about things that don't concern this place or your rotten sheep!'

Sir Bayard turned to stare out of the window, fortifying himself for what he knew was coming next.

'If you'd told me about inviting Bill before it was too late to stop it, Betty and Bernie need never have come here at all,' Sybil pointed out. 'As it is. . .'

'Well, at least *they* can't be feeling particularly sorry about how things have turned out,' Sir Bayard pointed out gruffly.

'Bay!' Sybil yelped. 'That's a perfectly rotten thing to say. And besides, you're missing my point. I do believe that wretched

Remington creature was actually intimating that, well, that there might be something more . . . *sinister* . . . going on here. About Bill's death, I mean.'

As she spoke, Lady Sybil was anxiously watching her husband's profile reflected in her mirror. She saw him stiffen then turn to look at her.

'Sinister?'

'Yes.' Lady Sybil took her courage firmly in both hands and straightened her shoulders. 'Firstly, she says she doesn't think it likely that Bill committed suicide. Then she seemed to find something interesting about Agnes's wretched sleeping powders being available to one and all. It's almost as if she suspects one of us of. . .' She forced herself to say it, and blurted out, 'Murdering Bill.'

She held her breath as she pretended to fiddle with her hair, but her eyes were fixed on her husband's reflection. And she felt a slight chill slide down her spine as she watched him smile gently.

'Well, my dear, who knows,' he said mildly. 'Perhaps one of us did. And if that's the case, let's hope that our gangling beanpole of an inspector doesn't twig, eh? Or else one of us will find ourselves in a bit of a tight spot.'

With fingers that had turned icy cold, Sybil reached for her compact and shakily dabbed fresh powder onto her cheeks. She forced a laugh. 'Oh Bay, you do say the silliest of things. *I* know when you're only joking, of course, but others might not, so please, Bay, do be careful what you say when we're in company. And speaking of which, our resident author has asked if we can fit one more in for lunch today. Apparently, Miss Coulton-James's young man is in the area. I said of course he should come.'

Sir Bayard shrugged. 'Why not? We seem to be inviting half the county to come and join in the fun. All it will take is for the papers to get hold of things, and I dare say we'll have reporters jumping out at us from the shrubbery next.'

*

Whilst the residents at the manor passed a lazy Sunday morning, the offices of Inspector Battle and Sergeant Jellicoe were a hive of activity.

The inquest to be held on Bill Endicott in the morning was all set, and all the witnesses they'd talked to in the interim had agreed to come and testify. The picture they'd built up of young Bill Endicott and his rather erratic way of life was, Battle suspected, clear enough to satisfy the coroner and jury that it was a case of suicide, but something about it nevertheless left him feeling a little uneasy.

Still, his superintendent had read the files and hadn't seen anything to worry about and had promptly told him not to borrow trouble. Traces of Veronal had been detected in the nearly empty glass, which had also contained traces of Champagne. The bottle of Champagne itself, however, had contained nothing but the vineyard's finest. A fingerprint test done on it had proved that only the dead man had handled it. So that was all plain enough. Endicott, the Superintendent had theorised, had decided to do away with himself, and do it in style. He'd opened a bottle of Champagne, laced it with the old biddy's sleeping stuff, and slipped gently off this mortal plane. And with that, he'd strongly hinted that he expected the case to be put to bed as soon as possible. It wasn't as if they didn't have enough 'real work' to be getting on with.

And with that, Battle supposed pragmatically, he would have to be content.

*

Arbie took himself off to the library after finishing his breakfast, and thus managed to get in half an hour or so of reading the Sunday papers in peace, before Val tracked him down.

'Here you are,' she said, slipping onto the sofa beside him and half-turning in her seat, the better to regard him. 'So, what do you think of Miss Remington then? She's not what I was expecting at all.'

'No.'

'I didn't like her much, did you?'

'Hmmmm? I've only just met her. I can't say I have an opinion yet.'

'Liar! One thing's obvious – she and Bill were proper friends, if not more than that.'

'Eh? How do you make that out? She said they occasionally bumped into each other, nothing more.'

'Exactly,' Val said with satisfaction.

Arbie shook his head at this and attempted to bury his face back into *The Times*.

Val, naturally, was having none of that. 'Did you see that look she gave poor Mrs Rowe? I wonder what that was all about?'

Arbie *had* seen it and was as mystified by it as Val, but had absolutely no intention of pursuing it further and mumbled something about taking a walk down to the village and walking back with Geraint.

Val, who had been very cross indeed when Arbie had so shamelessly wangled an invitation for the country solicitor to attend Sunday lunch at the manor, became grimly silent.

*

In the orangery, Daphne and her husband were lounging on the rattan chairs with a paper each on their laps.

'Do you know this Remington girl?' Roger asked his wife casually.

'No,' Daphne said. 'But I know her type.'

Roger sighed. 'Yes – our already awkward situation looks as if it might get worse before it gets better, doesn't it? I'll be glad when this blasted inquest is over, and we can all leave. It's Sir Bayard I feel sorry for.'

Daphne sighed. 'You'll not try and butter him up to be on your board of directors now, obviously,' she warned softly.

'Oh no – that'll have to wait,' Roger agreed at once. 'I'll be seeing him at that Chamber of Commerce bash next month – I'll approach him then. Once he's got a few brandies down him.'

Daphne nodded at this strategy. And then said quietly, 'Roger, you're sure no one here knows about . . . you know what?'

Roger lifted his head from his vague perusal of his paper and met her gaze. 'Oh, I'm quite sure. Don't worry, old thing, that won't turn around and bite us.'

Daphne sighed. 'I'm not so sure. Not now *that* girl has appeared.'

'The walking fashion-plate?' Roger scoffed. 'I can't see why she need worry us.'

His wife gave him an affectionate but impatient look. 'No, I can see that you don't. But mark my words, that girl's clever, Roger. And hard as nails. And there was something going on with her and Bill Endicott.'

'Going on? What do you mean?'

'I'm not sure,' Daphne said slowly. 'But I'm telling you this. She knows who Betty and Bernadette Rowe are. And she doesn't like the fact that they were invited here at the same time as Bill.'

Roger frowned. 'Yes. That does seem a bit rum! I can't think what Sybil was playing at, inviting them and Bill at the same time.'

'Oh, it wasn't Sybil,' Daphne corrected him. 'That business was all down to Bayard.'

Roger rattled his paper. 'It's still a rum do,' he insisted. 'I'll be glad when we can all get out of here. There's a decidedly odd feeling abroad in this house, Daphers old girl. And I don't like it.'

Daphne nodded and bowed her head back to her paper.

*

In Elizabeth Rowe's room, her daughter was perched on the edge of the bed, moodily watching her mother, who was sitting at her dressing table and regarding her reflection thoughtfully.

'Mummy, can't we leave tomorrow, right after the inquest?' Bernie whined.

'You know we can't. There isn't a train until Tuesday.'

'I'm sure Sir Bayard wouldn't mind asking his chauffeur to run us to a bigger station.'

'We're not asking him to do that,' Elizabeth said sharply. 'Don't you see, it would look as if we were running away?'

Bernie bit her lip, then swallowed the hasty words she wanted to say. What was wrong with running away, after all, when things became unbearable?

'Do you know anything about this woman who's just come?' Elizabeth changed the subject quietly.

'Samantha Remington? No, nothing. Except I think she and *that man* might have known each other rather better than she made out.'

Elizabeth gave her offspring a small, wry smile. 'You can hardly expect a pat on the back for discerning *that*, my dear,' she said dryly. 'It was rather obvious that they were – or rather had been – an item. Except, possibly, to poor Agnes. I don't think she's realised it yet.'

'Oh, she's such an innocent,' Bernie grumbled. 'She seems to think her goddaughter is a rose beyond compare, whereas to me she seems to have all the makings of—'

'Bernadette Rowe, keep a check on your language please,'

her mother reprimanded her sharply. 'You really must keep yourself under control. Remember, with the police still taking an interest in us all, we must be careful.'

'Sorry, Mummy. But really, this is the limit. I don't like the way things are going – I really don't. And that Remington female worries me. Oh, why did she have to come?'

'Agnes needs her to hold her hand at the inquest. And I must say, Miss Remington does seem to know how to handle her. I do so hate fuss and bother, and if Agnes mentions that silly book of hers one more time, I'm sure I shall scream.' Elizabeth broke off and gave a wry smile. 'Sorry, sweetheart, but my nerves are at stretching point too, as you can see. So, for taking Miss Warren in hand, we should at least be grateful to Miss Remington for that.'

Bernadette, however, wasn't convinced. It seemed to her that the newcomer already knew far more about the state of things here at the manor than she would have wished. 'Tomorrow is going to be a circus – I can just feel it,' she said, getting up and walking restlessly to the window and then looking out. 'Mumsy – they won't mention anything about us, will they? The police I mean, or the coroner?'

'Of course not,' Elizabeth said briskly. 'We haven't even been called to give evidence. And I doubt that they even know about Marcus. Nobody here will have told them. Sybil certainly wouldn't have.'

No, Bernie thought silently. But Samantha Remington just might. She was the sort of spiteful cat that would, just to make trouble.

Elizabeth Rowe regarded her daughter's tense back for a moment, then let her eyes drift back to her dressing table. She wasn't quite as confident as she'd made out that the inquest tomorrow would be all plain sailing, but she was quietly hopeful that a verdict of suicide would be returned by the coroner's jury.

But if, by some chance, the police had been more diligent than she expected, she was prepared to fight her corner. And if danger looked as if it was creeping their way, there were always ways and means of keeping herself and her daughter safe. Say, for instance, if the police should learn about Bill and Sybil's affair last year... And then there was Roger Potts-Gibbon and his own reason to despise Endicott. Oh yes – Elizabeth wasn't without weapons of her own, should she need to use them.

She had always preferred to walk the smoothest path in life, and she was well aware that the outside world regarded her as a demure, inoffensive lady. Mild-as-milk, her nanny used to call her. Well, and so she was, in normal circumstances. But Elizabeth, like all mothers, could become a tigress if the need arose to defend her cub and her den.

Quietly, she reached out and smoothed back a lock of dark brown hair.

*

Agnes Warren nodded approvingly at the simple black frock Samantha had selected from her wardrobe. 'Yes, dear, very discreet and tasteful. Which hat do you think . . . ?'

Samantha hid a sigh and picked out the least atrocious item of her godmother's headgear, then sat beside her at her dressing table and made a show of picking out a plain amber set of beads to complete the 'inquest outfit'.

She took a slow, careful breath. 'Aunty – I know you don't want to talk about it, but was everything . . . well . . . as you'd expect, when you and Bill first arrived?'

'Oh yes, dear,' Agnes said, casting the younger woman a nervous glance. 'I think Sybil was a little tense though. I got the impression that Bill had been invited by Sir Bayard, and Sybil hadn't known anything about it.'

Samantha Remington's eyes narrowed slightly. 'Ah, I see. And how was Bill behaving?'

'Samantha, dear, I didn't know that you knew Bill,' Agnes said, changing the subject a little, a slight catch in her voice making her cough. 'Did you know him very well, my dear?' Although her voice was mild, she was watching her goddaughter very intently out of the corner of her eyes.

'Hardly,' Samantha said crisply. 'Just well enough to know that he didn't strike me as the sort of man to deliberately swallow sleeping stuff.'

'Oh Samantha!' Agnes wailed. 'Don't say things like that. It almost sounds as if, as if . . . you think . . .'

Samantha, realising that if she didn't become more tactful she'd have an emotional wreck on her hands in no time, reached across and patted the older woman's stooped shoulders. 'Sorry, Aunty, I didn't mean anything by it. I just meant it was probably an accident of some kind, that's all.'

'Oh yes! That's what it must have been.' Agnes's thin shoulders wilted with relief. 'An accident of some kind. Yes, that'll be it,' she agreed, and nodded vigorously to herself.

Samantha watched her godmother with contempt and had to turn her face away sharply. It was just like her to try and bury her head in the sand like some silly ostrich! As if Bill, Bill of all people, could have accidentally taken poison!

When she was sure she had herself under control again, she held the amber beads up to the light and pretended to regard them. 'So, until Saturday morning then, everything here seemed normal?' she began again casually.

'Oh yes. Well, Bill was a little stiff around Mrs and Miss Rowe,' she said. 'And he spoke much more to Daphne Potts-Gibbon than to her husband, but then, Daphne is such a good conversationalist, isn't she? Clever, but not in a way that makes you feel stupid yourself. Such a kind lady.'

'Yes,' Samantha agreed flatly. 'Very kind.'

Inwardly, she was thinking furiously. She knew well enough why Roger and Bill wouldn't have anything to talk about – indeed, why they would have gone out of their way to avoid talking at all, if they didn't want to come to fisticuffs.

The thought of the pompous Roger trying to thump Bill on the nose or chin made her inwardly laugh. He'd have made mincemeat out of the financier. But then she instantly sobered. This was no laughing matter. Somebody in this house had killed Bill, of that she was sure. The question was – who? And why?

And how could she turn it to her advantage?

CHAPTER TEN

Geraint regarded the people gathered around the Sunday lunch table and found it easy to place them all. On the walk back from the village, Arbie had given him a comprehensive account of the doings at the manor, and he was more determined than ever to try and persuade Val to return home with him right after the inquest. He would not feel easy until she was safely back in the Cotswolds with her family, and not under the influence of Arbie, and this house of tragedy.

But, as befits an unexpected guest, he put himself out to be charming to everyone.

Lady Sybil was genuinely amused by the advent of Geraint onto the scene, for it had taken her no time at all to discern that the demure Miss Coulton-James was, underneath her non-committal smile, fuming about Mr Kirkwood's pursuit of her, and even more amused by their famous author's attempts to facilitate Mr Kirkwood's wooing of Miss Coulton-James. Funnier still was the country solicitor's suspicions of Arbuthnot Swift, who, would he but allow himself to believe it, was trying to be his greatest ally.

She had been able to stir the pot further by flirting gently with Arbie throughout the meal, which had thrown Geraint Kirkwood into further confusion and caused Miss Coulton-James's anger to simmer even further, adding significantly to the author's bemusement.

Her husband watched her antics with a knowing little smile, whilst Samantha studied the performance with a careful eye. Agnes was still going on about the merits of her wretched book, waving her pale hands about with such enthusiasm that Arbie had promised her he would devote the afternoon to reading Dr Schuber's philosophy on harmonious living with the greatest of attention.

Daphne, as always, could be relied upon to be a witty asset, and her husband played along with her, so that by the time the meal was over, most felt as if they'd come through it reasonably well.

'Bernie, shall we take a turn in the gardens?' Elizabeth Rowe was the first to rise, looking questioningly at her daughter, who lost no time in joining her. As they went out through the French windows onto the patio outside, Samantha's eyes followed them, her face bland.

'And I'll head for the library and read Miss Warren's book, as promised,' Arbie said, giving that lady a cheerful smile. Although he wasn't looking forward to leafing through the blasted tome, it at least gave him the excuse to have some time to sit in peace and think. 'Geraint, why don't you and Val have a game of tennis? I'm sure there's equipment in the pavilion, eh Sir Bayard?'

'Oh yes, yes, all sorts. Splendid idea – go and have a knock-about. Or there's always croquet.' He beamed approvingly at the couple. Val, who normally loved tennis, murmured a vague thanks, and Geraint, although he always lost at tennis to Val (but then, who didn't?), was more than happy to resign himself to defeat if it meant having her to himself for a couple of hours.

Agnes said she had letters to write and left the table, and was almost immediately followed by Roger Potts-Gibbon. Samantha followed him out at a little distance, which left Daphne and the

Chervilles still sitting at the table and discussing the latest plays making the rounds in London.

Out in the hall, Roger quickened his pace and almost sprinted up the stairs, managing to waylay Agnes on the first landing.

'Oh, Miss Warren, I was wondering if I might just have a quick word?' he said. Down below, in the hall, Samantha moved swiftly and silently up the stairs and paused beside a large vase set in a small recess that provided her with a good shadow to slip into.

'Oh! Mr Potts-Gibbon, you did scare me,' Agnes said, giving a little jump of fright, and patting a hand against her rather flat chest.

'Ah, I'm so sorry. Yes, I fear we are rather all on edge, aren't we?' Roger apologised. 'I won't take up much of your time. I just wanted to go over what we talked about on Friday night?'

Agnes Warren gave a nervous little start. 'Really? Must we talk business now? I'm not sure I can really devote my attention to such things . . .'

'Yes, indeed, and that's what I wanted to say,' Roger put in smoothly. 'I think, under the circumstances, we should just forget all about it. As you've pointed out, now is really not the time to talk business.'

'Oh, I am glad you feel the same way too,' Agnes said, nodding happily. 'And yes, let's just forget all about it. I'm sure that's for the best.'

Roger gave her a brief bow and continued to his room. Agnes turned at the next bend in the landing and carried on to her own room, a little frown of worry tugging at her sparse brows.

From her hiding place, Samantha watched the two of them go their separate ways, and then slowly turned and descended the stairs. She would have to find out what that was all about from Agnes later.

But right now, she had other things to do.

*

In the library, Arbie was causally dipping in and out of *The Art of Harmonious Living* by Dr Randolph Schuber. 'Extraordinary,' he muttered over the title of one chapter, and then found himself chuckling at some of the 'good' doctor's theories on how one could improve the quality of one's life.

'Man's a total charlatan,' Arbie muttered mildly to himself, and made a mental note to recommend the book to his uncle, who would appreciate it no end. Knowing Uncle, he'd probably set about writing a rival tome of his own, on the supposition that if there were enough fools in the world to buy Dr Schuber's work, there would certainly be enough left over to buy a book of his own. Idly, he mused on a possible title for his uncle's work. 'How to fleece fools and make a small fortune' perhaps. That would no doubt be accurate, but he suspected something far more subtle would be needed. How about . . . 'A rascal's guide to easy living'? But that was rather derivative of his own book titles.

He yawned and flipped to the middle of the book and began to read at random. Outside, he could hear the vague *thwock, thwock* of tennis balls being hit, and smiled happily. With a bit of luck, Geraint would be able to persuade Val to travel back with him, leaving himself free to find somewhere to stay in York and pass a few pleasant days on his own.

He turned to the next chapter and yawned sleepily.

*

Samantha found her quarry in the rose garden. Although it was still too early for any blooms, the last of the spring bulbs were still giving a nice show, and Bernadette Rowe had just raised her eyes from contemplation of some scarlet tulips when she saw the newcomer.

Instantly, she tensed.

'Hello there.' Samantha greeted mother and daughter blandly, and paused beside the bench on which they were sitting. 'The narcissi are quite lovely, aren't they? Pity they're almost over.'

'Yes,' Elizabeth agreed quietly. She cast a quick glance at her daughter and shook her head so slightly that Samantha, who was by nature a very observant person, quite missed it. Bernadette did not, and she sat back slightly on the bench and turned her face away from the two other women.

'I hope I'm not bothering you,' Samantha began insincerely.

'Oh, not at all,' Elizabeth returned, equally as insincerely.

Samantha wandered slightly to her left, ostensibly the better to see the floral display, but actually so that she could more easily observe the expressions on the faces of her companions.

'Have you known the Chervilles long?' was her opening gambit.

'Oh, I've known Sybil since we were girls at school. I was older than her, of course,' Elizabeth said.

'Ah, how lovely. It's so nice to keep up with old friendships isn't it? And do you know Daphne and Roger?'

'Not really.'

'I must say, our celebrity is rather an interesting chap, isn't he? Have you read his books at all?'

'Bernadette has,' Elizabeth admitted. 'I prefer to read biographies myself.'

'And Bill?' Samantha asked smoothly. 'You'd met Bill before, of course.'

'Only once,' Elizabeth said, and sensing her daughter tense beside her, moved her fingers to touch those of Bernadette's.

'Yes. I thought that might have been the case,' Samantha said. 'Bill and I knew each other quite well, you see,' she admitted candidly, watching them closely.

Neither woman looked surprised. 'His loss must have come as quite a shock,' Elizabeth murmured. 'Allow us to pass on our condolences.'

Samantha's lips twisted into a wry smile. 'Thank you,' she said dryly. 'I was rather hoping you might be able to shed some light on this whole business.'

'Oh? I can't think how we could do that,' Elizabeth said mildly.

'You were with Bill the last night he was alive,' Samantha said, rather brutally. 'What did he talk about?'

'Oh, nothing out of the ordinary, did he, Bernie?' Elizabeth said, glancing at her daughter, who shrugged and said nothing. 'Just the usual small talk. You know how it is.'

'Did he seem . . . normal to you?'

'Oh yes. He talked a lot with Mr Swift about his book and ghosts and things. He rather ribbed him a bit, but Mr Swift took it all in good part. Then later I believe they had a game of billiards. Really, we didn't converse much with him at all.'

'No, I don't suppose you did,' Samantha said, again very dryly. 'What time did he retire, do you know?'

'I'm not sure.' Elizabeth shifted slightly on her seat. 'I believe we went upstairs to bed before he did, didn't we?' She again turned to look at her daughter, who again did nothing more than shrug.

'I see,' Samantha said. 'I don't suppose you heard anything untoward in the night? No prowling about in the early hours, that sort of thing?'

'I would have told the police inspector who came on Saturday morning if I had,' Elizabeth said pointedly.

Samantha nodded. 'Of course you would,' she said insincerely. And with another dry smile, she turned and walked away.

Mother and daughter watched her in antipathetic silence.

*

Val served for the game and shot such a scorching ace across Geraint's bows that it hit the netting behind him with an almost shotgun-loud *whump*. The resident wood pigeon sitting in the elm behind it nearly lost its feathers clattering clumsily out of the branches and fleeing for its life into the protective arms of a large and distant Douglas fir.

'Well done, old thing.' Geraint, perspiring, breathless and rather red-faced, gasped his congratulations and staggered over to the wooden folding chair where he collapsed, rather than sat. He poured out two glasses of lemon barley water that the butler had brought out just before their game, and handed one to Val.

She sipped daintily whilst Geraint glugged his down gratefully and then poured himself another. 'You know, Val,' Geraint began, once he had recovered control of his breathing. 'Why don't you come back down with me after the inquest tomorrow? I've a pal picking me up at Oxford station, and we can take our time motoring back. Perhaps drop in for a spot of lunch at this little place I know near Stow...'

'I'll have to see what Arbie's doing,' Val cut in ruthlessly. 'He'll probably want to scout out the local beauty spots and then there's my weather research to conduct, and...'

Geraint sighed miserably and bowed to the inevitable. 'All right, all right. Do you think the Chervilles will mind awfully if I go and have a bath, do you think? There's only cold water at the inn.'

'Of course they won't,' Val said mildly, and watched his drooping figure as he exited the tennis court and made his way back to the manor. She'd only been sitting there idly for a few moments, however, when she heard a sound.

'Pssttt . . .'

She sat up quickly and looked around.

'Psssttt . . .'

The noise was coming from a patch of shrubbery behind her, just beyond the netting.

'Hey, lady . . .'

Val got up cautiously, and as she did so, a man slipped out of the foliage. He looked vaguely familiar, and it only took her a moment or two to place him. He was one of the passengers who had got off the train on Friday at the same time as herself, Arbie and the Potts-Gibbons.

He was dressed in a rather sharp, all-black outfit and wore a soft felt hat and a rather garish and hideous diamond-and-platinum tie pin. His shoes were far too pointed for good taste and gleamed far too much.

'Wouldn't do me a favour, would you?' this unprepossessing specimen asked.

'That depends,' Val said warily.

'Would you mind nipping up to the big house and asking his lordship if we might have a word? He knows me, and he knows what it's all about. Just tell him I'll stay here by the tennis courts until he comes. You can do that, can't you?'

Val, now thoroughly intrigued, admitted that she could do that, and made her way to exit through the wire gate. She kept him in her peripheral vision as she did so, and once he was out of sight, she began to run lightly towards the house, glancing once or twice over her shoulder as she did so.

It was not that she was particularly frightened of him, but she was a cautious girl, and nobody's fool.

She found Jardine in the hall and asked him where she might find Sir Bayard. The butler directed her to the 'study', where she found the Lord of the Manor rather noisily sleeping off his Sunday lunch in a green Chesterfield chair, with a copy of the local paper half-falling off his lap, and his English setter snoozing (even more noisily than his master) across his feet.

After she'd gently woken him, he looked distinctly startled by her news that a man desired a private word with him at the tennis courts, and then heartily laughed, telling her it was about a pedigree pup that he wanted to buy as a surprise for his wife, after which he shuffled off, looking red-faced and rather peeved.

'A shaggy dog story,' Val muttered to herself, after her host had departed. 'Really?'

The English setter, who'd elected to remain behind, gave her a knowing look in agreement, then settled his nose onto his paws and stretched out to continue with the serious business of sleeping.

Val set off to find Arbie, to ask him what he made of it all.

*

'Come on, if we're quick we can still get down the courts and hear what they're saying,' Val said a few minutes later, after having apprised Arbie of the latest developments.

Arbie regarded her with a wide-eyed stare. 'Spy on our host? My dear girl, have you gone completely doolally?' he asked bluntly.

Val had the grace to flush. 'It's not as if I *want* to,' she tried to defend herself. 'It's just. . . Well, I'm sure something's up, that's all.'

Arbie was sure that something was up as well, which, to his mind, was a very good reason for keeping his nose strictly out of business that wasn't his own. From her description of the visitor, he was as sure as he could be that it was the cove from the Job's Rest right enough, and in his experience, the less you had to do with *his* sort, the better.

'Come on, you must want to know what it's all about!' Val egged him on, starting to look cross.

'I don't, you know,' Arbie contradicted her flatly.

'Arbie, do you really think Bill Endicott killed himself?' she demanded, and then nodded at the look on his face. 'See! I can tell that you don't. And what's more, I think Samantha Remington believes it's murder too. And I shouldn't be surprised if Lady Sybil thinks the same thing.'

Arbie leapt up from the sofa, now genuinely alarmed. 'Val! You can't go about saying things like that,' he hissed, glancing at the doorway nervously. 'Besides, it's up to the police to sort it all out, not us.'

'Why? We've done it before, and very successfully too,' Val pointed out stubbornly.

'We had no choice then,' Arbie huffed, but he already had the sinking feeling that this was an argument he wasn't going to win. 'Here, we don't know any of these people. What's more, this time nobody's asked us to help, which means it really is nothing to do with us.'

'It's a good thing that the Good Samaritan didn't feel the same way about such things,' Val said, quoting one of her father's favourite biblical parables. 'When he came across someone suffering on the roadside he didn't hesitate to lend a hand.' Her chin came up. 'So, I for one am going to go and see what's happening between Sir Bayard and that strange man. But don't worry, I won't drag you into things. I don't mind doing it all on my own.'

And with that, she turned and left.

And Arbie, naturally, had to follow her. What else could a chap do? Only a cad would let a lady head off into potential trouble alone. Bitterly he wondered where Geraint was – surely it was now *his* job to keep Val out of trouble?

*

They could hear slightly raised voices the moment they got within distance of the tennis court, and Val quickly found a nearby bush in which to conceal herself. Arbie knelt down beside her, wishing he was off somewhere fishing. Or walking along a beach, or . . .

'I told you, that's all off now.' Sir Bayard's voice came through the shrubbery a little muffled, but still clearly enough to tell that he was angry.

The other man mumbled something in a much lower voice.

'Oh, don't worry, blast you, you'll get your money,' Sir Bayard grumbled.

Val shot Arbie a knowing look.

The man in black mumbled something again.

'How can I possibly know how much you might have made?' Sir Bayard hissed. 'I can only give you a reasonable amount, to make it worth your while coming here and to cover your expenses. Can't say fairer than that, can I? Look here, my man, I don't know what you have to complain about – you're still getting paid, and what's more, without having to do any of the dirty work. You should be pleased.'

The two men must have been pacing around for when the stranger responded, his voice was fainter than ever, and they couldn't make out their host's reply either.

Val indicated to Arbie that she was going to back out of the rhododendrons, so he obligingly scooted backwards to give her room, sitting on the slightly damp grass and no doubt getting the seat of his Oxford bags slightly damp in the process.

'So, what did you make of that, then?' Val hissed excitedly. 'I was right! Something is up. Was it blackmail do you think? I wonder what the stranger has on him?'

Arbie shook his head. 'Hold hard old bean, not so fast. It didn't sound much like blackmail to me.' He tried to curb her excitement. 'It sounded more like Sir Bayard had brought him here to do something, and he was just reassuring him that he'd get paid.'

'Yes – for "dirty work" no less,' Val pointed out triumphantly. 'You heard Sir Bayard say that for yourself. What other dirty work could he be referring to other than what happened to Bill?'

'Now hold on, old bean,' Arbie said, seriously getting the wind up now. 'Are you really saying that you believe Sir Bayard hired an assassin to bump off Bill? Because if so, I think you're letting your imagination run away with you.'

Val looked a little chagrined. 'Yes. I suppose it does sound rather far-fetched.'

'Even if Sir Bayard did have some reason for wanting Bill dead, why would he hire someone to kill Bill in his own home? That's just asking for trouble. And why pick on someone so . . . well . . . conspicuous to do it? Besides, our stranger didn't look the killer type to me. He looked more like the sort of cove who'd fleece you by selling you dodgy shares or a villa in Spain that doesn't exist, or shares in a goldmine that had long since run dry or something. In my experience, men of that type are far too fond of their own skins to risk it by going around bumping people off at weekend house parties.'

Val sighed. 'I suppose those are all good points. But even *you* can't believe that there isn't something weird going on at this place now,' she said, waving a hand at the beautiful manor house behind them.

Arbie nodded. 'No,' he agreed heavily. 'Something's not right somewhere, old bean, I'll grant you that. Val, I think you should leave tomorrow with Geraint. I really do.'

'Hah!' was all Val said to that.

*

In her room, Agnes finished writing the last of her letters to her friends in the WI and put them to one side for the maid to send down to the post. Then she rose and paced about her room for a while, which set her head to throbbing. And then she was vexed to realise that she was running low on lavender water, the only thing that would do when she felt one of her 'heads' coming on.

She knew Samantha had been given a room just a few doors down from her, and after tapping timidly at the door, pushed it open a crack and heard feminine voices issuing from inside. Pushing the door further open, she saw Lady Sybil first, sitting on a chair at the side of Samantha's dressing table, and then her goddaughter sitting directly in front of it and looking in the mirror.

'I just love your outfit,' Lady Sybil was saying, with apparently genuine admiration. 'Is it a Madeleine Vionnet?'

'Schiaparelli actually.'

'Wonderful. I have several pieces by the divine Coco, of course, but simply must add some by Elsa too. Do you have shoes by . . . Oh Agnes,' she broke off. 'I was just admiring your niece . . . er . . . goddaughter's fashion sense. Isn't it perfectly exquisite?'

Samantha, still brushing her long, long hair, half-turned on her stool and glanced at her latest visitor.

'What is it, Aunty?' she asked coolly.

'Have you any lavender water, dear? I have "a head" coming on and really a hankie soaked in lavender water and pressed against my temples is the only thing that does me any good.'

Lady Sybil and the very fashionable Samantha locked amused eyes. 'I'm afraid I don't use it, Aunty,' Samantha drawled.

'But I'm sure I can have some sent to your room, Agnes dear,' Sybil said hastily. One of the servants was bound to have some, after all.

'Oh, thank you, Sybil dear,' Agnes said, watching as Samantha finished with her hair and began to put it up in a chignon. 'Don't you need a maid to help with that, dear?' Agnes asked, fascinated with the ease with which the younger woman dressed her hair.

'I don't have a maid at home, Aunty,' Samantha pointed out dryly. 'We single girls have to learn quickly how to make do for ourselves.' And so saying, she reached for a headband in shades of peacock blues and greens, and then selected a long, fine silver-and-pearl hat pin to keep it and her chignon in place.

'How lovely,' Sybil said admiringly. 'It's a Charles Horner piece, obviously.'

'I wouldn't wear anything else,' Samantha agreed, re-setting the hat pin carefully and then checking it in the mirror.

'Well, I'll leave you two to it,' Sybil said, rising and exiting like a svelte cat.

Samantha watched her go, looking amused. No wonder she had caught Bill's roving eye last year. Of course, Samantha hadn't minded it since she knew it would come to nothing. Bill's silly little flings never did.

'Aunty, whilst you're here,' Samantha said, turning to regard the middle-aged woman still hovering uncertainly in the doorway, 'just what was it that Mr Potts-Gibbon talked to you about the night before Bill died?'

Agnes jumped a little and looked alarmed. 'Oh – good gracious, my dear, how do you know about that?'

'I'm starting to learn about a lot of things that have been happening here this weekend,' Samantha said, and patted the seat of the chair recently vacated by Lady Sybil. 'Do sit down, and let's have a proper catch-up, shall we?' she purred.

Still looking slightly alarmed, but unable to resist the demand in her goddaughter's snapping dark-brown eyes, Agnes sat down and began to twist her handkerchief nervously in her fingers.

'Oh, well, it was nothing really,' she began. 'It's just that Mr Potts-Gibbon is such a clever man, you know. Really, a self-made man – made his fortune himself, so I was told. Really, it was very good of Daphne to take him on, don't you think, when she could have had her pick of men who came from old money. Her mother was the daughter of an earl, you know. Still, he is *very* clever about money and such things, so when he wanted to talk over my investments . . .'

Samantha listened so attentively to what she had to say that after a while Agnes became quite animated and almost forgot that she was getting a headache.

CHAPTER ELEVEN

'And that's really all there was to it, dear,' Agnes concluded a little while later.

Samantha nodded. 'Yes, I see. Our Mr Potts-Gibbon *has* been a busy little bee, hasn't he?' she mused. 'I wouldn't be at all surprised if he hadn't come to this party purely to try and persuade Sir Bayard to agree to be a "name" on the letterhead of one of his enterprises. I have it on good authority that it's the sort of thing that he does. A frightfully well-bred friend of mine said he did the same to the Marquis of . . . Well, never mind all that. Let's just say I know quite a lot about our self-made man.'

'Do you, dear?' Agnes asked absently. 'I didn't know you knew him that well.'

'Oh I don't,' Samantha agreed. 'But after what happened a few years ago . . . oh, never mind. You wouldn't be interested. Let's just say that your "very clever" Mr Potts-Gibbon missed out on a very lucrative deal and he's probably still rather sore about it. Still, his loss was Bill's gain.'

'*Bill's* gain?' Agnes echoed, surprised. 'You mean Mr Endicott? I didn't know he was the kind of man who dealt in stocks and shares and things. I got the impression his family was independently wealthy, and he was pretty much a man of leisure.'

Samantha's fox-like face creased into a smile for a moment,

and then just as quickly became sombre again. 'Yes, he was very good at giving that impression, wasn't he?' she mused lightly. 'Oh well, never mind. I think I'll go and have a word with Sir Bayard. Do you know where he is?'

'Yes dear, I think I saw him in the garden a little while ago, near the tennis courts.'

'Ah. I'll see if I can catch him there then,' Samantha said, and giving her godmother's hand a brief pat, she got up and sashayed out.

Agnes watched her go, a small frown creasing her forehead. She looked and felt puzzled and was very out of sorts. And who could blame her? she thought resentfully. She'd had an awful, frightful shock, and now things felt very strange and all out of kilter, and she was so very afraid all the time. She had never been the kind of person who could cope with things very well, and she'd hoped that having Samantha beside her would steady her, but somehow, she felt worse, not better. She wanted nothing more than to go home to her lovely familiar house and her comforting maid and look out at her pretty view and pretend that none of the last few days had ever happened.

Restlessly, she began to fiddle with Samantha's things to try and distract herself. What was the point in being morbid? And, really, her goddaughter had such lovely things. A perfume bottle in the latest Art Deco style, with a cut-glass fan-shaped stopper in that lovely Bristol blue. And a splendid silver-and-black enamel cigarette holder – not that Agnes liked this modern fad of young women smoking, and she wished that Samantha hadn't picked up the habit. It was so unladylike. But then, the poor girl's mother had died when she was young, so she hadn't ever had the influence of a good woman in her life.

She sighed, and checked out a shade of lipstick which, well, really, was much too red. Almost *scarlet* in fact, and shuddering, she put it back down.

She was just reaching out to see what shade of powder her goddaughter used, when her elbow caught the edge of Samantha's beaded bag, and it fell to the floor, its contents spilling onto the Aubusson carpet. Agnes gave a little tut of exasperation and began to push the items back inside. She was just admiring the machine-turned pattern in a lovely shade of pink on the back of a hairbrush, when she noticed the opened envelope.

It was edged in red, and Samantha had made sure the letter stayed inside by tying a red ribbon around it. Which could only mean one thing, and it made Agnes's hopelessly romantic heart flutter.

A love letter! How thrilling.

Agnes had for years been secretly longing for the day when Samantha came to her and told her she was to get married at last. Agnes would be the matron of honour, of course, and would have to help her 'niece' pick out her dress and the colour of the bridesmaid's dresses, and what flowers to have in her bouquet, and the menu and . . . oh, such fun they would have!

Giving a quick, guilty look over her shoulder, she picked up the envelope and began playing with the ribbon. She wouldn't dream of undoing it, of course, but . . . oh drat! It had fallen off. Oh well, it wouldn't hurt to take just a peek inside. Just so that she would know the young man's name, and could reassure herself he was the 'right sort' and from a good family. She might even know him! Wouldn't it be wonderful if her clever, beautiful goddaughter had managed to snare a good match for herself? Maybe he even had a title? Wouldn't that be wonderful? If anyone could carry off becoming a lady, or even a countess, it was Samantha. Why, even Lady Sybil admired her style and élan.

And it wasn't being that naughty, was it? Samantha would

be bound to tell her all about her beau sooner or later – she always did end up telling her 'Aunty' everything. And why not? Agnes was the closest thing she had to a mother.

Feeling deliciously daring, Agnes opened the letter and began to read it.

She didn't realise that Samantha had left the door ajar, and that what she was doing was obvious to anyone who happened to be passing by.

*

It was late in the afternoon when a rather rattle-trap van pulled to a noisy halt on the outskirts of Middle Stratton. The faded lettering on the side of the van indicated that it had once hauled seed potatoes about, but if it still did so was a little less clear.

The man driving it turned off the engine, and the exhaust gave a little explosion in protest, the scent of slightly burnt oil briefly polluting the air. He wore a flat cap pulled low over his eyes and was dressed in a workman's outfit of dungarees over a shirt frayed at the collar and cuffs.

A passenger opened the door and climbed out.

'See you later then, guv'nor,' the driver said cheerily. 'Let me know when you need me.'

'I'll do that, Eli,' the passenger said heartily.

The driver nodded. 'You sure there's gonna be something in it for us?'

'Oh yes. From what my nephew said, I think we'll see some sort of action all right.'

The driver grinned, turned on the engine again, which coughed and complained but eventually caught, and then the van rattled off.

The man left behind stood looking around for a while, getting his bearings. 'Well, the boy was right about something.

This is definitely the back of beyond,' he muttered to himself, and started walking.

He was a fit but by no means young man, although he didn't look his sixty-one years. About five feet eight inches or so, he was neither fat nor thin and had slightly receding grey hair and eyes almost the same colour. He was carrying a rather battered suitcase, and as he walked, he whistled jauntily.

He found the inn with no difficulty, for a public house was one of his favourite places and he had all the instincts of a homing pigeon when it came to seeking out any available pleasure spots. For a moment he regarded the Job's Rest thoughtfully. At first glance, it wasn't particularly prepossessing, but he wasn't about to judge it until he'd tasted its beer.

According to his nephew, two other people were already staying there – a chap called Geraint who appeared intent on marrying one Valentina Coulton-James (so help him!) and another some sort of sharpie with a very particular dress code.

Which was, he thought, interesting enough in itself. Add some mysterious train that was up to no good, and a landlord who looked as if he'd passed through half the prisons in the kingdom, and there was definitely mischief to be had somewhere. Which was just how he liked it.

Arbie's uncle nodded to himself, then picked up his case and went inside. Like most buildings of this era, it was dark inside, with small windows and hidden wooden beams that could take your head off if you weren't careful. He approached the bar with an amiable grin.

He was wearing respectable but not fancy clothes and could have passed for a travelling salesman anywhere in the land. Which pleased him, but inevitably left him feeling a little insulted at the same time.

'Ah, landlord, a pint of your best if you please. And can a weary traveller find a room for the night?'

Amos Fairley pulled a pint of ale, watching the newcomer closely. 'Just one night?'

'Or maybe two,' Uncle said mildly, glancing around. 'Depends on how much trade I can drum up.' He thrust out his hand. 'Edward Roberton's the name,' he lied. Back in the village where he and Arbie lived, everyone simply called him 'Uncle'. And if nobody now remembered his given name, well, all the better as far as Uncle was concerned. 'And magazine subscription's my game,' he added, equally as mendaciously.

'I don't read much,' the landlord said hastily. 'And you can have the last room available if you want it. Ain't much to look at, but it's got a bed,' he added vaguely.

'Splendid! Could I get some victuals as well?'

Amos sniffed loudly. 'I suppose I could do some cold mutton, pickles and cheese.'

'Sounds like a feast fit for a king,' Uncle said happily, and settled himself down on the bar stool. He looked such a natural fit for it that Amos visibly relaxed, nodded once curtly and then pulled himself a pint as well, just to be sociable.

Amos hated to see a man drinking alone.

*

Monday dawned bright and cold with a touch of frost that added a sparkle of diamonds to the grass and hedges. These faux gems were quickly chased away by a strengthening sun, and robins, thrushes, chaffinches and a whole host of other feathered creatures were flitting about industriously, looking for grubs and worms to thrust into hungry, gaping mouths.

The inquest into the death of Bill Endicott was being held in the public saloon of the Job's Rest, being as it was the largest public space in the village.

The coroner was a man from the nearest town, one George

Maynard, who owned an undertaking business. Inspector Battle had come across him once or twice before in his career and was reasonably happy with his lot. At least the man could be trusted to keep things moving and put up with no nonsense from the public or witnesses.

Uncle, by dint of being under the roof already, was able to get a prime seat early on, but it didn't take long for the room to fill up. The death of a 'toff' from the local manor had been the talk of the village, and nobody wanted to miss out on any of the juicy details.

Outside, Arbie was in time to spot Inspector Battle approaching, and murmuring something to Val about going inside and saving him a seat, neatly intercepted the policeman.

'I say, Inspector, might I just have a very quick word with you?' Arbie asked anxiously. He then fidgeted a little under the sharp gaze the policeman gave him.

'I don't have much time, Mr Swift,' the Inspector pointed out from his lofty height, his eyes wary.

'Oh, no, I know, and I'm sorry. But I've only just come across something that I'd rather you knew about.'

'Oh? I do hope you haven't been up to your usual amateur sleuthing tricks, Mr Swift? I believe I told you before that we wouldn't tolerate any of that nonsense,' Battle said severely.

'No, I bally well haven't then!' Arbie said hotly, cut to the quick by the sheer injustice of the charge. 'In fact, if you knew the things I've had to put up with trying to keep Val *out* of things. . .' he began, then abruptly stopped.

'Ah. I see,' the Inspector said, beginning to look thoroughly amused now. 'Yes, I do think I begin to understand.'

Arbie flushed. 'Look, Inspector, can I just get this off my chest and then leave it all to you?' he begged earnestly.

'Indeed, you can, sir,' the Inspector said, beginning to look much more benignly on the younger man. 'So, what's it all about then?'

To the Inspector's astonishment, the author produced a book from under his arm and opened it at a marked page. 'Please, read the second paragraph down on page seventy-one.'

Instantly, the Inspector began to feel angry. 'Mr Swift, I have no desire to read your work right now, and . . .'

'It's not my work, blast you,' Arbie said, glancing around nervously. 'It's a perfectly awful tome by some charlatan doctor or other, that Miss Warren is currently infatuated with.'

'Oh yes, I vaguely remember from the constables' written reports that the lady was trying to thrust it upon all and sundry. Even the housekeeper.' The Inspector turned the book around so that he could read the title and tutted.

'Yes – and I got nobbled too,' Arbie said bitterly. 'But that's neither here nor there. Please, just read the passage,' he said, tapping the book at the appropriate spot.

The Inspector sighed but decided it might just be prudent to indulge him. Young Mr Swift might have been badgered into poking his nose into past police cases by the rather fetching and determined Miss Coulton-James, but there was no denying (to all appearances to the contrary) that the author must indeed have a very good head on his shoulders.

'Hmmm . . . all right, let me see,' Battle murmured and began to read out loud. '"*In order to clear your life of negative influences, it is a good idea to take a moment and set pen to paper and list all the things that are currently making you feel unhappy. Or which you perceive are making you unhappy. This will help clear your mind of extraneous influences and allow you to picture your difficulties in a more orderly manner. You can then set about thinking of ways and means to meet these dark clouds that are blocking your spiritual sunshine and allow you once again to emerge into the light of fulfilment . . .*" Good grief, what twaddle!' the policeman broke off in disgust.

'Oh yes, utter twaddle,' Arbie agreed amiably. 'Wrapped

up in sound common sense, in a way. But that's not the point. Doesn't anything about that strike a chord with you, Inspector?'

Battle nodded, for he had been known to use his brains on occasion. He looked at the author shrewdly. 'You're thinking of Mr Endicott's suicide note.'

Arbie nodded. 'You know, that struck me at once as being odd, and the more I've pondered on it, the more it worries me. For a start, it had no salutation. Not even a cursory "to whom it may concern". And it wasn't signed. All it really consisted of was . . .' He nodded at the book.

'A list of things that were making him unhappy. Yes,' the Inspector said uneasily. 'You're thinking Mr Endicott had read this bilge and had simply jotted down a list – probably as a jape or a joke. I can see how that could have happened. This Miss Warren of yours had probably induced him to read the odd chapter or two, just as you have.'

'Well, that wasn't exactly . . .' Arbie began, but the Inspector had just seen the coroner enter the inn.

'I'm sorry, the inquest is about to begin. Thank you for bringing this to my attention, Mr Swift, but I'm not sure that it gets us very far. And I can imagine what my superintendent would have to say about it should I try and present it to him as evidence of any kind. Firstly, we have no proof, only surmise, that Mr Endicott read this book at all. And even if he did, it could well be that, after having sat down and written out this list, even in jest, he might have begun drinking and become maudlin and fallen into a real depression about it.'

'That's still not what . . .' Arbie began, but already the Inspector was thrusting the book back into his unwilling arms.

'Come along, Mr Swift, we'll probably both be amongst the first to be called; better not keep the coroner waiting.' And with that he strode off, leaving Arbie trailing miserably in his wake.

*

The inquest into the death of Mr William Endicott began dead on time (no pun intended) and was conducted at a rapid and orderly rate. As he'd predicted, the Inspector was called to the stand first and gave a concise but full account of the events of that morning; of being called to Cleeves Lea Manor, on finding the deceased in the library and of interviewing Sir Bayard Cherville and his guests.

At this, the people in the packed room turned to ogle an uncomfortable-looking Sir Bayard. Neither Lady Sybil, Daphne and her husband, nor either of the Rowes were present as the police had their statements, and it was deemed that they had witnessed nothing of importance. (And if Sir Bayard had used his position to shield the majority of his guests from unnecessary unpleasantness, nobody – and certainly not Battle's superintendent – was going to make a fuss.)

After the Inspector had finished giving his evidence, it was the turn of the doctor who gave a rather dry and complicated account of his findings, which, boiled down to the nitty-gritty, confirmed that the young man had died of an overdose of Veronal, a common sleeping aid. Traces of it had been found in the dregs of a glass of Champagne that the deceased had consumed sometime around midnight.

There then followed a report from the scientists outlining the technical evidence, which made nearly everybody's eyes cross.

The note found beside the body was then read out loud by the coroner, after he'd solemnly informed the jury that an expert had concluded that it was indeed in the deceased's handwriting. Agnes, sitting beside a grim-faced and wildly elegant Samantha Remington, gave a little sob of distress on hearing this, and a little murmur of sympathy ran around the room for her. The housewives of Middle Stratton, it seemed, were unanimous in their support for the dowdy little woman who had been forced to attend the inquest. No doubt most of them had maiden aunts of their own, who – though generally deemed to be a nuisance – nevertheless induced a certain feeling of fondness and familiarity in the family bosom.

Arbie was called next, and there was a murmur of interest as the famous author took the stand. He'd dressed in country tweeds and looked every inch the gentleman as he gave his name, address, occupation and then a brief explanation of his presence at the manor. At the mention of the local ghost, there were some smiles, some 'oohs and ahhs' and a general feeling of approbation. The village of Middle Stratton was rather proud of the ghostly Jethro Hoskins.

The coroner quickly guided Arbie into giving his account of the finding of the body and what he'd done afterwards, and when he'd finished, Mr Maynard was gracious enough to commend Arbie on his intelligence in calling in the police immediately and making sure that the scene was secured and untampered with.

Next to be called to the stand was Agnes.

Trembling visibly, she took her seat next to the coroner and looked at him like a terrified rabbit.

Mr Maynard sighed inwardly and put on his softest voice.

'Now, Miss Warren, we won't keep you long. This is a very unpleasant business, and a lady such as yourself is bound to feel the strain, but if you can just bear up and be brave and answer my questions simply and plainly it will soon be over.'

'Oh, thank you, sir!' Agnes said gratefully.

'Now, we've heard that Mr Endicott died of an overdose of Veronal.'

Agnes drew her breath in sharply and nodded. She'd worn her best gloves in honour of the occasion, but her hands were twisting a handkerchief in her hand so agitatedly that it was in danger of tearing.

'And we have heard Inspector Battle's report that you regularly took Veronal and had brought your supply to the manor that weekend. Is that true?'

'Oh yes, sir,' Agnes admitted, barely above a whisper. 'I've always had trouble sleeping.'

'I'm sorry to hear that, Miss Warren. Now, when the Inspector talked to Lady Cherville, she recounted how another guest, a Mrs Elizabeth Rowe, had found Veronal in the bathroom. Was that yours?'

'Oh, I think it must have been,' Agnes said, her voice beginning to waver. 'I know I had some in my bag that I keep beside my bed, but I may well have left some in the bathroom too. At home, you see, I always put it in my bathroom cabinet, and I do perhaps do things out of habit without realising it and . . . Oh, I know it was wrong of me, but I never imagined someone else would take it! How could I?'

She began to sniffle alarmingly, and Mr Maynard hastily swept on.

'Nobody could know or suspect that, dear lady,' he reassured her. 'And no blame is being attached to you. We're simply trying to establish that Mr Endicott, who would have used the bathroom also, could have found the powders in the same way that Mrs Rowe did.'

'Oh yes. Well, I'm sure you know best,' Agnes said. 'Please, is that all?'

Wisely, Mr Maynard agreed that it was and dismissed her with a gentle thank you. Normally he would have censured any witness strongly about leaving personal medication lying around, but he was no fool. Not only would that have put the backs up of everyone in the room, but it would have reduced the lady in question into a quivering wreck. And Mr Maynard would rather not have quivering wrecks in his courtroom.

After that, Mr Endicott's father was called to the stand. Ernest

Endicott was a very upright gentleman, dressed like a banker and was rather stiff in his manner, but he was clearly grieving. Mr Maynard handled him deftly.

'I understand that you were somewhat estranged from your son, Mr Endicott,' he began, after checking Inspector Battle's written report.

'Yes, I'm afraid that's true,' Mr Endicott senior admitted. 'He'd lost his mother a little over a year ago, and he was an only child, and I'm afraid she rather spoiled him. He felt her loss keenly. I'd been trying to get the boy to settle down to a career for a long time, and I'm afraid, after his mother died, I rather lost patience with him.'

'He, er, regularly approached you for living expenses, I believe?' Mr Maynard said delicately, again consulting Inspector Battle's report on his interview with the dead man's father.

Ernest Endicott's shoulders drooped a little. 'Yes. So much so, that six months ago I told him it was the last time I would give him any more money. I told him he was a grown man and needed to buckle down and shift for himself, like every other man in this country.'

At this there were many nods from the hard-working men in the room, and quite a few from the even more hard-working women also.

'I see. And how did your son react to this ultimatum?'

Ernest shrugged. 'In his usual carefree manner. He told me cheerfully what I could do with my "piffling" handouts and informed me that a friend of his had offered him a position and he would take it up.'

'I see. This would be . . .' Here Mr Maynard shuffled through the Inspector's report. 'This would be Mr James Deering? Let me see . . . yes, he owns a fleet of garages and sells cars?'

'Yes. He gave Bill a job as a salesman. Sports cars, that sort of thing. Apparently, he did rather well at it,' Ernest said with pride. But then his shoulders stooped a little. 'Well, at first, anyway.'

'At first?'

The dead man's father sighed. 'The trouble with Bill is . . . er . . . was . . . is that he was easily bored. He never could stick at anything. He had brains enough to do well at school, but never really applied himself. It was always the same story. He'd get these great ideas, which if he'd stuck at them would have worked out, but he'd just lose interest. I've since been in contact with Mr Deering and he tells me that Bill picked an argument with him, and Mr Deering had no choice but to give him his marching orders. I didn't blame him,' Mr Endicott senior put in hastily. 'It wasn't the first time he'd lost a perfectly good job.'

'I see,' the coroner said, his disapproval obvious. 'I'm sorry if this is a painful question, Mr Endicott, but was your son prone to depression at all?'

'I wouldn't say so, no,' the man said, straightening up stiffly.

'But he *was* prone to mood swings, would you say? The police have been diligently questioning your son's friends, and they all seem to indicate that he could be moody. And the argument he had with the man who'd been kind enough to give him employment would seem to indicate a man of, shall we say, an uncertain temper?'

'Oh, he was always up and down I suppose,' Mr Endicott admitted reluctantly.

'Did he drink much?' Maynard asked casually.

'Yes. In my opinion, more than he should have. He always seemed to crave adventure of some kind, and as result, he lived a rackety kind of existence. He went through money like it was water. Feast or famine, that was Bill,' his father said sadly.

After dismissing the last witness, the coroner then went into his summing up. He painted a picture of Bill Endicott as a rather unstable young man, prone to fits of temper and mood swings, who drank too much and lived a rather reckless, shambolic life. He pointed out the note left behind. He pointed out the easy access the deceased had to a common sleeping prescription. He pointed out the fingerprint evidence on the glass and bottle of Champagne that showed only the dead man's prints. And he asked them to consider their verdict.

Nobody was surprised when, after a whispered consultation, the foreman of the jury returned a verdict of suicide.

*

Sir Bayard returned to the big house via his Rolls-Royce, and by a bit of dextrous handling, Arbie had persuaded Val to return with him.

Now, spotting his uncle retiring to one of the benches in the back of the pub's garden with a pint of ale, he joined him surreptitiously under the shade of a large horse chestnut tree.

'Hello, Uncle,' he greeted him softly, glancing around. But most of the villagers, now that the excitement was over, were dispersing back to their homes and jobs, and none seemed to notice the two men conversing quietly in the shadows.

'Hello, my boy. What did you make of the doings then?' Uncle asked curiously, nodding towards the inn. 'Seems to me like a suicide verdict was inevitable.'

'Oh yes, I suppose it was,' Arbie agreed flatly.

His uncle regarded him thoughtfully under his somewhat bushy eyebrows. 'Don't believe it then, boy?' he asked, genuinely curious. Secretly, he was rather chuffed with the way his nephew had solved two previous cases of murder but he'd been very careful not to show it. For a start, he didn't wholly approve of the boy mixing with the law in the way that he did, and for another, it alarmed him to think of Arbie swanning around in the company of murderers. The boy was bright enough, but lacked experience in the ways of the world, and he'd be relieved when some woman took him in hand and put a stop to it all.

Arbie sighed. 'I think it unlikely Bill killed himself,' he admitted. 'But that's not why I asked you to come up here, as you know,' he said. 'It's that other business that worries me. This blasted train. What's it up to, Uncle? That's what I want to know.'

'Ah yes – the devil's train. I've been keeping my eyes peeled and my ears flapping. Been getting round some of the locals too. They all know about it, right enough, and none of 'em will venture into the valley on certain nights.' He nodded sagely and took a sip of his ale.

Arbie wasn't surprised by his relative's quick work. If anyone could ferret out nefarious doings, it was his uncle. 'Any ideas?'

'Oh, my boy, it's as plain as a pikestaff!'

'Is it?'

''Course it is. Use your head, lad. We have a little out-of-the-way place in the back of beyond, not six miles from a deserted coastline. We've got a railway network that connects with all the big cities for miles around. We've got an ex-mariner taking up a position as a landlord in a tumble-down inn that barely makes a profit. Connect all the dots, and what do you get?'

Arbie sighed heavily. 'Smuggling?'

Uncle nodded happily and rubbed his hands together gleefully. 'Right you are. Smuggling – stands to reason. That Amos Fairley would have been a pirate had he been born a few centuries ago, and no mistake. As it is, I reckon he's got something going with some of his dodgy sea-faring mates. Dark of night, and well away from the prying eyes of the customs men, they haul their goodies onto this train of yours and send it speeding down the line to be dispersed hither and yon.'

'Any ideas what they're smuggling?'

'Well, it could be anything. Booze, cigarettes, anything that carries a heavy duty. But after having observed our none-too-friendly landlord for the last twenty-four hours or so, my bet is on booze. Think about it – if he's ever raided, and they find a stock of booze in his cellars, he can always claim he'd been stockpiling it for his business. France isn't that far away, and those Frenchies like their wines and cognacs and what have you. Good stuff, too, it is,' he said approvingly, having downed more than his fair share of such wares in his lifetime.

Now he rubbed his hands in glee. 'With a bit of luck and some smart thinking, lad, we should be able to land ourselves some crates of the best brandy and spirits on the market. Or rather, on the black market! Save one or two good specimens for our own cellar and then sell on the rest. A nice little earner if ever there was one.'

'Uncle!' Arbie yelped. 'You're supposed to be here to help me keep out of trouble – not land me in any more of it!'

CHAPTER TWELVE

Two hours later, Arbie was walking along one side of the railway tracks, his uncle on the other.

Arbie's thoughts were not happy ones. He'd been orphaned young and raised by his uncle, and they both lived together in what had once been a chapel back in his home village of Maybury-in-the-Marsh. Uncle, who fancied himself – among other things – as a bit of an architect, had spent years re-structuring it into something truly unique. (Arbie was ten by the time he managed to track down the only permanent bathroom in the edifice.) He remembered his childhood with fondness though, as it had been an incredibly happy one. His uncle's relaxed (some interfering busybodies might have said 'scandalous') approach to child-rearing had suited them both, and he had never felt any cause for complaint with his lot.

Except for what he always referred to as his uncle's forays into the wilder side of life, which sometimes left him baffled, anxious and, once or twice, quite frankly terrified. Holding down a regular job had never been something his relative had ever contemplated, which Arbie understood only too well. (He himself had the same aversion.) Because of this, Uncle had had to make ends meet in a variety of different ways. He was, for instance, a talented painter, and several galleries regularly sold his daubs. But Arbie often wondered uneasily about the 'copies' he made in the 'style of' various collectable artists for some of his friends; friends who were never let into the house, but only into his barn-like studio.

Then there were the 'little windfalls' that came his way, the origins of which were never fully explained. There were other little curious peccadillos he could also mention, the majority of which induced in him the same reaction – anxiety. And given his guardian's somewhat hit-and-miss approach to the law, there had been moments in his life when he fully expected the village constable to come and cart Uncle away.

That it had never happened (yet) Arbie put down to a combination of his relative's innate cunning, spectacular luck, and his extremely convoluted way of doing things.

And here, he thought morosely, was yet another example. Although he'd managed to talk his uncle into agreeing that after they'd scouted around a bit and were sure they had a reasonable idea of the ins and outs of the devil train's activities, they would hand all their findings over to Inspector Battle. Whether that policeman would show any gratitude for their efforts was another matter, and one he didn't want to dwell on too closely. But he was still left with an uneasy feeling that there would be a hitch in the proceedings somewhere.

And that the hitch, moreover, would somehow end up benefiting his uncle. He could only hope that, yet again, his relative's expertise in avoiding any unpleasant (and legal) consequences would hold steady, and that whatever he was planning to do would not result in him, Arbie, having to find bail money.

It was, therefore, not surprising that as he moodily walked along the line, carefully inspecting the ground for any signs of activity that suggested a stopping point where the train was met by a cart or any other kind of vehicle, Arbie was heartily wishing that he hadn't given in to his craven cowardice and called in his uncle for reinforcements after all.

Really, he told himself savagely, he should have known better!

'There's some disturbance here, boy, but I'm pretty sure it's just a crossing place for sheep,' his uncle called to him from the other side of the track.

'Righty-oh,' Arbie replied listlessly, then lifting his head from his perusal of the ground, glanced around nervously. He'd been doing so ever since they'd started their inspection, but so far he'd seen no one. But that didn't mean that someone might not be watching them through binoculars right now before reporting back to the unsavoury Amos Fairley. And his uncle's cheerful assertion that if they *were* spotted, they could always claim to be looking for the ghost of Jethro Hoskins, didn't exactly fill him with confidence.

Call him wildly pessimistic if you liked, but somehow, he didn't think the landlord of the Job's Rest would be inclined to believe it.

He could see, a few hundred yards farther up and set a little back from the lines, a ramshackle wooden building, well-fallen into a state of disrepair. At some point it might have been a shepherd's hut, or maybe it had been some kind of equipment storage shack for the railroad. Whatever it had been, nature was well on its way to reclaiming it, for an ash sapling was growing happily in and out of one of its walls, whilst moss and lichen had turned what remained of the slate roof tiles a dull green.

By the time he'd come parallel with it, he could see that the door was missing altogether, and the glass windows were all broken, with ivy beginning to straggle its way inside.

'Better check that out,' his uncle called over to him. 'Looks too small to be any use to our smugglers, mind. You won't fit a huge amount of booty in there, but they might use it for something else. You never know. If they have, they might have left some clue behind.'

'All right,' Arbie sighed, eyeing the hut with displeasure. His uncle continued walking, and Arbie reluctantly left the tracks and made for the door. As he did so, a sudden chill wind seemed to rise out of nowhere and made him shiver. At the same time, he became aware that he could hear no birdsong.

Had that just happened, or had they been quiet for some time, and he'd just not noticed?

Then he saw, painted on the side of the hut, the railway's initials, making it a definite adjunct to the railway company, and he paused nervously. The building (such as it was) was certainly old enough to have been in proper use in Jethro's day. Perhaps it was a lineman's little shack, somewhere he could go to get out of the bad weather in the winter months, and maybe make himself a brew of tea?

Perhaps Jethro had even been in there on the night of the fateful storm, seeking shelter before leaving it to do his duty and check on the state of the bridge farther down the line?

Another chill breeze swept over him and now the silence seemed portentous, even ominous. He swallowed hard and told himself not to be such a nincompoop. It was broad daylight after all and his uncle was only twenty or so yards further on down the line. And nobody had ever reported seeing the resident ghost in daylight hours.

Nervously, he approached the door and cautiously stuck his head inside. It was dark in there, for ivy had indeed invaded the interior, and its lush evergreen leaves had shut out most of the ambient light. There was a very faint smell of old oil. Some rickety wooden shelving, lined with various tins, jars and boxes containing who knows what, had been added underneath one of the windows, and some old hessian sacking, lying rotting in the damp corner at the back, gave off a scent musty enough to make him cough slightly. It was at that point that a wood pigeon, who regularly roosted in the hut at night, became aware of an invading human presence. He'd just been out in the fields, gorging himself on a mound of spilled seed, and now his crop was pleasantly full.

The sudden appearance of one of those odd, two-legged predators had been the last thing Arbie was expecting and was very unwelcome indeed. Like the rest of his kind, he was a big, clumsy bird, inclined to panic and make a racket when disturbed. He immediately stretched his wings and prepared to fly out of a broken window, but in his desire to be gone, one of his legs caught an empty oil can and sent it spinning. Alas, on the way down to the ground, it hit various other precariously balanced objects on the shelves below it, sending a whole cascade of noisy tins onto the floor.

Arbie, who only caught a glimpse of some vague, grey-tinted shape that loomed suddenly up into the air, heard the loud clattering and gave a yelp of fear, his imaginative mind leaping at once to a single conclusion.

Poltergeist.

Poltergeists were notorious for throwing things around, moving objects and making weird, knocking noises (and were the most faked of all phenomena), but he hadn't been expecting to find one here in the middle of nowhere, and such an active one at that!

For his part, the poor wood pigeon heard the odd, two-legged predator make a sound that he didn't like one little bit. It was not the sharp crack that came from the stick-like things they sometimes pointed at birds, making them fall out of the sky, but rather more like a sound sheep made when it was in distress.

Frantically, the pigeon furthered its desperate efforts to escape, and in doing so, its flailing wings knocked out a piece of loose glass from the window that it was scrambling to get through and it shattered noisily.

Arbie, who was now in the process of removing himself from

the doorway, recognised the tinkling of glass and instinctively ducked. He now had no doubts that the poltergeist inside the shack was of a particularly vicious nature and was trying to lacerate him!

He gave another wild bleat of panic and began to run.

The wood pigeon, witnessing this further evidence of alarm and fear from the top predator, was now quickly going beyond mere pigeon-brained panic into something approaching downright feathery hysteria.

Arbie, nearly falling over his feet in his haste to get out of range before being pierced through by a shard of projected glass, stumbled and yelped again. During his research, he'd come across tales of people who had encountered poltergeists and been so badly affected by the experience, that they'd sickened and even died. One thing was for certain – he wasn't going to look back. He had absolutely no desire to see whatever it was that might now be chasing him. Why risk looking over his shoulder and perhaps seeing something so monstrous that it would turn his hair white overnight?

By this point, the pigeon had managed to get leverage on the window frame and was already flapping his wings with fury so that he could force himself through the ash sapling that was blocking his way. Arbie, hearing the snapping of twigs coming from behind him, put on an extra burst of speed – which was truly impressive, as he was already dashing away at a rate of knots that would have astounded (and wildly pleased) the track and field coach at his old school.

Whatever hideous thing had been in the shed, Arbie was now convinced, was trying to get out! And probably wanted to eat his liver.

Now, the innocent wood pigeon – had he been able to hear or understand Arbie's thoughts – would have been truly astonished to hear himself being described in such a way. True, he was a fine specimen of wood-pigeon-hood, having been around for two summers and therefore knew his onions all right, but given the chance of fight or flight, he would always choose flight.

Thus, when he saw the fearsome two-legged predator running for his life in what the bird instinctively realised was a state of mortal terror, the poor pigeon nearly fell out of the sky in fright himself. One thing was for sure – whatever awful danger had been present in his normally safe roosting spot, he wanted nothing to do with it.

The wood pigeon was no fool.

By the time Arbie drew level with the comforting, fellow human presence that was his uncle, he'd managed to get a hold of himself enough to reduce his headlong flight into what looked like a slight jog.

His uncle looked across at him questioningly. 'What's up with you, lad? You look like you've seen a ghost,' he said with a grin.

Arbie, who was rapidly gaining control of himself once more, forced himself to grin back. He knew he'd never be believed if he tried to explain his near miss. But more pertinently, he knew that his uncle would insist on them going back just so that he could see the poltergeist for himself!

And that Arbie was not having.

'Very funny, Uncle,' he managed to say, around his noisy panting for breath.

'Anything interesting in the shed then?' Uncle asked next.

'No,' Arbie warbled quickly. 'Nothing at all.' But the skin on the back of his neck was still crawling, and not for all the tea in China would he be induced to turn and look back at that shed.

To his relief, his uncle merely shrugged and carried on walking doggedly. 'If we don't see any signs of a rendezvous point in the next couple of hours, we'll try further down the tracks tomorrow.'

'As you like, Uncle,' Arbie agreed readily, still rubbing the back of his cold neck with a shaking hand.

From the safety of the branches of a beech tree, the wood pigeon watched the two-legged predators recede into the distance, his chest feathers puffed out to generate some much-needed warmth after such a fright.

One thing was for certain. He was going to have find another roosting spot.

*

By the time he got back to the manor, Arbie had already decided he would not tell Val about the haunted railway shack. He'd also decided he was not going to do another ghost watch either. He'd had enough for one trip.

Tomorrow he was going to make his excuses and he and Val would catch the first train out.

That was the plan.

CHAPTER THIRTEEN

Tuesday morning saw Arbie down early for breakfast, his packed bags ready and waiting for collection in his room. He'd chickened out of telling Val last night that they would definitely be leaving today – and not staying on to do more work on the book – preferring to wait until the last minute to let her know so that she'd have less time to complain about it and attempt to talk him out of things.

So when she came downstairs she was her usual self and Arbie, having eaten his fill, cravenly told her that he'd see her outside in the gardens later and wandered outside. It was another beautiful day, but he had no eyes for the glories of spring. Instead, he made his way slowly through the rose garden, to where a bench was placed beside a small ornamental pool.

He was feeling a little guilty at abandoning his uncle, which, he knew, was ridiculous. His uncle had been getting himself in and out of scrapes long before Arbie had ever been born.

Back in the house, all the guests had now assembled and were chatting desultorily over the bacon and eggs. The Rowes were happy to be leaving and trying not to show it, and Daphne and her husband were likewise inclined, but perhaps hiding it better. Even the Chervilles, whilst still the epitome of hospitable hosts, were secretly relieved at the prospect of the house emptying and freeing them from their social obligations.

Only Samantha Remington failed to appear at the breakfast table, leaving Agnes to apologise for her. This she did in her usual manner, saying that she thought her 'niece' rarely ate breakfast and had probably asked her maid to just bring her tea in bed and she hoped nobody minded.

Oddly enough, nobody did.

Within a quarter of an hour, the breakfast room was empty.

*

Outside the garage, Sir Bayard's Rolls-Royce was being cleaned by the chauffeur, in anticipation of its trips to the railway station, and Arbie was just watching an early yellow brimstone butterfly flitting amongst the primroses, when a horrified scream rent the air.

Arbie jumped out of his skin whilst simultaneously jumping off the bench and began to race towards the sound. As he did so, the scream turned into a blood-chilling wail.

'She's dead. She's dead. Help! Help, come quick. She's dead!'

The voice he recognised instantly as belonging to Lady Sybil. He thought it was coming from one of the side terraces that surrounded the house, and he shot up the main shallow steps and hared off to the left, where he could still hear his hostess's repeated wails for help. As he did so, his mind was racing.

She was dead.

But which 'she'?

He sensed swift movements coming from another part of the garden, which were beginning to intersect with his own and turned his head slightly, relief flooding through him as he saw it was Val. She was safe! And with her, just managing to keep up with her, was Geraint, who must have just arrived to call on Val. The third person – who was unable to keep up with their speed – was Daphne Potts-Gibbon, falling farther behind with every step but still gamely running towards the sound of Sybil's continued laments.

But Arbie was ahead of them all as he rounded the side of the house, instantly taking in the scene ahead of him. The terrace was a relatively small one that overlooked a lawn housing a pretty fountain set within a small ornamental pond. But he was not quite the first to arrive on the scene of the tragedy, however.

He expected to see Lady Sybil, and she was there, pacing up and down and wringing her hands. She saw Arbie round the corner of the house and began to approach him, relief flooding her face, then almost immediately she turned and looked behind her. She then staggered back and ran towards the French windows, reaching out with her hands to someone stepping through them. A moment later, Arbie saw that it was her husband.

'Hold hard, old girl, what on earth's the matter?' Sir Bayard asked, his tone gruff with alarm.

As Arbie pounded closer, his eyes went to the figure slumped over a white wrought-iron table. She was sitting on the matching chair, her long brown hair spilling over her face and down the sides of the table, almost reaching the ground.

By the time he reached her, he was walking slowly and cautiously. He could feel Val and Geraint crowding in behind him and he held out both arms instinctively to prevent them from coming any closer.

Sir Bayard was helping his wife to collapse onto a chair. She had begun to sob quietly. From inside the house, through the open French doors, he could hear Elizabeth and

Bernadette Rowe's agitated voices, and a few moments later, the masculine voice of Roger Potts-Gibbon asking them what was going on.

Cautiously, careful not to touch a thing and feeling just slightly sick, Arbie approached Samantha Remington's slumped form. She appeared to be unconscious, and at first, he couldn't understand why Lady Sybil had been so sure that she was dead. It was more likely, surely, that she'd either had a fainting spell, or been taken ill, or . . .

And it was then that he saw it. Sticking out of the nape of her neck, but almost flush to her skin, was a complicated and twisted piece of silver with a single pearl attached in the middle. No man who'd ever had to wait for a woman in a hallway whilst she pulled on her coat, gloves and hat could possibly have failed to identify it.

It was the ornamental top of a hat pin.

Arbie swallowed hard. These, he knew, invariably had long, thin and sharp spikes attached to them, to secure the fabric of the hat to the hair of the wearer. Which meant that the length of that spike must now lie buried deep within the base of Samantha Remington's skull.

Lady Sybil had been right all along. She was mostly definitely dead.

'What is it?' he heard Val ask tentatively behind him.

'It's Samantha,' Arbie said, his voice sounding a little odd in his ears. He turned to look at Val over his shoulder and gave her a wobbly sort of smile. 'I'm afraid she's dead, old bean.'

Instantly, Geraint put an arm around her and tried to pull her away. And after a quick glance at Arbie's pale face, she allowed herself to be led to the end of a terrace, where a low stone wall, prevented anyone from falling the few feet into the flower beds below. There they both sat down in miserable silence.

Arbie turned and looked towards the Chervilles, catching Sir Bayard's appalled eye. The Lord of the Manor patted his wife's shaking shoulders, straightened up and marched over. There he stood beside Arbie looking down at the second person to die in his house within the last few days.

Through the French windows the two Rowes and Roger stepped, looking around in bewilderment. By now Daphne had gained the terrace also, and catching sight of her, her husband walked to meet her. Whether by accident or design, he didn't look towards the table and chair that held its grisly burden.

'Hello, Daphers,' Arbie heard him murmur. 'What on earth is going on? Was that Lady Sybil shouting?'

Arbie tuned out the explanation being given to him and instead turned to his grim-faced host.

'Sir, we need to call Inspector Battle again,' he said urgently. 'Nothing must be touched. It would be best if everyone went back inside and perhaps . . . hot cups of tea?'

Sir Bayard nodded, looking relieved at having something to do. 'Yes.' He tugged his tweed jacket down a little more firmly and stuck out his chin. 'Yes, you're quite right. Quite right. I'll ask Jardine to get the tea organised. We must get the ladies away from here. Will you telephone the police?'

Arbie nodded.

Sir Bayard raised his voice. 'I think we should all retire to the lounge. There's been a dreadful . . . accident, and I'm afraid Miss Remington is . . . er . . . has passed away.'

At this, there seemed to come a collective, swiftly drawn breath, and then a blank silence.

'Has anyone seen Agnes this morning?' Sir Bayard asked vaguely, looking around.

'She hasn't come down yet,' Sybil managed to mumble. 'She's nearly always the last. I suppose someone should go up and tell her, but . . . oh my, I can't face that right now. She'll be down soon anyway, and we can break it to her then.'

Elizabeth Rowe gently told her daughter to 'come with me, dear,' and Roger said something comforting to his wife. Geraint ushered Val towards the open French doors, careful to put the bulk of his body between himself and the dead woman, so that Val wouldn't have to see her.

Arbie waited until they'd all gone, then glanced around. To his relief, he spotted the chauffeur and a couple of gardeners, who had also raced to the scene in response to the cries of the mistress of the house. They were loitering around the ornamental pond, looking unsure and uneasy.

'Ah, would you mind?' Arbie said, beckoning to the chauffeur and the two men, who approached reluctantly. 'I just want you to wait here whilst I go and telephone the police. Don't come any closer than you are now, and don't, whatever you do, touch anything. I just need you to watch over Miss Remington until I return, and make sure no one, er, disturbs her. Understand?'

'Right you are, sir,' one of the older gardeners said, doffing his cap.

Arbie nodded and raced around to the front, which was the nearest entrance into the hall and thus the telephone booth. Once inside the little wooden cubicle, he got the operator, and a short while later, was speaking to the local police station and asking for Inspector Battle. To his frustration, he was stolidly informed that Inspector Battle had returned to the larger town from whence he'd come, and Arbie was obliged to inform the constable on duty to bally well send for him, sharpish.

'Tell him there's been another death at Cleeves Lea Manor,' he said flatly. 'And tell him, this time, there's no mistake. It's murder.'

At this, predictably, the constable on the other end began to squawk and kept Arbie on the line for several tiresome minutes, answering questions that could have waited. Eventually he was able to hang up the receiver and began to cross the hall.

He could hear muted conversation issuing from the lounge, but just as he was passing the large grandfather clock, he heard movement coming from above and behind him. His nerves were so tense that as he swivelled, his hands, already clenched into fists, were starting to come up in front of him in a pugilistic gesture of defence. But it was only Agnes Warren, turning the last bend in the staircase and hurrying down, her little patent leather shoes making tappity-tap sounds as she descended.

She saw him, and her worried face cleared a bit. 'Oh, Mr Swift! Is everything quite all right? I was in my room, and I thought I heard dear Lady Sybil crying out. I hope she's all right? She hasn't fallen, has she? I had a little fall down some steps last year, and . . .'

Stoically, Arbie let her querulous voice wash over him as she related the many inconveniences caused by a twisted ankle. All the while, though, he was wondering just how he could possibly tell her about the fate that had befallen her much-admired goddaughter.

Then Val was there. With her sharp ears, she'd heard Agnes's voice in the hall and had come to his rescue. Arbie watched with relief as she approached the worried woman and gently put a hand on her arm. 'Miss Warren, why don't you come with me?' she said quietly, her blue eyes soft with sympathy. 'I'm afraid there's been a terrible accident,' instinctively she co-opted Sir Bayard's description of the recent events, 'and you're going to have to be very brave.'

At this, Agnes went rather pale. 'Oh. Oh. Is it . . . is it truly very bad?' she whispered.

Val took her arm and let the other woman lean on her. 'Yes, my dear, I'm afraid it is,' she said gently. Patting the hand on her arm, she gently guided the woman towards the lounge.

Arbie, with profound gratitude, watched them depart, then went back outside to relieve the chauffeur and the gardeners from their guard duty.

He could only hope that help wouldn't be long in coming.

*

The first person to arrive was the same local doctor who had called before, no doubt alerted by the constable to get himself to Cleeves Lea Manor as fast as he could. Arbie heard his car coming up the driveway and moved to the end of the terrace so that he could wave at him frantically and divert him to where he was most needed.

Luckily the doctor saw him and instantly stopped his car, collected his bag and began to half-run towards him, his eyes alert, his mouth a slim, grim line.

'What now, young man?' he asked briskly, on arrival.

Wordlessly, Arbie beckoned him further down the terrace and deliberately lagged behind as the medical man, spotting the woman half-lying over the table, rushed to her side.

Arbie looked determinedly away. A woodpecker was hammering away at the bark of an ailing sycamore tree, and he watched its antics as closely as any avid bird-watcher would have done. It was a yaffle, and its lovely green plumage and red-tinted head glowed like jewels in the morning sun. He was so determined to remain engrossed in the lovely sight, and not think of the horror behind him, that when the doctor touched his arm, he started.

'Sorry, er, doctor, I was miles away. Did you say something?'

The doctor looked at him keenly, diagnosed mild shock, and wisely refrained from giving him the standard advice. 'Well, she's gone,' he said instead.

'Yes. I know,' Arbie said listlessly.

'I'll wait here with you until the police arrive,' the doctor said, heading for the same low wall that Val and Geraint had sat upon earlier. Arbie, glad of the company, went with him and the two men were sitting in companiable silence when the local constable pedalled up the drive on his old black boneshaker, some five minutes later.

He spotted Arbie and the doctor on the wall and abandoned his bicycle and trotted over to them. He took a quick look at the body on the terrace, turned rather pale, swallowed hard once or twice, then started questioning Arbie.

Wearily, Arbie set about satisfying his curiosity, and it was whilst the constable was scribbling diligently in his notebook, that a car appeared around the bend in the drive. With relief, Arbie recognised it as belonging to the Inspector. It swept past them to the main entrance of the house, however, and it was a few minutes later before Battle and Jellicoe stepped through the French doors and slowly approached the dead woman.

After a brief inspection, Battle turned, gave the two men sitting on the wall a long, thoughtful look, and addressed his sergeant. His words carried clearly across the warm, still air.

'Telephone headquarters and tell them they need to send everyone they can. This is now officially a murder investigation.'

After the Sergeant had hurried off, the Inspector walked across to the doctor and Arbie. He stood in front of them silently, his great height and their low wall forcing both men to look up at him, as if looking up at the moon. But even though the Inspector's face was as enigmatic as the man in the moon, Arbie had no trouble reading it.

'You're going to re-open Bill Endicott's case, aren't you?' Arbie said, more as a statement than a question.

The Inspector regarded the young writer thoughtfully for a moment, and then slowly nodded. 'Oh yes,' he said, surprisingly mildly. 'I think so. Don't you?'

*

The Inspector turned to the doctor. 'I realise you've only just arrived, doctor, but is there anything you can tell me now?'

The medical man stood up and glanced back at Samantha Remington. 'I can only tell you what you can see with your own eyes, I'm afraid. The nape of her neck was pierced by what looks like a hat pin at an upward angle, which would mean that the metal spike would have entered the base of the brain and probably killed her instantly. That's why there's nothing more than a drop or two of blood on the back of her neck, since her heart would have immediately stopped pumping blood. Bad news for you, I assume, since I doubt whoever did it would have got much blood on them, if any at all. I can tell you she was still warm to a certain extent, which leads me to believe that she's been dead less than an hour – certainly not more than two. From my very preliminary examination, I can see no other wounds, so there's no outward evidence that she was able to put up a fight for her life with her attacker.'

He shrugged helplessly. 'As the rest, it's pure speculation. From the position of the body – which I don't believe has been moved or interfered with – I suspect the poor young woman was sitting at the table, and her killer came up behind and . . . well, did their business. It's to be hoped that the victim never knew or perhaps even felt what was being done to her.' The doctor gave a little shake of his shoulders. 'Once you've delivered her to the mortuary and a proper post-mortem can be carried out, your own man will doubtless be able to give you a full report. Now I really must get on – I have two patients waiting for me back at my surgery.'

'Of course – thank you, doctor.' The two men watched him leave the terrace and head back to his car, and a somewhat awkward silence took up residence between the Inspector and Arbie. Then the tall man folded himself in half and sat down on the wall next to the writer, sticking his long, long legs straight out in front of him, otherwise, Arbie surmised, his knees would have been higher than his ears.

He gave a soft sigh. 'I've been talking to my colleagues in your home district, and those on the coast, where you were so helpful to them before.' This was said with such dryness that Arbie could have sworn he could feel desert sand pooling around his feet. 'They told me that you're the observant sort, so during your time here, you've probably been using to good effect your eyes, ears and, presumably, what must be that very fine brain of yours.' The Inspector's lips twisted into what might have been a smile. 'And may I congratulate you on the fine job that you do of keeping the latter so very well concealed.'

'Thank you,' Arbie managed, with dignity.

The Inspector sighed again, then appeared to resign himself to the inevitable. 'All right,' he said briskly. 'Tell me.'

Arbie blinked. 'Er, tell you what exactly?'

'What you've seen, what you've heard and what you think,' Battle said patiently, clearly beginning to wonder if his colleagues from down south had been pulling his leg about his companion's unexpected and baffling prowess.

'Oh. Sorry. Yes. Righty-oh,' Arbie said, scrambling to put his thoughts in order. 'I suppose the best thing to do is to start with the people here,' he muttered, indicating the house behind him, 'and then add in the extras, so to speak.'

Battle made no attempt to take notes, seeming to be rather more interested in the state of his feet than anything else. Arbie couldn't help but be impressed by the colossal memory the man must have.

'Well, here goes,' Arbie said, 'but just remember these are only my own private thoughts and conclusions. I have no proof of anything really – and certainly not what you chaps would call evidence.' Seeing the Inspector nod solemnly down at his feet, Arbie took that as a sign that his warning had been noted. 'It seems to me that Sir Bayard and his wife are not quite on the best of terms. Right from the start there was a bit of an atmosphere between them – you know what I mean? Nothing you can get a hold of, just the odd look, or the occasional bite to the tone that indicates all is not hunky-dory.'

'Any idea what it was all about?'

'I'm not sure, but Bill told me over our game in the billiards room that his invitation to the party came from Sir Bayard, as opposed from Lady Sybil, which seems to be the usual drill. It's certainly the case that all the other guests' invitations came from the lady of the house. I think, if you question the servants, you'll find that she didn't know about him coming until the very last minute. I dare say they'd have had to scramble to get an extra room ready and warn the cook about having an extra mouth to feed, and so on.'

The Inspector shot a glance at the younger man. In truth, despite his colleagues' warnings to the contrary, he had not expected to be much impressed with Mr Swift, and having to rapidly rearrange his expectations was leaving him feeling mildly grumpy.

'And from that you deduce what?' he asked cautiously, still not convinced that this opening gambit wasn't a fluke.

'Oh, well, you know, it struck me that Sir Bayard must

have had a specific reason for wanting Bill Endicott here this weekend. He's the sort of chap who normally leaves all the social stuff to his wife – as most husbands do, I've noticed. So, for him to step out of line, as it were, seems odd. Especially as his wife was so obviously angry about it.'

'She was?'

Here, Arbie shuffled a little on the wall. 'Well, according to Miss Coulton-James she was, and I've found Val is really good at knowing about this sort of thing.'

The Inspector's lips twitched. 'Yes. I imagine that she is. Did you – or Miss Val – come to any conclusion as to what it all meant?'

Arbie nodded glumly. 'Yes – we both rather thought that it was possible that Mr Endicott and Lady Sybil had become, er, rather friendly of late, and that her husband didn't much like it.'

'You think he brought Endicott down here to have it out?'

Arbie shrugged helplessly. 'Now there you have me, old sport. To me it seems an odd sort of thing for a chap to do. If you expect to have a flaming row with your wife, why would you invite a house party down for the weekend and then pick a fight right in the middle of it?'

'Hmmm. Unlikely, I grant you. And yet Sir Bayard had reason to resent Mr Endicott, and Mr Endicott dies.'

Arbie sighed. 'Yes. But I have a feeling that he wasn't the only one who had a bone to pick with poor Bill.'

'Oh?'

'I may be wrong, and this is pure speculation, but I think the Rowes had something against him as well. I noticed right from the start when we arrived that they and Bill studiously avoided each other. Not one of them ever instigated a conversation with the other, and the ladies wouldn't meet his eye. Not that he ever cast it their way.'

'The mother and daughter, eh? It'll be interesting to see if they admit to any connection with him when it's their time to be questioned more fully. Next?'

'Daphne and Roger Potts-Gibbon?' Arbie shrugged. 'As far as I know, they weren't acquainted with Endicott, but again, they didn't have that much to do with him either. You have to remember, I was only here for one night before Bill was . . . er . . . you know, so I didn't really have time to find out anything specific. Having said that, I certainly can't see the daughter of an archbishop having anything to do with . . . well . . . all this,' he added, waving a hand vaguely at the silent woman by the table.

'No,' the Inspector agreed, 'but you can never tell. Who's left?'

'Miss Warren,' Arbie said simply.

The Inspector contemplated Agnes Warren in silence for a moment, and then, simultaneously, both men sighed.

'Anyone else?'

'Well – me and Val,' Arbie said, honour-bound to be fair. 'But I promise you, neither one of us had ever met any of the people here before now. Oh, apart from Val once meeting Daphne at some sort of church do, years ago.'

'Hmmm. Now for these extras you mentioned. I have to say, I'm intrigued.'

'Yes. Right. Well, let's start with the stranger staying at the Job's Rest, shall we?' Arbie began, then added hastily, 'but I don't mean the older man who arrived this Sunday. I mean the man who arrived at the same time and on the same train as we did, on the Friday. There's something suspicious about him, right enough.'

'Oh?' For the first time, the Inspector's general air of gloom lifted. 'What about him?'

Arbie told him of witnessing Sir Bayard sneaking into the

inn to talk to him and then, later, of the same man sneaking around the manor gardens and asking Val to go to the house to ask Sir Bayard if he could meet him by the tennis courts. He also – rather red-faced – admitted to lurking in the bushes close by with Val, and the few snippets of conversation that they'd overheard.

When he was finished, the Inspector's eyes were wide open and very thoughtful. 'He sounds as if he might be known to us already. His type usually come to our attention sooner or later. Passing fraudulent cheques or setting up some small con game or other. I'll get my sergeant to nip down to the inn sharpish and find out who he is and see what reason he gives for coming to an out-of-the-way spot like this. You say there was another visitor?'

Arbie, who had been dreading this moment, took a deep breath. 'Yes. My uncle. I called him and asked him if he might like to come up and join me for a couple of days. There's, er, good fishing around here,' he added lamely.

The Inspector, whose nose for lies and half-truths rivalled that of a prized truffle hound catching a whiff of black gold, glanced sideways at him, and then returned to his usual contemplation of his shoes. Then he smiled slightly and gave a little nod. It wasn't unusual for people mixed up in violent death to get the wind up and call for their mummies. Or in this case, their uncle.

'I see,' he confined himself to saying blandly. 'Anything else?'

'I don't think so.'

'No? What about that young man who seems to be paying very assiduous attention to Miss Val?' Battle asked.

'*Geraint?*' Arbie said, his voice rising a little in surprise. 'Oh no, Inspector, you're barking up the wrong tree there. Val's papa, that is, the Reverend, is trying to facilitate a match between Val and Geraint, and neither one of them took too kindly to Val insisting on continuing her work with me. I assure you Geraint only came up here to keep an eye on . . . er, that is, came here to ensure that Miss Coulton-James was . . . er . . . is . . . I mean. . . Oh dash it!' Arbie finished, having talked himself into a corner and seeing no clear way out of it.

Battle (who was not without a heart, despite all appearances to the contrary) took pity on him and helped him out. 'I think I get the general picture, sir. The lady has a mind of her own, and Mr Kirkwood suspects that your relationship with his intended might not be strictly professional.'

Arbie, going a deeper shade of red, began to assiduously contemplate the state of his own feet. 'He's quite wrong, of course. She's like a sister to me,' he muttered. 'Really. I wish the silly ass would see sense and stop looking at me as if I was Bluebeard's right-hand man.'

But Battle was not interested in Arbie's woes. 'Now, about this morning,' he continued briskly. 'Can you tell me your own movements and what you know of everyone else's?'

'Yes – right. Well, I came down to breakfast early and finished early, so whilst the others were still eating, I went out into the garden. I must have been sitting overlooking the lake for . . . I don't know. Twenty minutes or so.' In short order he told the Inspector about seeing Val, Geraint and Daphne running to join him on the terrace, which presumably meant that they must have been walking or sitting in another part of the garden. He then described Sir Bayard being first on the scene, coming through the open French windows, and then hearing the Rowes and Roger talking out in the hall, and finally Agnes coming down last of all.

'And you saw or heard nothing unusual at all before hearing Lady Sybil scream?' Battle asked, without much expectation of anything useful.

Arbie shook his head. 'Sorry – no.'

'And now for Miss Remington. What did you make of her?'

Arbie took a fortifying breath. 'Well – to be frank, from what Miss Warren said about her, I think we were all expecting her to be a rather prim and proper young lady, making her own way in the world, and very competent and all that. In our minds – well, mine anyway – I sort of had a mental picture of a librarian crossed with a school mistress. So, when she first walked into the room – well, we were all surprised.'

'In what way?'

'Oh, by how striking she was, I suppose. Clothes, hair and whatnot, very elegant and chic and stylish. But mostly because she had this aura of confidence about her, almost of insolence, somehow. As if she had the world by the throat and knew it. It's hard to describe really. Val thought she was as hard as nails, and I daresay she was right. But I'll tell you something – she was dead sure that Bill Endicott hadn't committed suicide. And what's more, in my opinion, she was determined to get to the bottom of it.'

'Ah!' the Inspector said with satisfaction. 'Now we're getting to it.' The murdered lady, the Inspector surmised, must have known Endicott very well indeed to be so sure of his character. And if Endicott had, indeed, been murdered, then her determination to poke around might well have been enough for a killer to want to put her out of the way before she became too dangerous.

'In which case, it's more imperative than ever that I interview everyone concerned and see if we can't trip somebody up.' And with that he got up abruptly and walked towards the open French windows, where he bellowed for the village constable to come and stand guard on the terrace and to alert his sergeant that his boss wanted him.

Arbie prudently took this opportunity to slope off from

under the policeman's eye, and went to find Val. He needed to persuade her and Geraint to keep quiet about seeing the devil's train, and was reasonably confident that he could do so. Geraint, as a sobersides solicitor, would not be anxious to get the reputation as a man who saw hallucinations or ghostly machinery. And Val, he knew, would agree to keep quiet – for a price.

And that price, he mused despondently, would be that they'd conduct their own investigation into the two deaths.

*

As expected, Val agreed not to mention anything about the devil's train to the Inspector, unless he asked her directly about it, in which case she wouldn't lie. Arbie, though, thought it unlikely that Battle would pay much attention to any village gossip that might come his way about ghost trains, when he already had so much on his plate. Geraint also agreed to keep quiet, as Arbie had known he would, but he wasn't happy about it.

They had just finished their whispered consultation in one corner of the hall when the Inspector, coming in through the main door, spotted them and beckoned them to join him. Nervously, they followed him into the lounge, where all the others were already gathered.

They fell silent as they spotted the Inspector's looming form, presenting a sea of anxious, pale faces towards him. 'If you wouldn't mind taking a seat,' Battle said, glancing at Val, Arbie and Geraint, who quickly clustered together for comfort on one of the large Chesterfield sofas.

'I will, of course, be taking detailed statements from each of you later,' Battle began, 'but first I want to get a clear picture of where everyone was this morning, and what they were doing.'

He knew it wasn't good practice to question witnesses en masse like this, but he was a man who was prepared to put the rule book to one side if his instincts told him to do so. And something was telling him that this disparate group of people felt no loyalty towards one another, and he was willing to bet that, should he unearth some worrisome little facts, they would soon be at each other's throats.

And who knew what revelations that might lead to?

'I also want you to be very frank with me, as I'm going to ask each of you if you've noticed anything at all out of the ordinary about this weekend party, and if so, to tell me what it was. It doesn't matter if you believe it has nothing at all to do with either Mr Endicott's death, or that of Miss Remington. If anything at all odd or unusual has happened, I want you to tell me about it. Am I making myself clear?'

The people in the room darted nervous glances at each other, but all of them reluctantly conceded to the authority in the Inspector's voice.

'All right. I've already got Mr Swift's movements. Sir Bayard, as head of the household, I'll begin with you. Can you tell me what happened from the time you woke up until the time you stepped onto the terrace and saw that Miss Remington had been murdered?'

At the word 'murdered' Agnes gave a little cry and a ripple of unease circumnavigated the room, but Sir Bayard, who was seated beside the grand piano, stood up gamely and cleared his throat.

'Of course, Inspector. Well, I awoke, bathed and got dressed and came downstairs to breakfast. Mr Swift left the table first, followed by Miss Coulton-James and Daphne, who left to look at the tulip display on the west lawns. It was such a nice day, I decided to have a chat with the gardener about the availability of new potatoes, those being grown in the greenhouses, that is, for lunch, then came back, intending to go to my study. I was crossing the hall when I heard my wife shouting for help. It seemed to me to be coming from the east terrace, so I went through the nearest room which had a door leading on to it – which is the library, don't you know – and stepped through. I saw Mr Swift running along from the far end of the terrace, and then my wife staggering towards me. Er . . . I'm not sure what else I can tell you.'

'Did you hear a woman call out any time *before* hearing your wife's shouts?'

'No, sir, I did not.'

'Did you see Miss Remington at any time this morning?'

'No, sir, I did not. She didn't come down to breakfast.'

'Thank you. And now for my last question – has anything at all about this weekend struck you as odd?'

Here the Inspector watched him closely, for he was pretty sure that being summoned from his house to have a chat with an unexpected visitor at the tennis courts should be classed as unusual.

The Lord of the Manor, however, looked him in the eye and said earnestly, 'I'm afraid not, Inspector. Everything seemed to be much the same as the parties before. I mean, not about Endicott of course . . .' he added, going a shade red.

'Yes, Mr Endicott's death, I think, we can all agree was out of the ordinary.'

Sir Bayard seemed to go redder still, then sat back down in his chair, looking relieved that his stint was over and done with.

'Mrs Potts-Gibbon?' The Inspector turned to the woman seated beside her husband. She looked pale but composed.

'Well, Roger and I awoke about seven thirty or so. The maid brought us tea. We came down together around about an hour later, I should say. We didn't linger long over breakfast, neither one of us having much of an appetite. Over the table, the talk turned to the wonderful gardens here, and Miss Coulton-James remarked on the tulips, and I agreed that, since we had plenty of time before our train was due, I should like to see them, so we went outside. A young man, that one,' she nodded a polite smile at Geraint, 'joined us about five minutes later. He told us he'd just walked up from the village. He is an acquaintance of Miss Coulton-James and was, I think, rather keen that she should return to her home, as all the rest of us were set to do. We were just looking at some rather splendid scarlet specimens when we heard Lady Sybil's cries. We all three ran towards them. I'm afraid I'm not as young or as fast as my companions, so I arrived at the terrace a little behind them. Mr Swift was there, and very kindly prevented us from seeing . . . well. . . And then I heard and saw Roger coming through the French doors and he joined me.'

'Very succinct, Mrs Potts-Gibbon, thank you. And have you noticed anything odd about the weekend party? Any members of it behaving in an unexpected way, perhaps? Or unusual sounds in the night? Raised angry voices?'

'Oh no, nothing like that,' she said, her gaze level.

'Mr Potts-Gibbon?'

Roger coughed, then like Sir Bayard, stood up. 'Well, it's like Daphers said. We woke up, washed, dressed and came down to breakfast. Then she left to see the garden and I stayed on to read the papers. I moved from the breakfast table to one of the chairs, which was quite comfortable, and I was still reading when I heard the commotion outside. I couldn't quite tell where it was coming from, so I went out into the hall and had a bit of a look around. Then I saw Mrs and Miss Rowe standing in the doorway to the library, so I went up to them and asked them if they knew what was up, but they didn't seem to know either. But I could hear some voices coming through the open French windows, so

I went across and saw Daphers, a little out of breath, standing some way down the terrace. So I went to her and that's pretty much that.'

'Had you seen or heard anything of Miss Remington that morning?'

'I'm afraid not, no. She must have got up early and gone to the terrace to take the air. None of us use that terrace much, I think, so she might just have wanted some peace and quiet.'

'Hmmmm. And has anything struck you as odd – Mr Endicott's situation excepted – that gave you pause for thought?'

'Can't say anything did, old man. Sorry.' And with that he sat back down next to his wife. The Inspector's sharp eyes noted Daphne reach out and take her husband's hand in her own and give it a gentle squeeze.

'Miss Coulton-James?'

Val's story was very simple. She awoke, went down to breakfast, went out into the gardens with Mrs Potts-Gibbon, where Geraint met up with them shortly thereafter, and then they heard the screaming. She hadn't seen Samantha Remington either.

Geraint's story was even shorter – he'd breakfasted at the inn and enjoyed the walk up to the manor and had been delighted to spot Val in one of the gardens and had joined the two ladies in their admiration of the tulips. Lady Sybil's scream had brought him to the terrace, along with Val and Mrs Potts-Gibbon. Since he wasn't a member of the weekend party, he didn't know Samantha Remington even by sight, and didn't know much about the other guests either.

The Inspector nodded, then braced himself a little, and turned to Agnes. 'Miss Warren?'

Agnes was seated, rather like a collapsed bag of flour, in an armchair. A large handkerchief was being used assiduously, and her pale face had tear streaks running down the cheeks where her face powder had been washed away. Her nose and eyes were red. She was dressed in some sort of drab brown outfit that did nothing for her but which the Inspector instinctively knew had cost more than his monthly salary – considerably more, probably.

'You must have seen your niece, or goddaughter, Miss Remington, this morning?' he asked gently and hopefully.

But instantly Agnes shook her head. 'Oh no, I'm so sorry, Inspector, but I didn't. Samantha was in the habit of rising early – she worked for a living, you know,' she added, with a pathetic mixture of pride and defiance. 'But I'm afraid I've always been the opposite. I can never seem to get out of bed much before ten o'clock. It's very lazy of me, I'm sure, and I do try to be good and—'

'Oh, I'm sure a lot of people feel the same way,' the Inspector said, anxious to cut her off before she could regale them with more self-imposed confessions about her faults. 'I understand, from what others have told me, that your niece knew Mr Endicott?' he said next.

'Yes – I didn't know that until Samantha mentioned it. But then, they were both of an age, and lived in York, so perhaps it's not surprising that they ran in the same set.'

'She never talked to you about Mr Endicott?'

'Oh no, Inspector,' Agnes said, her voice definite. 'Until she came here, I had no idea they were acquainted.'

'She seemed very sure that Mr Endicott wouldn't commit suicide. Would you say that was a fair comment?'

'Oh, dear, I couldn't possibly say,' Agnes said, looking anxious. 'I myself feel sure that what happened to poor Mr Endicott must have been a dreadful accident. A nice young man like that, with so much to live for—'

'Yes, I see,' the Inspector cut in hastily. 'Perhaps you can tell me what you did this morning?'

'Well, I woke up, and the maid brought me a nice cup of tea. Then I had a bath, and I dressed, and I came downstairs, and met Mr Swift in the hall. Oh – I should have said, whilst I was dressing, I thought I heard a woman shouting and calling out something. Anyway, when I went downstairs, Mr Swift told me something awful had happened, and Miss Coulton-James was kind enough to tell me about . . . about . . .' Her lower lip began to wobble, and the Inspector again hastily changed the subject.

'You're doing very well, Miss Warren. Now, can you tell me, had Miss Remington confided in you anything about her thoughts of Mr Endicott's . . . er . . . passing?'

'Oh no,' Agnes said, shaking her head fearfully. 'Dear Samantha knew that talking about bad things always upset me. Dr Schuber's book tells us we must eschew the negative and only dwell on the good and positive things in life, that way it's much harder for us to become depressed or downhearted. Although . . . oh dear, it's so hard to find anything cheerful to think about now, isn't it?'

The Inspector cleared his throat loudly. 'Quite so. Quite so. And has anything struck you about this weekend as untoward or odd, Miss Warren?' he asked, and prepared himself for a rambling, probably mainly incoherent litany of utterly irrelevant gossip. To his immense surprise then, the lady merely tilted her head to one side, frowned, shot a glance towards Daphne and Roger Potts-Gibbon and went a little pink.

'Well, the only thing I found odd . . . well, actually, it was Samantha who thought it was odd and asked me about it, was Mr Potts-Gibbon talking to me about an investment opportunity. Which I'm sure was perfectly all right and all that,' she added hastily, her words almost falling over themselves, so anxious was she not to offend. 'I didn't think it odd at all, and I'm only too glad to have the advice of clever men of business, like Mr Potts-Gibbon.'

'I think I can help you out there, Inspector,' Roger said, standing up. 'It's all right, Miss Warren, don't worry yourself. I'll explain.' He turned to the Inspector and nodded, as if trying to establish the fact that they were both men of the world and knew what made it go around all right.

'I'm setting up a new venture to add to my current businesses – in car manufacturing actually – since I'm convinced that's the future. I'm converting some of our bicycling-making plants and I'm looking for investors. I mentioned this to Miss Warren and asked for the name of her man of business so that I could put together a portfolio for him. That was all. Naturally, after the tragedy of finding Endicott, I later told Miss Warren not to worry about such things, and we agreed to simply forget about it.'

The Inspector nodded, his face bland. 'I see. Thank you, sir.'

'Mrs and Miss Rowe?'

Elizabeth and Bernadette Rowe's story was, perhaps, the simplest of them all. They had adjoining rooms and were in the habit of waiting for each other to finish washing and dressing before going downstairs. They went down to breakfast together and left the table at the same time and had then gone to enjoy the ferns and other tropical plants in the conservatory, whilst they too waited until it was time to catch their train. There they had both heard the faint sound of screams and had hurried back to the house where they got as far as the door to the library, where Mr Potts-Gibbon had joined them.

Like everyone else, neither of them had seen Samantha Remington. Neither of them admitted to noticing anything odd about that weekend, or any of their fellow guests acting in any way out of the ordinary.

Mrs Rowe did all the talking, with her daughter only adding

the occasional firm nod or shake of the head, as if to underline her mother's account.

Then the Inspector turned slowly to Lady Sybil.

That lady was sitting stiff and upright in a chair. The doctor had offered her a sedative before leaving, but she'd refused to take it, and now her chin lifted as she was forced to look up high to meet the towering Inspector's gaze. She was wearing something very chic, and her hair was dressed splendidly. She looked every inch the Lady of the Manor, and a rich man's pampered darling. Her blue-green eyes blazed magnificently.

'I know you've had an awful shock, my lady,' Battle began. 'But if you could bear to just run through things for me?'

'Of course. I woke up, bathed and dressed. I followed my husband down to breakfast, but didn't have much appetite, and left the breakfast room not long after Miss Coulton-James and Daphne did. I went to the orangery, where I wanted to check on the state of the forced soft fruits. I then had a word or two with one of the gardeners there, then made my way back to the house. I went via the east terrace, intending to pass through the library and into the hall, as it's the shortest way to get back into the main house from where I was. When I reached the terrace, though, I saw Miss R-Remington,' she stuttered slightly, and took a deep breath. 'I thought she was sitting in an extraordinary manner, and for a moment it reminded me of the way we used to sit as girls at our school desks when we didn't want a classmate to see what we were writing; you know, all hunched over, to stop anyone copying our exercise books.'

Sybil gave her head a brief shake. 'It's odd, isn't it, the things one thinks of when we we're presented with something so bizarre? I saw at once she was lying with her face on the table, and that long, long hair of hers. . .' Again, she paused and took a deep, fortifying breath. 'Anyway, I went to her and . . . yes,

I'm sure I called out her name. I think I may have asked her if she was feeling faint and if she would like some smelling salts or something, but then as I got closer I s-sa-saw the thing in her neck and. . .' At this point she flung out her hands. 'Oh, what's the use of denying it? I rather lost my head. It was just the shock of it . . . seeing that lovely hat pin and slowly coming to understand what it meant. . . I just remember screaming like a silly little chit and then shouting out "murder" or "help me" or some such banal thing, like a character in one of those ghastly, awful plays. After what seemed an age, I saw Mr Swift coming towards me, and I started to go to him, and then my husband stepped through the door, so I went to him instead. And, and, and if you d-don't mind, Inspector, I now feel all done in. I really don't have to say any more, do I? Not right now?' she asked, and the appeal in her beautiful aquamarine eyes would have done for a lesser man than Felix Battle.

As it was, he only partially granted her request, however, for he wasn't yet quite done with her. 'Yes, that's perfectly all right, Lady Sybil, I won't ask you any more about Miss Remington just yet. But do you know of anything odd that has happened during this weekend party? Anything at all, no matter how random or unimportant it might seem?'

'No. Oh, well, only the pearls,' Lady Sybil corrected herself vaguely.

Val, who was sitting directly behind Bernie Rowe, saw her friend stiffen to attention.

'Your pearls?' Battle repeated blankly.

'Yes. I mislaid them. I can't think how, but I must have done, because I couldn't find them where I always kept them. Perhaps I just missed them in the jumble of other boxes, because when I went back to look for them later, I found them. I expect my maid had been swapping things around again without telling me.'

But she didn't look convinced, and Battle thought that this was a lady who didn't easily lose sight of her valuable jewels.

'I see,' he said quietly, although he didn't, not altogether. But if they weren't actually stolen, he told himself, they probably weren't relevant. 'Very well. All right. We'll be taking formal statements all today, so I know you're all anxious to be off home, but if you could keep yourselves available here in the house until at least tomorrow, I'd be obliged.'

Everyone agreed, without much enthusiasm, to stay within the confines of the house or garden, and Battle nodded and took himself off to the library, where he would commit his thoughts to paper, and make a list of things he needed to get done, sooner rather than later.

CHAPTER FOURTEEN

In the library, Battle made himself comfortable at a table and began to arrange his thoughts.

Why is Roger P-G pursuing Miss Warren for money? Get the financial boddos to check out the state of his company. Might the financial genius be in trouble after all? If so, had Endicott invested heavily with him?

Find out who's staying in the local inn and why Sir B. seems to be as thick as thieves with him. Possible blackmail? And get my opposite number in York to sniff around and see if there's any truth to the rumour that Endicott and Lady S. might have been more than friends just recently. Crime of passion? Also, see just how well Endicott knew Samantha Remington. Both their 'set' and friends need to be closely questioned. (Ask Superintendent for more men. He won't like it though!)

Ask Lady S.'s maid about those pearls going missing. Did someone attempt to steal them and then get the wind up and put them back because police were called to the house? Get someone in records to check if there have been any other robberies at fancy house parties lately, and check against guest list. Possible we have a high-class jewel thief on our hands? If so, why kill Endicott and Remington? Maybe one of them was part of a gang?

Get on to our people in Woodstock and get a background check made on the Rowe women. Any connection at all to Endicott or Samantha Remington?

Same for the P-Gs. (Must tell them to tread carefully though – I don't *want the Superintendent getting angry phone calls from any muckety-mucks high up in the church!)*

Find out just how wealthy Miss Agnes Warren is, and the state of her financial portfolio. And has she made a will – and if so, how much would Samantha Remington have received?

At this point the lofty Inspector was interrupted by his sergeant who wanted to know who he'd like to have hauled in first for a formal interview and did the Inspector want to get himself to the Job's Rest and nab the mysterious man there first?

The Inspector did.

An hour later, Miss Remington's body was discreetly removed from the premises, a process which, mercifully, went unobserved by the remaining guests in the house.

*

Uncle, who had a sixth sense when it came to the proximity of trouble (especially the trouble that accompanied members of the constabulary), spotted the approach of the Sergeant from his bedroom window almost immediately, and instinctively nipped down the back stairs and hared it out of the back door of the inn.

He had no reason to suppose that the Sergeant had any business with himself, but why risk it?

Besides, he needed to get in touch with his pal who had driven him up here and was now patiently waiting in the nearby coastal village to hear from him. For, unless Uncle missed the signs, the landlord was busy preparing another journey for that ghost train of his, and this time Uncle wanted to be ready for him.

Arbie's relative had been far from idle since arriving at Middle Stratton. He'd already contacted another old friend who'd lived his life on the railways and had taxed his brains vis-à-vis the fire-breathing train. His opinion was that the discharge of fire (as opposed to steam) from the smokestack was possible, and probably the result of the use of the basest of 'slack' by the fireman (as opposed to proper coal) and with the addition of the odd chemical element or two. One of which was probably sulphur, resulting in the inevitable stink his nephew had detected after the train had passed by. This made sense, because for centuries, sulphur had been associated with Old Nick and Hellfire, Uncle knew, and its incorporation into the devil's train was a nice little touch that was guaranteed to keep the more superstitious members of the public well away from the smugglers and their midnight activities.

He'd also been studying the local maps thoroughly, following the railway line all the way from the coast to the other end of the valley, where – he'd discovered – there ran a short piece of disused track. Even better, this line came with a convenient tunnel situated barely a mile from the old terminus of a stone quarry that had long since been worked out and abandoned.

And this tunnel, Uncle was convinced, was just the place for a devil's train to 'disappear into thin air' for an hour or two, well out of sight of prying eyes.

Before the advent of the iron horse, of course, the old way of getting the stone to market had been via the canal network. And the nearby canal system now interested Uncle considerably, for it could carry a barge right into the heart of any number of nearby cities. And whilst policemen could (and often did) patrol the roads for any suspect lorries, vans, carts or trucks to check their contents, how many of them would think of stopping a barge, meandering at the pace of the horses pulling it along a distant waterway in the middle of the countryside?

Uncle had to hand it to Amos Fairley and his chums. They were no chumps!

After hiding in the garden long enough to spy the Sergeant leaving with his prey, Uncle made his way to the village shop.

There he sent a seemingly innocuous telegram to his pal on the coast asking about the uncertain health of their fictitious Aunt Edna, and how they needed to go up and see her, which in fact was a pre-arranged code for them to meet up later that night.

Uncle wanted to reconnoitre several spots that he'd marked as possibilities on his map, and he wanted to do it under the cover of darkness. And with the help of his very useful mate (and his even more useful van) he was confident that the next run of the devil's train might not work out quite as smoothly as Amos Fairley and his crew might expect.

*

After ascertaining that the Inspector was alone, Sergeant Jellicoe ushered his man into the library, announcing, 'Mr Whittaker, sir' in a droll voice.

Alerted by the tone, Battle looked up and a smile of recognition wreathed his face, changing his usual appearance from that of a dyspeptic heron to that of a very self-satisfied heron indeed.

'Well, well, well, if it isn't Max Wolverton,' Battle said, rising slowly to his feet. 'Let's see now – pickpocketing and cardsharping is your game, if I remember correctly. Didn't I have the pleasure of feeling your collar a couple of years ago?'

'He was registered at the inn under the name of Whittaker, sir,' the Sergeant said meaningfully.

Battle nodded, looking at the unhappy man with a gleam in his eye. 'Which means you're up to no good, as usual, laddie. So, take a seat and tell me what brings you to this neck of the woods,' he began, with patently false bonhomie. 'Funny, I wouldn't have said that murder was your usual game,' he added slyly.

At this, Max Wolverton gave a little yelp of dismay. 'Here, don't go saying things like that, Inspector. Have a heart, why don'tcha? You know violence and me ain't even nodding acquaintances, like. And you've no call to get so high and mighty either. I'm here on legitimate business, I am,' he whined self-righteously.

He slithered into the chair opposite the Inspector's and removed his black fedora with a flourish. He then ostentatiously adjusted his silver-mounted cufflinks, trying to look impressive and unworried. He failed on both counts. Probably because he was remembering the last time that he'd had occasion to meet the six-foot-six gangly inspector, which involved a rather distressing use of handcuffs shortly followed by a six-month stretch at His Majesty's pleasure in Halifax.

'Now why do I have grave doubts about that, Sergeant?' the Inspector said, casting an amused eye at his equally amused sergeant.

'Can't imagine, sir,' Jellicoe said, playing up to his superior.

'Well, start imagining it then,' Max said, with far too much confidence for either policeman's liking.

'Cut the waffle,' Battle suddenly roared, making the man in black jump nervously in his chair. 'What are you up to? Come on – out with it.'

At which, Wolverton, alias Whittaker, speedily obliged him. 'I was invited down here by his nibs, wasn't I? Sir Bayard Cherville, the man himself. So put that in your pipe and smoke it!'

'Huh,' Battle said disbelievingly, but inwardly his mind was racing. 'And just why would the lord of a manor like this' – he indicated the lovely room around him – 'invite the likes of you into his home? You'd have the silver out of it and off to a fence in three minutes flat.'

'Here, I resent that! As a matter of fact, I was supposed to dine here with all his other lah-di-dah guests last Saturday night, I'll have you know. All above board and everythin'. I've even got a proper invitation.'

'Of course you have,' the Inspector drawled, leaning back in his chair and regarding the specimen before him with deep distaste. 'And I'm the Queen of Sheba.'

'No, straight up. It's back at the pub,' Max said, holding out his sensitive, long-fingered hands in a gesture of appeasement. Those hands, both policemen knew, had served him very well in the past.

'And what did Sir Bayard want you to do? Pick his guests' pockets?' the Sergeant jeered.

'No, he didn't then,' Max contradicted. 'He wanted me to set up one of the party and expose him as a card cheat.'

And then, very satisfied at the sensation he had caused, he allowed a cat-like smile to cross his face, which unfortunately for him, was a face far more suited to a rat-like grimace. 'And I'd have done it too,' he boasted, for a moment forgetting who he was talking to. 'Any Tom, Dick or Harry could learn to cheat at cards if they take the time to practise.' He gave a little sneer. 'But it takes a real artist like me to plant cards on someone else. But I'd a done it all right. And your fancy Sir Bayard offered me a nice little bundle to do it too. I don't know what he had against this fellah, but take it from me, his nibs was out for his blood, right enough.'

'A likely story,' the Sergeant snorted, but a quick look at his superior told him that Battle was thinking hard. As, indeed, he was.

It wasn't hard for Battle to believe that, out of his wide range of acquaintances, Sir Bayard might know some no-good but aristocratic sort who sailed too close to the wind and could have put him in touch with the likes of Wolverton. But, for the moment, the name of this contact didn't interest him. The name he wanted was that of someone else entirely.

'Who?' he said sharply. 'Who did Sir Bayard want you to set up as a card cheat?'

Max Whittaker shrugged. 'If I tell you, I get to skate, yes? No harm, no foul? It's not as if I've done anything wrong. . .'

'Yes, fine, you get to walk away free and clear,' Battle said, loath as he was to do it. But, as the slimy little toad had just pointed out, he hadn't done anything illegal. Yet.

The man in black gave a small sigh, and then relaxed in his chair. 'Fair enough, Inspector. It was a chap called William Endicott.'

*

In the lounge, Val caught Bernie's eye and nodded to a window seat in the back of the room. Bernie whispered something to her mother, who nodded, and then the younger woman moved to join Val.

Once they were seated, Val peered at her closely. Bernie had dark smudges under her eyes, and despite her clever use of face powder, she could see that underneath it she was as pale as milk. What's more, she could tell that her new friend was 'living on her nerves' as her granny would have said.

'Hello, old bean,' Val began cheerfully. 'How are you bearing up?'

'Oh, I'm all right,' Bernie lied bravely.

'Balderdash,' Val said, careful to keep her voice down. 'I was sitting right behind you when Lady Sybil said something about her pearls going missing,' she said bluntly. 'And you nearly jumped out of your skin. Listen, Bernie, I warn you, you've got to be careful. Keeping secrets in this sort of situation is no good. The police will find everything out. I know, I've been in on murder cases before.'

'You have?' Bernie gasped. And then listened, her big blue eyes widening ever further as Val related her two previous brushes with murder, and the results thereof.

'So you see,' Val concluded, 'Arbie and I are already on the case. And it's no use trying to bamboozle us!' she told her sternly – and rather more emphatically than was really warranted. 'The best thing you can do is come clean. If you tell me what's bothering you, and if it has nothing to do with the murders, then perhaps I can help you.'

Val took a deep breath, and said, rather uncertainly, 'You didn't kill Samantha, did you?'

'Of course not,' Bernie squeaked/whispered. 'I didn't know the woman from Adam!'

'What about Bill Endicott?'

Bernie stiffened. 'I didn't kill him either,' she denied, far more flatly.

But Val, sensing prevarication, narrowed her eyes thoughtfully. 'But you *did* take Lady Sybil's pearls, didn't you?' she said. It was a total shot in the dark, and she was half prepared for her friend to give her a piece of her mind. Instead, after a moment, Bernie's shoulders slumped.

'Yes, I did,' Bernie admitted, making Val almost fall off her chair in shock. For although she had instigated the confession, she had, in truth, never expected it to come to anything.

'You did!' Val squeaked/whispered. 'Bernie! Why on earth. . . You're the last person I would have expected to be a thief.'

'I'm not a thief,' Bernie hissed, looking angry, then appalled, and cast a quick glance her mother's way. She was not at all reassured to find that lady looking their way with a very tight, anxious and ominous expression on her usually sweet-natured face.

'I never intended to leave the house with them.' Bernie leaned closer to Val. 'I only moved them from Lady Sybil's bedroom and put them . . . somewhere else.'

Val looked as nonplussed as she felt. 'Somewhere else?' she repeated. 'But why? And where did you put them?'

'I hid them in Bill Endicott's room,' Bernie said miserably.

Val's jaw dropped and for a moment, she simply couldn't think what to say. She looked around and caught Arbie's eye but he, traitor that he was, quickly dipped his gaze back to the paper he was reading and looked set to stubbornly remain in his chair until the woodworms had eaten it out from underneath him.

Crossly, Val turned back to her friend. 'What on earth did you do that for?' was the only thing she could think to ask.

'Because I was hoping that Lady Sybil would miss her pearls and kick up a fuss and a search would be made, and then they'd be found, of course,' Bernie said, as if it was obvious.

Val blinked, but gamely followed the thought through to the logical conclusion. 'You mean – you wanted him to be accused of stealing them?'

Bernie, looking mutinous, nodded.

Val, thoroughly thrown now, stared at the other girl, wondering how she could have been so mistaken about her. She'd instinctively felt that Bernie Rowe was a good egg, and now to find out that she was capable of such underhanded rottenness made her feel distinctly wrong-footed.

'But, Bernie, *why*?' she asked helplessly.

At this, Bernie looked back at her, her blue eyes shimmering with unshed tears. 'Because he killed my brother, Val,' she said simply.

'Hush!' A voice interrupted them, making both women jump. Val looked up to see Bernie's mother. Elizabeth Rowe pulled one of the Queen Anne chairs from underneath a nearby table and set it down in front of the two young women then sat in it. 'Bernadette, be quiet,' Elizabeth said, her tone unusually harsh. 'Miss Coulton-James, I would be obliged if you would excuse us for a moment.'

And even Val, who had thought she could hold her own

against anyone, felt herself quailing under the angry eyes of the normally mild-mannered Mrs Rowe.

'Oh, yes, er, of course,' she muttered, and got up from her seat and headed straight for Arbie. Sitting down next to him, she reached out and clutched his arm, making Geraint glare at them from across the room.

'Arbie! You'll never guess what Bernie has just been telling me,' Val hissed, and began to whisper in his ear.

At this further sign of intimacy, Geraint loped the length of the room and stood glowering down at them. Val, piqued, waved a peremptory hand at him to sit down, and continued talking. And Geraint, after a few moments, began to simmer down as he took in the startling information Val was relating.

When she'd finished, Val said breathlessly, 'Well? What do you think we should do?'

Arbie shrugged. 'We should tell Inspector Battle of course,' he said. 'What else?'

'Arbie, you beast!' Val said, looking and sounding so cross that it made Geraint's battered heart sing with happiness. 'You can't! She told me this in confidence.'

'This is a murder case,' Arbie said.

'She said that Bill killed her brother! We have to find out what she meant by that first. We have to . . .'

'This is a murder case,' Arbie repeated.

'Don't be such a, such a, such a . . . an ass!' Val, almost beside herself with anger, hissed at him. 'We can't just turn Bernie over to the Inspector. He'll arrest her. Geraint, back me up on this.'

At this, her ardent swain's mouth fell open in despair. Hitherto, he'd almost dreamed of this moment – the moment when Val would see Arbuthnot Lancelot Swift in his true colours. The glorious moment when the scales fell away from her lovely eyes, and she saw the man for who and what he really was. And always, in these wonderful daydreams, Geraint pictured himself coming to her rescue, standing stalwartly by her side, and rescuing her from her folly.

So, he wanted to scream out loud in frustration that his beloved should choose, of all things, to ask him, a solicitor, to keep vital information from the police about an active murder investigation! He simply couldn't do it. He'd be disbarred. His relatives would disown him. He'd face social disgrace and. . .

Val, reading the look on his face, all but stamped her foot in exasperation. 'Men!' she hissed, and getting up, flung herself across the room, her back stiff with outrage.

Geraint watched her go with utter dismay.

Arbie merely sighed. Tomorrow, he needed to go into York and make certain enquiries. After which, if his guesses were proved to be correct, he should have something solid with which to help guide the Inspector towards the truth of who and what lay behind the killings of Bill Endicott and Samantha Remington.

He wasn't much looking forward to being proved right, though. In fact, he would feel a whole lot better if he was barking up the wrong tree altogether.

*

Elizabeth Rowe listened with a heavy heart to her daughter's confession about her plan to 'ruin' Bill Endicott by branding him a thief. She had been so busy making her own plans to settle her old score with Mr William Endicott that she had failed to realise that her child had made independent plans of her own.

Plans which could have resulted in her disgrace – or even a prison term – if she'd been caught in the act.

'I want you to promise me that you'll say nothing about the necklace to anyone else. I'll go and speak to Miss Coulton-James and explain about Marcus, and I'm sure she'll understand that you acted foolishly, and that you're very sorry. She's a nice girl, and her father is a vicar, so she'll understand about forgiveness. I'm sure I'll be able to persuade her to keep it all to herself.'

'But what if that beanpole of an Inspector finds out?' Bernie said nervously.

'There's no reason he should. Besides, after I've spoken to him he won't give you a second thought.'

'Mother! What do you mean?'

'Never you mind,' Elizabeth Rowe said calmly, but somehow her face looked almost like that of a stranger. 'You just promise me to keep quiet, and don't talk to anyone else about anything at all. Promise me!'

'All right,' Bernie said meekly. But as she watched her mother join Val and began to talk quietly to her, Bernadette Rowe couldn't help but shiver. She had never seen her mother's face look as it had just moments ago. Why, oh why, had they had to come to this place? And why had William Endicott had to be here? Feeling tears threatening to spill, Bernie got up and hastened out of the room.

Daphne Potts-Gibbon noticed, of course, and followed the distraught young girl's exit with her eyes. Then her eyes sought out the girl's mother, who was talking earnestly to that nice girl Valentina. Then, slowly, Daphne looked towards the figure of her husband, who was standing smoking cigars with Sir Bayard and discussing horse racing.

Daphne sighed gently.

CHAPTER FIFTEEN

Barely ten minutes after Max Wolverton had departed (in rather a hurry) Sergeant Jellicoe knocked portentously on the library door. On hearing the Inspector's grunt, which he interpreted to mean that he was to enter, he ushered in Elizabeth Rowe. 'Excuse me, sir, the lady has asked if you can spare a few minutes.'

The Inspector regarded his visitor rather thoughtfully, as he'd completed his formal interview with the lady not an hour since. 'Of course,' he said, and catching the pleading look in his sergeant's eye, beckoned him to remain.

'Inspector. I've come because I have something to add to my statement,' she said simply, accepting his invitation to sit down on the chair opposite him. 'I have to confess to being rather more reticent than, perhaps, I should have been.'

'That sometimes happens in police cases, Mrs Rowe,' the Inspector said, not unkindly. 'I'm sure you'll feel better for telling the truth now. Please, take a seat.'

'Oh, I haven't lied to you, Inspector,' Elizabeth corrected him, somewhat chidingly. 'I would never do that. It's more that I haven't been as . . . expansive with you as perhaps I might.'

'Ah, that can happen too,' Battle conceded graciously.

'Thank you. It concerns my son, Marcus,' the lady began briskly. Despite doing her best to look and sound business-like, both policemen could easily detect the strong emotion that lurked beneath her stiff-backed and blank-faced exterior as she sat erect in her chair.

'Yes?' Battle asked politely. He had no idea where the lady was going with this opening gambit, but he was prepared to be patient.

'Marcus died last year during the Henley regatta. He was younger than my daughter, Bernadette. He was up at Oxford, at the time.'

Battle sighed gently. 'I'm very sorry to hear that, Mrs Rowe.'

'He and his friends had gone to Henley, not to take part in any of the official races, you understand, but just to enjoy themselves. He and this group of his friends all rowed, so it was only natural that they hired a boat to go out for a few hours, on a stretch of river some distance away from the official routes and courses. Just for their own amusement, you understand.'

'Yes, I see.'

'I was later told by one of the lads in the boat with him that they were timing themselves, seeing how close they could get to the best times that were being set by the official teams. One of the lads was younger even than Marcus, but most of them had been at Oxford some years ago and were reliving past glories, I expect.'

Here Elizabeth paused and settled herself more firmly on the chair. Her gaze was directed at the fireplace, where an arrangement of daffodils and sticky buds had been placed in front of the unlit grate. 'I was told that one of the rowers "caught a crab" – at least, I think that was the phrase used. I know nothing about rowing, you understand, but I was told that he mishandled the oar somehow, and instead of going into the water smoothly, it went in at the wrong angle and instead of slicing through the water cleanly, it blocked the passage of water, making the oar judder. He nearly lost his oar, and the movement of the boat was upset, making it rock and flounder momentarily. I'm afraid the rest of the rowers laughed at him about this, or jeered at him or something, and he got rather angry about it, and started a bit of a ruckus that only made matters much worse.'

The Inspector caught his sergeant's puzzled eye and gave a slight shrug. He didn't think the lady was telling the story simply to hear her own voice, and his slight frown indicated to his underling that patience was required.

'The rower at fault started a bit of a play-fight with his accusers, and, not surprisingly, the boat overturned. They were unlucky in that it happened as the boat had just gone over a submerged fallen branch from a tree. Anyway all the men went into the water. One of them was Marcus. He could swim, of course, but only as well as most boys do that learned to swim during their childhood years. That is, he rarely used a swimming pool or swam in the summer months just for fun. As it turned out, he was the least experienced swimmer of them all.'

She looked down at her hands, and took a long, slow breath. 'All the men in the water were now pretty annoyed with the man who'd started it all, of course, and there was a bit of a free-for-all with the man who'd caught the crab making the most fuss and taking it in turns to try and "duck" his adversaries under the water, so nobody noticed that Marcus wasn't amongst them. And by the time one of them realised that he was in difficulty, he was already facedown amongst the willow branches of the tree. They thought he had become trapped under the net of smaller branches and hadn't been able to get clear. Oh, they were very quick, and the oldest one, who was in training to be a doctor, dived under and got him free, and then they all rallied around to tow Marcus to the shore. And the one training to be a doctor and another one trained in first aid did their best to resuscitate him, but . . . Well, it was too late.'

'I'm very sorry to hear about such a tragedy for your family,' Battle said solemnly.

Elizabeth Rowe gave him a brief, cool smile. 'Thank you. But you're wondering why I should tell you all this now. I can see it on your face. It's because, Inspector, the name of the man who'd caught the crab on the boat that day was William Endicott.'

Jellicoe drew in a sharp breath, and the Inspector's eyes opened a fraction wider. 'I see. And you blamed him, naturally.'

Elizabeth shrugged helplessly. 'One tries not to, in such circumstances. One tries to be a good Christian and forgive. We . . . *I* tried for a long time to come to terms with the fact that it was an accident – an awful accident, but . . . yes. I'm afraid we . . . that is, *I* did blame him. I couldn't help myself. He showed so little remorse at the inquest, you see. He acted as if the whole thing wasn't his fault at all – that everyone was just having a bit of a lark, and how was he to know what would happen? It was clear to everyone that he was just trying to gloss over his part in it. Even the coroner thought so, for he had some very sharp words for him.'

The Inspector allowed himself a moment to digest this information, then leaned forward in his chair a little, watching the other woman closely. 'In that case, Mrs Rowe, I'm surprised that you agreed to attend this weekend party. Why did you?'

'Oh, we had no idea that Mr Endicott had been invited,' Elizabeth said at once.

The Inspector gave her an astonished look. 'Didn't know? But surely Lady Sybil, your close friend, knew all about your tragic loss? I can't see her inviting you and Mr Endicott . . .'

'Oh, but she didn't, Inspector,' Elizabeth said earnestly. 'Believe me, she was most apologetic, almost distraught, when she learned that her husband had invited him without telling her.'

'Ah yes, I remember now,' the Inspector said grimly. Hadn't young Mr Swift told him as much? At the time, though, he hadn't understood the importance of that piece of information. Now he had to wonder why the Lord of the Manor would have made such an immense social gaffe. For he must have heard from his wife about her friend's awful loss, and the cause of it. Or maybe he was one of those men who only listened to his spouse with half an ear, and the information she related barely registered?

Or then again. . .

'As you can imagine, it made for a rather strained atmosphere,' Elizabeth said dryly.

'Yes, I can well imagine. What was Mr Endicott's reaction when you and he became aware of the, er, mistake?'

'Well, what *could* we do?' she asked helplessly. 'We avoided conversing with each other as best we could, and I told Sybil that Bernadette and I would be leaving at the first opportunity, which was to be on Saturday morning. But . . . well, obviously, circumstances dictated otherwise.'

'Yes. With the discovery of the body of the young man you held responsible for your son's death,' the Inspector pointed out.

Elizabeth nodded and forced her eyes from the fireplace towards the policeman. 'Yes. And now you must be wondering if I was responsible for that death. After all, I was one of the people who knew of Miss Warren's Veronal being in the bathroom cabinet and could easily have taken some. And I had a motive. Perhaps now you can understand why I never mentioned our . . . my connection with the dead man before now. I was hoping to be spared from this understandable suspicion.'

'Indeed,' Battle admitted. 'So, I hope you'll understand if I ask you straight out. Did you murder Mr Endicott?'

'I did not.'

'You must have been sorely tempted though,' the Inspector said softly. 'You find yourself, through no fault of your own, having to share a roof with the man responsible for your son's death. That would have tested the nerves and stamina of anybody. It would be understandable if you tried to exact revenge.'

Elizabeth Rowe smiled slightly at this and inclined her head. 'You're quite right, Inspector. I did want revenge. And I plotted to have it. But,' she held out a hand as both policemen gave a startled reaction to this confession, 'it didn't include murder. Even if I was the kind of person who demanded a tooth for a tooth and an eye for an eye, there was never any question that William Endicott *murdered* my son. He caused his death, yes. But it wasn't with malice aforethought. The evidence at the inquest made that quite clear. Although I *was* human enough to want revenge, I wasn't *inhuman* enough to believe he deserved to pay with his life. Not his literal life, anyway.'

Elizabeth sighed and returned her gaze to the fireplace. 'No. I planned instead to ruin the life he was so obviously enjoying. You see, after Marcus's funeral, I asked around about William Endicott, and the picture I got was of a man who liked living high, but not working for it. A reckless gambler, a chaser of women, a lazy, shiftless . . .'

She heard her voice rising with contempt, and took another long, careful breath and brought herself back under control. 'In short, Inspector, he was enjoying himself far too much, whilst my boy . . . Anyway, I planned to – what's that common phrase – yes, "put a spoke in his wheel". That's what I was going to do. By the time we'd finished with him, Mr William Endicott wouldn't be quite so pleased with himself, and the way his life was going, I promise you.'

'We?' Battle said quietly, and saw the woman stiffen. 'You said, by the time "we'd" finished with him. . . Was your daughter in on this plan to ruin him?'

'Don't be ridiculous, Inspector,' Elizabeth said sharply. 'Bernadette is still little more than a child.'

The Inspector thought this was stretching it a bit, but before he could express this view, the lady was talking again.

'No, I kept my daughter in total ignorance of my plans. When I said "we" I was referring to the other person here at the manor who had reason to want to see Mr Endicott brought low.'

'You mean Sir Bayard?' the Inspector said smugly.

'Oh no,' Elizabeth said, looking genuinely surprised – even shocked – and shattering the Inspector's smugness instantly. 'I mean Roger Potts-Gibbon.'

*

Roger entered the library like a wary dog, suspecting he was about to be given a smack across the snout, rather than be fed a juicy bone.

'My turn for the thumbscrews, eh, Inspector?' he began, his false joviality at odds with the sheen of perspiration that gleamed on his forehead. 'I have to come clean first, and tell you that Elizabeth, Mrs Rowe that is, warned me she was going to confess all to you, and that, er, my name might arise.'

'Did she now?' the Inspector said, not best pleased. Giving his suspects time to come up with a good story was not something he generally approved. 'Let's hear it then. Exactly what grudge did *you* have against the dead man?'

The blunt, no-nonsense question made Roger grimace, but he didn't let it put him off his stride. If the Inspector wanted to keep things brisk, he would oblige him!

'A couple of years ago, he was responsible for me losing out on a very lucrative business deal,' Roger said flatly, unable to keep the anger out of his voice, even now. 'I was at my club one night, and the miserable weasel was there as a guest of another member, and he manged to get a hold of some information about shares that I was negotiating to buy from a wealthy American industrialist that would have. . . Well, never mind all that. The little rat sold the information to my closest competitor, who, as you'd expect, nipped in and undermined me with the American millionaire and secured the good deal for himself. I learned Endicott was to blame when my competitor got drunk at a big bash in Mayfair about six months later, and a good friend of mine overheard him boasting about how he'd put one over on me, and what part he had played in it.'

'I see. I take it the loss was quite significant. Was it enough to put you in severe financial difficulties?' he asked shrewdly.

Roger flushed. 'It wasn't quite as bad as all that. I wasn't staring bankruptcy in the face or anything so dire. But it did cause me a rather lean year that should have been dripping with fat instead,' the businessman conceded coolly. And met the Inspector's gimlet stare with one of his own.

'Which means you must not have been very pleased to arrive here at Cleeves Lea and find Endicott already ensconced with his feet under the table.'

'You have a gift for understatement, Inspector,' Roger remarked dryly with a smile that didn't quite reach his eyes.

'Mrs Rowe told me that she intended to make Mr Endicott's life less comfortable for him, but refused to tell me how she planned to do this. Instead, she insisted that I ask you.'

Roger shrugged. 'That was sporting of her,' he said with a nod of admiration. He would wager that not many women could weather this policeman's manner and stand up to it. 'Very well. After missing out on the American deal, you'd better believe that I made it my business to keep an eye on Mr Endicott and his activities.'

'With the intention of doing him one in the eye at the first chance you got, no doubt,' Battle slipped in slyly.

If he was fazed by this, Roger Potts-Gibbon showed no signs of it. Instead, he coolly lit a cigarette and nodded. 'As you say –

with the intention of doing him one in the eye.' He blew a leisurely smoke ring and then gave a wry little laugh. 'But that was easier said than done. I soon learned that Endicott was a drifter, moving from one job and place to another. One moment he seemed to live high on the hog, the next hand-to-mouth. There were always women in his life, naturally. When it comes to his sort, young, charming and good-looking, there always are, aren't there? At times that man was little more than a damned gigolo. And of course there was gambling, and no doubt other dirty little deals like the one he pulled on me. But there was nothing meaty enough that I could get my teeth into. Nothing I could do to really make him come a proper cropper.'

'That must have been very frustrating for you, sir,' the policeman commiserated drolly. 'I can only imagine how very tempting it must have been for you to exact a more permanent revenge, when you found him here, right under your nose, so to speak.'

'Yes, I thought you might see it that way,' Roger said grimly, watching a smoke ring rise into the air in front of him. 'But I can assure you, Inspector, that I have too high a regard for my neck to risk putting it into a noose over the likes of Endicott. Besides, I couldn't do that to Daphers. Daphne is worth ten of me,' he added softly. 'And that's probably flattering myself. I would never bring shame to her door.'

'Very nice sentiments, I'm sure, sir,' Battle said, unimpressed. 'So, just what *did* you and Mrs Rowe intend to do? And how long have you two known each other?' he added sharply.

'Oh, we don't know each other,' Roger said, and seeing the sceptical look cross the policeman's face, he shook his head. 'No, honestly, we'd never met before this weekend. You can ask around about that all you like,' he said, his confidence too genuine for Battle to doubt him. 'But like I said, I was very interested in anything to do with Endicott, and I paid some grubby little man to sniff around and compile a dossier on him, and one of the things the private detective uncovered was his role in that tragedy at Henley. So when we arrived here, the name Rowe rang a bell. To cut a long story short, I approached her, and we tentatively swapped our stories and . . . Well, let's just say, we both firmly agreed that something needed to be done about Mr William Endicott.'

'Yes, so you and she keep saying,' the policeman said, fast losing his patience. 'But if you didn't kill him – and I'm reserving judgement on that, naturally,' Battle put in dryly, 'just what was it you had planned for him?'

Roger smiled coolly. 'Well, just for starters, we intended to spike his latest plans to live on easy street, Inspector.'

'And what plans were those exactly?' Battle asked, very much interested.

'Why, to leech off Agnes Warren, of course. What else?'

*

'Do you believe him, sir?' Jellicoe asked after Potts-Gibbon had left, closing the library door softly behind him.

The Inspector shrugged. 'You mean, do I think Endicott was sucking up to our rather naive spinster lady? Probably. Potts-Gibbon is not the first to mention how Endicott seemed to be paying her special attention, flattering her and playing up to her. Lady Sybil mentioned it in her formal interview, as did one or two others. But they put it down to Endicott just hamming it up as the handsome, available young man-about-town. I don't think they thought it amounted to anything other than him amusing himself with a silly, rather plain middle-aged woman.'

'Hmmm,' Jellicoe said. 'But from what we're learning about him, I wouldn't be surprised if Mrs Rowe and Mr Potts-Gibbon had the right of it. I could just see him talking the poor woman out of some of her money. And by the way, sir, the reports have been coming in all day, and Miss Warren is very well off indeed.'

Battle nodded wearily. 'Hence Potts-Gibbon approaching her with a business deal to keep her ready cash tied up.'

'And Mrs Rowe was going to pretend to invest in his scheme as well, to reassure Agnes that it was all on the up and up, and save her from being fleeced' – Jellico nodded – 'which, if Endicott hadn't died, and they'd pulled it off, would have made him as mad as a hornet I reckon. Oh, Miss Warren might still have indulged him with a few trinkets, but she wouldn't have stretched to holidays abroad or new cars, or whatever it was the swine was angling for.'

Battle gave a rare smile. 'That is, if we believe them.'

'You don't, sir?'

'I think, Sergeant, that everybody in this blasted house seems to have had a good reason for wanting the man dead,' Battle said, exasperated. 'The Lord of the Manor, because Endicott had been messing about with his wife. Lady Sybil, because she was afraid Endicott would spill the beans, or even try a spot of blackmail on her. Elizabeth and her daughter to avenge Marcus Rowe. Roger to have his revenge for all that lost loot – and he was a man who struck me as having a very healthy love of loot. Now even little Miss Warren might have a motive, if she found out the big bad wolf was after her savings, so she's not ruled out either. So far as I can tell, only our famous author, his assistant and her lovesick swain have no motive for wanting Endicott dead.'

'What about Samantha Remington, sir?' Jellicoe pointed out. 'How does she fit into all this?'

Battle sighed. 'Yes – that's the burning question, isn't it? Everyone and their great aunt Fanny had a motive for bumping off Endicott. But what did Miss Remington do that made her killer ensure that she also had to shuffle off this mortal coil? Granted, I think we can take it as read that she and Endicott were rather more than mere acquaintances. And even if she was highly motivated to prove he hadn't killed himself, she'd barely been here two minutes. What on earth could she have found out in that time that put the wind up the killer and made him or her decide to put her out of the way?'

'But everyone says she was a hard and smart woman, sir,' the Sergeant pointed out diffidently. 'Perhaps Endicott confided something to her *before* coming here? Perhaps he knew he was in danger? Or maybe, he knew he was going to do something that might put him in danger, and he told her about it as a sort of insurance policy? The answer must lie there somewhere, surely?'

'Yes, possibly, but which of them are we talking about? The Chervilles? Or that alliance between the Rowe women and Potts-Gibbon? In light of all this new information, let's take another look at what they all said they were doing at the time Samantha Remington was killed.'

Battle drew his notebook towards him and flipped back through it, though he didn't really need it as an aid to his memory, for Arbie had been correct to admire the Inspector's reliance on his recall.

'Lady Sybil now,' Battle mused. 'She claimed she was in the orangery. She was first to find the victim, and as you know, it's always worth taking a close look at *them*,' he said darkly. 'Her stated movements might well have been correct right up until the last minute, when instead of merely discovering the woman dead, she spots her alive and well and sitting at the table, but then creeps up behind her and does the deed.' He snorted in disbelief at his own words. 'And, of course, just happened to have the murder weapon on her!'

He looked up at his sergeant sharply. 'The maids who were looking after Miss Remington and Lady Sybil both confirm the hat pin belonged to the murdered woman, and not to the lady of the house?'

'Yes, sir. Which means, whatever else it was, the murder of Miss Remington must have been premeditated. Whoever did it must have gone to her room and pinched the hat pin with malice aforethought.'

'Unfortunately, that doesn't help us much. Everyone we've spoken to has commented on the murdered woman's fashion sense. They'd all have seen her wearing fancy hats and known about her hat pins.'

Jellicoe nodded gloomily. 'Is it just me, or does the murder weapon suggest that it was a crime more likely to have been committed by a woman, sir? I mean, a hat pin . . . somehow I just can't see a man using it.'

'Then you haven't been around long enough, Sergeant,' Battle told him briskly. 'I knew a case where a woman who you wouldn't have thought could kill a fly, took a sledgehammer to her cheating husband. And I knew a case where a sixteen-stone ditch-digger used a dainty little stiletto-style letter opener – a memento of Venice no less – to neatly fillet the man who'd stolen ten shillings from him.'

Jellicoe, abashed, fell silent.

'So, what about Sir Bayard?' Battle said, more to himself than to his now slightly resentful sergeant. 'I can see him, just, killing Endicott. A man with a beautiful wife can be driven to any extreme when his pride and vanity are hurt. But killing the woman? Why? Even if she'd somehow got on to him, a man as powerful as Cherville would more likely either try and pay her off or put his faith in fancy lawyers and take his chance with a jury. It isn't often a jury will convict a muckety-muck, you know, Sergeant. They feel it goes against the natural order of things.'

'Yes, sir. What about Bernadette Rowe?' Jellicoe, forgetting to sulk, put in hopefully. 'To my mind, that little miss isn't as innocent as she makes out, with them big blue eyes of hers.

What if Miss Rowe killed Endicott and the Remington woman caught on to her? There was nothing to stop her from stealing the hat pin and killing her to keep her quiet. And her alibi for the time of the second murder was only that she was with her mother all the time.'

Battle gave another little snort. 'Yes, and we both know what *that's* worth! After losing one child, that woman would do anything to keep her last chick safe.'

'Who else? Daphne Potts-Gibbon was with that Miss Coulton-James and her swain, so her alibi is all right. Unless she killed Miss Remington before joining up with them. The worst of it is, nobody knows how long the woman was sitting out there before she was killed. Any one of them might have done it!'

For a while the two policemen were silent. Then Battle gave a heavy sigh. 'This case is beginning to feel as if it's getting bogged down,' he admitted gloomily.

He might not have felt quite so gloomy, though, if he'd known about the current activities of one Mr Arbuthnot Swift.

*

Arbie, from his seat in the train, caught sight of that most wonderful of sights, York Minster, in the warm April sunlight. Its square tower and wonderful stained-glass windows lifted the spirit, even from a distance.

From the train station, he caught a taxi to the city hall, where he filled out a form allowing him to peruse the 'births, deaths and marriages' registers of the good people of the county. But even as a helpful clerk settled him down at a table with ledger upon ledger to go through, and he sneezed in the dust lifting off so many turned pages, he wavered between two paradoxical thoughts.

One thought went – *please don't let me have to trawl through too much paperwork before I find what I'm looking for*; and the other thought went – *please let me be wrong and get to the end of the day with nothing to show for it.*

But it was the first of his silent laments that came up trumps, and less than half an hour later, Arbie left York behind him a wiser and much sadder man. Moreover, a man who had a lot of thinking to do, and a very hard decision to make.

By the time he'd arrived back at Cleeves Lea, he was running very much true to form, and had decided to sleep on it, in the vague hope that when he woke up, the problem would have gone away or solved itself.

*

That night, Uncle slipped from the Job's Rest and met up with his friend, who was waiting just outside the village with his van. Both men were in high spirits, and fully intended to be in even higher spirits before the night was over.

That night, the devil's train thundered once more through the valley, unaware that it was being tracked to its lair.

CHAPTER SIXTEEN

Arbie awoke the next morning feeling like something no self-respecting cat would even *dream* of dragging into the house. He hadn't slept well, and as he rose and walked drearily to his bedroom window, he wasn't particularly surprised to find that no miraculous solution to his problem had materialised overnight.

There was nothing for it but to dump the whole mess in Inspector Battle's lap and have nothing more to do with it. He . . .

A small *ping* came from his closed window, making him jump back instinctively, then, more cautiously, he peered down and espied his uncle standing there, about to throw another small pebble to attract his attention. Seeing his nephew appear, he tossed the little stone to one side and beckoned him down instead.

With another unhappy sigh, Arbie quicky dressed and trotted down, using one of the side doors to avoid the notice of the servants. His past experiences of his uncle's various exploits had long since drummed into him the need for discretion.

Outside, it was a crisp, cool morning, with a bit of low-lying mist that the sun was just attempting to burn off. He found his uncle restlessly pacing up and down. 'Ah, there you are, boy. I just popped over to say cheerio. I'm off.'

'Back home you mean?' Arbie asked, dismayed.

'Yes.'

'How? There's no train as far as I know for hours yet,' he complained.

'Oh, don't worry about that, I've got a lift with a friend,' Uncle said vaguely, beginning to walk casually away down the driveway. Instinctively, Arbie began to trot after him.

'What friend?' he asked suspiciously.

'Oh, just a mate.'

'Uncle!'

'What?'

'I thought you were going to help me with the train?'

'Oh that. Shouldn't worry about it if I were you,' his relative said airily.

By now thoroughly alarmed, Arbie quickened his pace. In doing so, they reached the end of the drive neck-and-neck, where a rather disreputable van, purporting to sell seed potatoes, stood waiting. The canvas back was tied down and Arbie could see someone's elbow – presumably that of his uncle's friend – sticking out of the open window.

'But things are just coming to a head here,' Arbie complained. 'About the murders, I mean.'

'Oh yes?' Uncle said, clearly uninterested. 'Know who did 'em, do you? And why?'

'As a matter of fact, I do,' Arbie said coldly.

'Well done. You've got brains right enough, boy, always knew it,' his uncle said, patting him heartily on the back.

By now they'd reached the rear of the van. 'Aren't you forgetting something, Uncle?' Arbie said ominously, making the older man look at him curiously.

'Me? No, I don't think so.'

'I thought we were going to track the smuggler's route so that I can inform the local police about it,' Arbie reminded him, his voice now frigid.

'Not so loud!' Uncle hissed at him, casting the open window on the driver's side a nervous glance. Clearly, he didn't want his mate to run away with the idea that he and the law were on friendly terms. 'And what smugglers? That turned out to be nothing, boy. Nothing at all,' he said heartily.

Arbie gave him a disgusted look, and deftly untied one of the ties on the canvas flap and tossed a corner back. Uncle gave a hiss of alarm, looked around and frantically tried to cover it up again. But not before Arbie had got a good look at the crates piled up there – and the labels on the side.

'Cognac. Whisky. Port. Sherry. Champagne. Wine. Quite a haul I see,' Arbie mused. 'I didn't know your friend was in the wine trade,' he added sardonically.

'Sssshhh, keep your voice down, will you?' Uncle told him, grumpily grabbing the ties from his hand and reattaching the canvas securely.

'You followed the train, didn't you?' Arbie said, but in a near-whisper now. 'And snaffled some of the booty for yourselves. Let me guess, it happened when they were busy unloading the stuff from the train and were in the process of loading it onto – what? Carts?'

'Never you mind what they loaded it onto!'

'They'll realise some of it is missing, you know,' Arbie said craftily. 'And if they find out about you and your truck here. . .' He mimed cutting his throat with a finger.

Uncle winced and went a shade pale. 'They won't find out, will they? How can they?'

'They might. You were staying at the ringleader's inn, after all. When he finds you gone, don't you think he'll be suspicious?'

'He thinks I'm a commercial traveller, and I told him last night that I was leaving early.'

Arbie shook his head. 'I don't know, Uncle. Amos Fairley struck me as a canny sort. He might put you and these missing crates of his' – he tapped the back of the van significantly – 'together. But if the local police catch the gang in the act and nab them, you'll be as safe as houses.'

Uncle scowled.

'Come on, Uncle, you know it makes sense. Tell me the route and the details and I'll pass them on to the Inspector. I know it goes against the grain, but the likes of Fairley and his gang could be dangerous, Uncle.'

'Oh, all right,' Uncle said, giving in ungraciously. 'As it happens, I think they're transporting the goods by barge, so it's not as if they're going to make a quick getaway. I reckon even the local police around here can be trusted to make a search of the canal within a thirty-mile radius and pick 'em all up in one fell swoop.' Uncle grinned gleefully at the thought. 'Come to think of it, the bottle boy at the inn this morning told me that the boss was going to be away for the next few days, so I reckon that Amos himself has gone off on the barge this time, to keep an eye on his investment. He won't trust any of his gang out of his sight now, not after they somehow managed to lose a couple of crates! He'll be convinced they've hidden it somewhere to sell on and line their own pockets.'

With a sigh, he pulled out a pencil and a notebook and drew a rough map showing the route of the train, the position of the tunnel and even the start of the route the carts took on their way over the hills towards the canal.

Arbie took it gratefully, then watched wistfully as his uncle climbed into the van. He'd been hoping that his uncle would stick around now that things were about to get sticky, and he felt a bit like an abandoned pup, left on the roadside.

The owner of the elbow stuck his hand out and waved it jauntily, but he was careful not to show Arbie his face, and then the van drew away.

Reluctantly, Arbie turned back to the house and slipped back in through the side door. As he did so, a hand clamped around his arm and gripped tightly.

Arbie let out a little yell of fear.

'Ssshhhh,' he was admonished for the second time in five minutes. This time it was Val doing the shushing. 'What's going on? Why are you sneaking about?' she demanded.

'Did anyone tell you that you have a very suspicious nature?' Arbie complained. It was a trait of hers that he'd always found very annoying, especially when he was doing something suspicious. 'And I'm not sneaking about . . .' he began to deny hotly, then realised that he had, indeed, been sneaking about, and sighed. 'I've just spoken to Uncle. He's going back home.'

'Typical of him – deserting us in our hour of need,' Val said fondly. She rather liked Arbie's uncle, although she'd never admit as much. 'Is he all right?'

'Oh *he's* just fine,' Arbie said bitterly, picturing his uncle merrily on his way back home with a truck load of twice-stolen booze that he would sell on, then live high on the hog for the next six months or so. 'It's me who's the one in a bind. As usual.'

'Self-pity is so unattractive,' Val said automatically, then did a double take. 'Wait – what sort of a bind?' she added, her voice rising sharply. 'Whatever it is, I'll get us out of it,' she promised.

'Oww!' Arbie said, for her hand, still clasped around his forearm, had clenched compulsively and her strong fingers were digging into his flesh.

'Oh, don't be such a baby,' Val said, letting go. 'Now come on, confess. Why are you in a bind?' she demanded. And then, looking more closely at his face, and seeing that his misery was real, went pale.

'You know, don't you?' she said quietly. 'You've worked out who killed Bill and Miss Remington?'

Mutely, Arbie nodded.

Val swallowed hard. Although she had to admit to herself

that she loved her past adventures with Arbie, hunting ghosts and catching killers, she couldn't deny that she didn't love at all the feeling that came with knowing that you were responsible for seeing someone suffer the awful and fatal consequences of their actions. The law, she knew, was remorseless.

'Who is it?' she asked tremulously.

Arbie told her.

*

Inspector Battle arrived back at the house promptly at nine, a mental list of priorities uppermost in his mind. He was met at the door not by the butler, however, but by Arbie Swift.

'Hello, Inspector. I was wondering if I might just have a word? It's important,' the young man said diffidently.

Just as Val had done not long before, the policeman took one look at the author's face and changed his itinerary on the spot.

'All right. Let's go to the library. It seems appropriate,' he added grimly.

Arbie supposed it was as good a place as any and slumped down onto the sofa in front of the coffee table. It was in the chair opposite him that Bill Endicott had died, and he did his best not to look at it.

'Right then – let's have it,' the Inspector said. His face, voice and manner gave no indication of what he was thinking or feeling.

'All right. Well, er . . . I suppose I should start by saying that I have very little in the way of actual evidence to show you,' Arbie began uncertainly. 'But, well, I've been thinking. . . And I might well be wrong in my thinking you understand, but, well, the thing is. . .'

The Inspector, who'd sat through his fair share of first-time reports from green-as-grass constables, sighed. 'Start at the beginning, sir, and then keep on going,' he advised with what might have been a near-friendly twinkle in his eye. Or might not. 'What's the first thing that gave you a nasty little feeling inside that things weren't as they should be?'

Arbie nodded at him, grateful for the olive branch. 'Right you are. Well, it was the set-up in this room on the morning I found Bill. There were things about it that just didn't sit right with me. Let's start with the Champagne for starters.'

The Inspector, for the first time since the interview, looked surprised. 'The Champagne?' he repeated uncertainly.

'Yes, the Champagne,' Arbie repeated firmly. 'It struck me as incongruous. I mean, when someone mentions Champagne to you, what's the first thing you think of?' he asked, eager to hear the other man's honest opinion.

'Oh, well, a celebration I suppose,' Battle said promptly, then frowned a little. 'You have it at special occasions. Yes, I think I see what you mean,' he added.

'Yes. I could see right enough what it was *supposed* to look like,' Arbie admitted. 'A chap leaves a suicide note, then sits down and swallows a lot of sleeping stuff with a drink. But that Champagne worried me. It wasn't . . . *right*. See here, Bill and I were much of an age, and had the same sort of childhood and upbringing in a general sort of way. And I tell you straight, if things ever got so bad that I decided to end it all, I'd bally well want a stiff drink – or two or three – first. Whisky or rum maybe.'

'But not Champagne. Unless, of course,' Battle played devil's advocate, 'you were a dissolute young man with a warped sense of humour. Then you might say to yourself – "only the best will do" and filch the Lord of the Manor's finest fizz.'

'Y-yes,' Arbie conceded. 'You might. But the Champagne was just the start of it. I then read the suicide note.'

'Yes, which wasn't a suicide note at all,' Battle mused. 'Since the inquest, I've borrowed that *How to Live Harmoniously* book from the library and read it from top to bottom.' He gave a little shudder.

Arbie gazed at him with real pity in his eyes. 'My dear chap! I do call that going above and beyond the call of duty, I really do.'

The Inspector shrugged. 'Be that as it may – I've come to the same conclusion that you did. Young Endicott, to please Miss Warren, had just scribbled down a whole list of his woes, and some enterprising killer came across it and saw its potential as a suicide note.'

'Exactly! So then I wondered – why would Bill come down to the library at all to kill himself? He had a perfectly decent bedroom in which to do it. Which brought me back to the Champagne.'

'Not following you now,' Battle said simply.

'Well, my first thought was, like you, that Champagne is usually quaffed when you are celebrating something special. So – what if he'd arranged to meet someone in the library to celebrate something? The simplest explanations are often the right ones, aren't they, and that would fit with all the facts, wouldn't it?'

Slowly the Inspector nodded. 'All right. For the sake of argument, let's say that that's what happened. He had an assignation with someone. You're thinking it was his killer?'

'I think that's a fair assumption.'

'All right,' the Inspector agreed equitably. 'Following on with your scenario then, Endicott and his killer presumably had something to celebrate?'

'Yes.'

'And the killer slipped the Veronal into his drink?'

'Er, no.'

'*No?*' The Inspector stared at him intently. 'Now you really have scuppered me,' he said. 'Tell me exactly what you mean by that?'

Arbie cocked his head thoughtfully to one side, then nodded. 'Actually, Inspector, I'd rather show you. Do you mind swapping places with me for a moment?'

The Inspector rose (and rose) to his six feet six inches, whilst Arbie got up to allow him to take his place. 'Now, if Bill died in that chair' – he pointed to the armchair opposite – 'and we have no reason to suppose that he didn't (why, after all, would the killer want to go lugging him about?) then the most likely place for his killer to sit to enjoy their cosy "celebration" would be opposite him on the sofa, yes?'

Battle, not to be rushed, took his time to look around at the various other seating arrangements on offer before regarding the chair, the table and his own position, and slowly nodded. 'Yes, I think that follows all right.'

'Okay,' Arbie said. 'Now, I'm going to go and fix a drink – let's say, open and pour some Champagne, which I have taken from the cocktail cabinet. Watch me and see if anything strikes you.'

And with this, Arbie walked to the drinks cabinet and did, in fact, pour two drinks. Not Champagne, but two whisky-and-sodas. 'Your back is to me all the while, yes?'

'Yes,' came Battle's voice from behind him.

'But look at what's right in front of you – or at least, almost in front of you but set at a slight angle.'

'Well, the fireplace and the mirror. . . Swift! The mirror! *I can see everything that you're doing*,' the Inspector said, a definite note of excitement in his voice now.

Arbie nodded complacently. 'Yes, I had occasion to notice that the first night I was here.' He brought back the two drinks, set them on the table, then looked unhappily at the 'death' chair, and said to the Inspector, 'Er, do you mind if we swap back again, old sport?'

The Inspector – now definitely with a twinkle in his eye – moved back to the chair where Endicott had met his end and unconcernedly parked his own end in it. Meanwhile, Arbie resumed his old place on the sofa.

'Now – what do you think of that?' Arbie asked and took a rather large gulp of his drink. Now they were getting to the nitty-gritty, he felt badly in need of a restorative to see him through.

'I think that whoever was sitting on this sofa would have seen what anyone at the bar had been doing with the drinks. Which would include any hanky-panky about slipping sleeping drafts into one of the glasses. And if Bill Endicott had been the one doing the watching, there was no way that he would have just tamely gone ahead and drunk what was offered to him,' the Inspector concluded flatly.

'Which means?'

Battle smiled grimly. 'Which means Bill Endicott *hadn't* been the one doing the watching. He was the one doing the pouring.'

'Yes. So now where are we?' Arbie mused. 'Bill arranges to meet someone here. He's careful to have Champagne ready, as well as the fatal dose of Veronal. He fixes the drinks, doctoring just one of them, and then comes back with the two Champagne flutes, to his companion. And, as you say, no way would anyone in their right mind then drink the glass that Bill hands over. So, Inspector – put yourself in the shoes of that person. What do you do?'

Battle settled a bit more firmly in his chair. 'Well, if it was *me*, I'd be very tempted to take the rat by his throat and make *him* drink it.'

'Yes. But you're a big, strong man. What if you weren't?'

Instantly, the Inspector ran down his list of suspects. Sir Bayard would have a go – or would he? Bill was younger and fitter, and that might make him think twice. But no, his own ego would make him believe that he could take the blighter on.

Roger Potts-Gibbon now – he wasn't so sure about. But certainly, none of the ladies would dare try it.

'It has to be a woman,' Battle concluded flatly. 'And a woman would have to use guile. Do something to distract the swine and then quickly switch the glasses over.'

'Yes – and that's exactly what she did. Then, after Bill succumbed, she only had to take the second glass away with her, and it looked as if Bill was drinking alone. But which woman? That's what had me stumped.'

'Now it's my turn to share,' the Inspector said slowly. 'Reports have been coming in. We now know for sure that Lady Sybil and Endicott had a fling last year. We know Mrs and Miss Rowe had a reason to want to see him dead. And Potts-Gibbon also.'

'Y-yes,' Arbie said. 'But why would any of *them* have agreed to meet Bill down here to celebrate something? What would any of them have to celebrate with the likes of Endicott?'

Battle frowned. 'Hmmmmm. That's a bit of a facer and no mistake.'

'Yes. That's where I was too.'

'But not for long, Mr Swift, I take it, eh?'

'No. There were several other things that caught my eye and began to make me wonder. And then, of course, along came Samantha Remington,' Arbie said heavily. 'And the second murder.'

Battle slowly reached for his own whisky and soda and took a small sip. If his sergeant had been there to see it, he would have been scandalised, but Jellicoe hadn't yet arrived.

'Yes.' The Inspector nodded. 'Right from the start it seems she suspected that the so-called suicide was no such thing and made no secret of the fact that she was going to make it her mission to find out the truth of the matter. Which is what got her killed, of course.'

'Er . . . no, I don't think it did actually,' Arbie corrected him reluctantly. Then added quickly, 'Or at least, *if I'm on the right track*, what really got her killed was the fact that it was becoming clear that Endicott and Samantha were lovers. And, perhaps more importantly, had been for some time. Tell me – am I right?' he asked eagerly. 'You must have had inquiries made about that by now?'

Battle nodded. 'Oh yes – we're confident that they were an item, and had been, as you say, for some little time. But what I don't understand is why you think that should make any difference. If your theory is right, the person who killed Endicott did it, as good as damn it, in self-defence. I'm not sure a prosecution QC would see it that way, but I wouldn't be surprised if the court of public opinion saw it differently – and a jury too, when it comes to that. But this killing of the Remington woman . . . that was cold-blooded and with malice aforethought. That was quite different.'

'Oh yes, I'm not arguing with you there,' Arbie agreed. 'Although I don't think it was done in cold blood, you know, Inspector. If I'm right, it was exactly the opposite, in fact, and done in very hot blood indeed. In fact, in a positive inferno of jealousy and rage.'

Battle leaned forward a little on his chair. 'Go on.'

'Well, the way I see it is this; Endicott was killed by a woman. She killed him because she saw him trying to kill her! She was left with no choice but to do what she did – change the glasses around and then watch him die. But I keep coming back to that Champagne. *Why*, I asked myself, did Endicott and the mystery woman meet up to drink Champagne? What were they toasting? Tell me, Inspector, in your opinion, what do men and women usually make a great deal of fuss over?'

'A romance,' Battle said promptly. 'A love affair of some sort. So we're back to Lady Sybil then? They rekindled their liaison?'

'Under her husband's nose and in his house?' Arbie objected. 'I don't think even Endicott had the brass neck for that!'

'Well, it certainly couldn't have been either of the Rowe women. They detested him.'

'So who's left?'

At this, Battle went a little pale. 'Oh no! Don't tell me the archbishop's daughter did it,' he said harshly. 'I just can't picture Daphne Potts-Gibbon looking twice at someone like Endicott. Let alone taking him for a lover.'

'Me neither,' Arbie agreed hastily. 'But what if the celebration was a bit more formal? Champagne, after all, is traditional at engagements – or to celebrate marriages.'

'But – *who*, man?' the Inspector demanded, his frustration beginning to show. 'There's nobody left. I've eliminated all the women.'

'No,' Arbie said miserably. 'You haven't. You said it yourself. Who's left?'

Swiftly, the Inspector ran quickly through the guests of the weekend party. And then his expression froze. 'You can't mean . . .'

It was at this point that the door was opened so hard and fast that it banged back against the wall like a gunshot, making them jump. Arbie leapt to his feet, closely followed by the Inspector, and both men turned as one to look at the pale and trembling maid who'd just entered, and was breathing quickly.

'Please, sir, you're to come at once,' she implored. 'Something's happened. It's Miss Warren, sir. She's taken something – oh sir, that nice young woman, the vicar's daughter, thinks she's going to die!'

*

The two men raced into the hall, the maid trailing after them. 'She's upstairs in her room, sir. I've already called for the doctor, but he's on another call and they're trying to track him down. . .'

Her wails were left behind as the two men shot up the stairs, Battle leading the way. He'd been given a floor plan of the house by Sir Bayard yesterday, so he knew the general direction of the room belonging to Miss Warren.

Another maid was standing outside the open door, wringing her hands uselessly as the two men swept past her – and came to an abrupt halt.

Lying on the bed, Agnes Warren was moving about fitfully. Her face was flushed and damp with perspiration. Sitting beside her was Val, who cast them a look of anguish. 'I didn't realise she had any of it left,' Val said, near to tears.

'Veronal?' the Inspector asked harshly.

Val nodded. 'I think so. She must not have handed it all over to you but kept some back,' she said, indicating a familiar bottle lying on the floor beside the bed.

'How long ago did she take it?' Battle asked, walking over to the bed.

'I don't know,' Val wailed. 'When Arbie told me what he suspected and took you off to the library, I thought it would be best if I came up here to check on her. She must have taken it before then. She seemed fine at first, even pleased to see me, and we just sat and talked about things like the weather, and where I might like to go on my holidays and – oh – just silly things like that. Then I began to get the feeling something wasn't right – she was too restless and nervous and at the same time, sort of . . . I don't know, I can't explain it. Almost serene somehow. But then she began to slur her words and sort of . . . wilted. That's when I helped her onto the bed and summoned a maid and asked her to call for the doctor. Oh, this is awful!'

The Inspector looked down from his vast height at the woman on the bed. 'Miss Warren – Miss Warren, can you hear me?' he said loudly.

'Yes – but you sound as if you're standing far away,' she replied faintly.

The Inspector obligingly raised his voice even further. 'Miss Warren, have you taken some sleeping powder?'

Her head, lying against the pillow, nodded slightly. 'Yes. I want to die. I don't want to hang. I've been so dreadfully afraid I might hang . . . I knew you'd find out eventually, you see. You're so clever. It's too terrible. I can't face the court or the papers or . . . that final walk at dawn,' Agnes said, and began to weep slow, silent tears that fell down her cheeks one after the other.

Val looked aghast at Arbie, who walked unsteadily to a nearby chair and sat down abruptly. The Inspector shook his head. Although it wasn't professional of him, he found himself wishing that the doctor wouldn't arrive in time, for in his heart, he agreed with the stricken woman that it would be better to end things this way. At least she'd save herself from the horror of a trial and having to watch the judge don the black cap during sentencing.

But he still had his duty to do.

'Miss Warren, did you kill William Endicott?'

'Yes. I didn't want to. But he was going to kill me. I saw him – in the mirror. It suddenly came to me in a flash – he wanted my money. Not me. Never me.' Her voice was fading in and out, but still clearly audible to himself and the other two witnesses.

'You met him in the library when everyone else had gone to bed. And you saw him put something into your glass of Champagne?' Battle asked, clarifying the situation whilst at the same time giving her less talking to do.

The woman nodded.

'Do you know why he tried to poison you. Miss Warren?'

'She's not Miss Warren, Inspector.' Arbie spoke up at this point, making Val look at him in surprise. 'It's Mrs Endicott, isn't it?' he added loudly, for the older woman's benefit. 'I found a copy of your marriage to William Endicott in the public records. You were married just over two weeks ago, weren't you?'

The woman on the bed gave a faint moan. 'Yes. I was so happy. We never told a soul – we wanted it to be a surprise.

For everyone. We were going to announce it here. . .' Her eyes closed and she gave a little sigh.

'Miss War— Mrs Endicott, can you hear me? Please try to stay awake,' the Inspector said urgently.

The woman on the bed gave a little sigh, and her eyelids fluttered. 'I'm so tired, and you're so far away now. . .' she complained.

'What about Miss Remington? You killed her too, didn't you?' the Inspector said quickly.

Agnes nodded. 'Yes. I found a letter in her bag. I read it. I shouldn't have . . . it was from . . . *him*, to her,' she said and began to cry again. Hopeless, weary tears. 'It broke my heart – the lovely, loving things he wrote to her. Because I knew that he meant them. It was *her* that he loved, never me. I hated her then. Really *hated* her. So much so, I just had to kill her. Because when he'd said those same things to me, I knew that they had been nothing but lies. She could have had anyone, but I thought he was mine. It just wasn't fair. . .'

And those were the final words she spoke, for despite the Inspector's efforts, she never opened her eyes again. And the doctor was, indeed, too late to save her.

*

The inquest into the death of Agnes Warren was mercifully short and inevitably attended by a plethora of sensation-seeking reporters.

The woman in question would have hated it.

Immediately following it, the Rowes and the Potts-Gibbons were finally free to go to the railway station where they could catch a train and head back to their homes, but Sir Bayard asked Arbie and Val to return to the manor for a while and take a later train themselves.

Arbie was in no doubt as to what the Lord of the Manor wanted from him, and once they were all seated in the lounge, and sherry and sandwiches had been served, he braced himself for the inevitable questions.

But it was Lady Sybil who spoke first. 'I still can't believe it,' she said, shaking her head, her remarkable aquamarine eyes shining like those of a cat. 'I mean – *Bill* of all people. And *Agnes*! What on earth was he thinking?'

'He was thinking of her money, dearest,' Sir Bayard said grimly. He looked tellingly at his wife, who flushed, and looked away. 'I'm right, aren't I?' He turned to Arbie. It had come as a distinct shock to the Lord of the Manor to learn that this rather lethargic-looking author was something of a noted amateur sleuth, but he'd had it from no less a source than Inspector Battle himself that this was indeed the case.

'Oh yes, I'm afraid so,' Arbie agreed.

'What do you suppose the fellow's plan was, exactly, though?' Sir Bayard asked, and then added with a flash of heat, 'and why the deuce did he have to do it all here at Cleeves Lea of all places?'

'Oh, I think his plan was probably relatively simple and straight-forward, Sir Bayard,' Arbie said. 'I'm only guessing, of course, but I imagine that if things had worked out as he expected, then we'd have found Agnes dead on that Saturday morning, and he'd spin us some tale or other. He'd probably admit that they were man and wife, but then say something along the lines of how he'd come to realise that he'd made a dreadful mistake, and that he'd told Agnes that evening that he intended to get out of it somehow. Then go on to speculate about how the thought of going through with a divorce or face the scandal of a separation had been too much for her. And that Agnes, deciding that she couldn't face the humiliation of her position, had decided to end it all instead.'

Val shook her head in wonderment. 'Did he really expect us to believe all that?'

'Why not?' Arbie argued sadly. 'We hadn't known Miss Warren – I mean, Mrs Endicott – all that well, but even we could see that she was a highly strung lady, and a very respectable one at that. She wasn't someone who would have been able to take the scorn or pity of her friends in her stride, let alone the slings and arrows that the wider and unkind world would have flung her way.'

'You're quite right,' Lady Sybil said quietly. 'If faced with ruin she *would* take the easy way out. As in fact, she did.'

Val looked at Arbie. 'I still don't see how you put it all together. What gave her away?'

'Oh, it wasn't any one thing you know,' Arbie said sadly. 'It was just lots of little things. Like her gloves for instance.'

'*Her gloves?*' Lady Sybil repeated, astonished. 'What about them?'

'Well, I noticed when we first arrived that she wore gloves all the time – even indoors. But after Bill died, she stopped wearing them at all. And I wondered why. Now, I think it was to hide the fact that she had been wearing a wedding ring and she didn't want to give the game away until the happy couple could announce it formally.'

'She could have just taken the ring off,' Sybil said dismissively, but instantly Val shook her head.

'Oh no – she wouldn't have done that,' Val said firmly, her blue eyes bright with unshed tears of pity. 'She loved him you see. To her, he was everything. Put yourself in her place; she had probably started to accept the fact that she'd never marry, never know love. And then, out of the blue, this charming, handsome man comes into her life and tells her that *he* loves her, and *he* wants to marry her. And does so. That wedding ring would have been the physical proof that all her dreams had come true. That it was all real. Oh, she must have been so happy. For a short time, anyway. No, she'd never have taken that ring off. Wild horses wouldn't have made her.'

As Val discreetly wiped her eyes with a handkerchief, even Lady Sybil had to swallow hard and look away. 'Poor Agnes,' she murmured. 'Poor, silly Agnes.'

'But afterwards, once she was over the shock of her husband trying to kill her, *then* she was able to take the ring off,' Arbie agreed. 'In fact, she probably hated the sight of it. And she certainly would have hated it after she'd discovered that her goddaughter and her husband were in love with each other.'

'You think they were in on it together then?' Sir Bayard enquired gruffly.

Arbie shrugged. 'I suppose it's *possible* that Samantha Remington didn't know that Bill intended to kill her godmother,' he said, chivalrously but rather doubtfully. 'But she *must* have known that her lover was romancing Agnes – I can't see someone as clever and sharp as she was, not knowing about *that*. Perhaps, as far as she was concerned, the plan was simply for Endicott and Agnes to get married and then Bill would share the spoils with her discreetly. Agnes would have handed her financial affairs over to him because that's what married women do. And it would be easy enough for Bill to set up Samantha in a better place. Buy her jewels. A car.' He shrugged.

'Pure rot,' Lady Sybil said emphatically. 'I believe she was in on it all the while. In fact, I don't blame Agnes for killing her – not one bit. I think I'd feel the same way.'

'Sybil!' her husband said, scandalised, but Sybil merely shrugged one shoulder defiantly.

'But what else made you suspect what was going on?' Sybil demanded, looking at Arbie with new eyes. 'It couldn't have been just that?'

'Oh no. There was also the way that Bill acted around her

that first night. Playing up to her. Of course, I realise now that he *had* to do that to keep her sweet. Remember, as far as Agnes was concerned, he was paving the way for the big announcement that she was his wife. But most of all, it was the so-called suicide note that convinced me that I was on the right track.' And here he told them about how he'd waylaid the Inspector just before Bill's inquest and shown him the relevant passage in Dr Schuber's awful book.

'The problem was – I could see Bill playing up to Agnes in a general way, as he did with all the ladies,' Arbie swept on. 'A little flattery here, a little gentle flirting there – that was second nature to him anyway. But to put in a real effort? To go to the trouble of studying the book, and then indulge Agnes's obsession to the point of literally following one of Dr Schuber's daft directives? No – that I just couldn't swallow. Not unless there was something far more solid behind it. And a man keeping his rich wife happy until he could kill her and inherit her fortune—'

'Don't! It's too awful,' Val interrupted him with a shudder. 'Let's not talk about it anymore.'

'Quite right, my dear,' Sir Bayard said firmly. 'Another glass of sherry before you go?'

*

Two hours later, Arbie, Val and Geraint (who'd met them at the station after settling his bill at the Job's Rest) were sitting in the first-class carriage of the late afternoon train as it pulled away from the halt, leaving Cleeves Lea behind them.

The weather had turned nasty, however, and dark storm clouds were gathering away to the west, blotting out the light and sending a brisk, cool wind blowing across the fields.

'Well, I'm glad that's all over,' Geraint said, settling in his seat and glancing moodily out of the window. 'Murders and suicides and whatnot – ugh! And there's something funny happening at the inn as well. The police were all over the place, searching the outhouses, and the landlord has been arrested apparently, though nobody's saying what it's all about. What a place! I'll be glad to see the back of it.'

He reached out and put his hand over Val's, who was sitting beside him and had been resting her digits on the edge of the seat. Gently, she inched her hand out from under his.

Geraint scowled across to the opposite seat to see if Arbie had noticed. But that gentleman appeared to be innocently looking out at the passing scenery.

Arbie was, in fact, musing that soon they'd be coming to the bridge where a train had plunged down into the valley far below, all those years ago. 'I say, it's a pity we didn't get to see Jeth . . .' he began when he was almost jerked out of his seat as the train suddenly braked.

'Now what!' Geraint said querulously, opening the window and sticking his head out. As he did so, fat raindrops blew into his face. He quickly drew his head back in and shut the window, just in time, before the rain began to fall in a deluge. 'Seems there's some sort of hold-up on the line,' the country solicitor huffed. 'That's just what we need,' he added, taking out his pocket-watch and glancing at it. 'I was hoping we'd be on time.'

Val leaned across to Arbie and smiled at him. 'Are you feeling all right, old bean?' she asked. 'This trip was a bit rotten, wasn't it?'

'Hmmm, it was a bit,' Arbie acknowledged. 'You know, Val, I've been thinking. This getting mixed up in murders and all that. Don't you think it's time we . . .'

Before he could finish, however, the door to the compartment rattled open, and the conductor looked in. 'Sorry about the delay, folks, we'll be starting off again soon enough. Seems the driver thought he saw a red light ahead warning of danger. We've got someone walking along the line now, just to make sure there's nothing to worry about. See!' he added, as the train gave a little jolt and began to slowly gather speed again, but proceeding with caution. 'We're off again.'

The conductor withdrew and went on down the corridor, spreading apologies and explanations to the other passengers in his wake.

But Val hardly heard him. Instead, with her eyes aglow, she looked out of the window at the storm now raging outside, then leapt across to sit next to Arbie and grab his arm in excitement. 'A red light signalling danger! And they thought they saw a lantern – and in a storm! And just as we're about to come to the bridge! Arbie, *don't you see what this means*?'

Arbie saw the look of excitement and happiness in her eyes and gave a little nod. 'Oh yes, old bean,' he said with a rather wistful smile. 'I see what it means all right.'

Discover Val and Arbie's first mystery

Oxfordshire, 1924. A scream rings out across the village of Maybury-in-the-Marsh. The lady of the house has been found dead at the Old Forge. But with all the windows and doors to her room locked, how – and by whom – was she killed?

Arbuthnot 'Arbie' Swift, author of *The Gentleman's Guide to Ghost-Hunting*, is investigating a suspected spectre at the house, and now the more pressing matter of murder falls to him too.

With old friend Val, he uncovers a sorry tale of altered wills and secret love affairs. When events take another sinister turn, Arbie must use all of his sleuthing skills to catch a killer and crack a most ingeniously plotted crime...

Join Val and Arbie for their second mystery

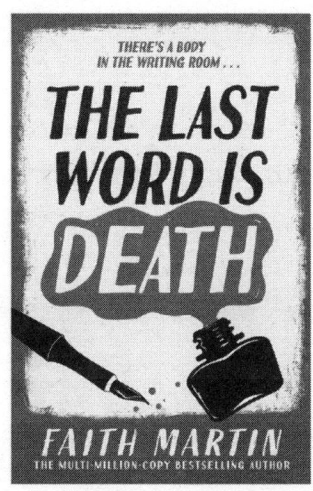

Arbuthnot 'Arbie' Swift arrives at Dashwood House, a glamorously modern hotel in the up-and-coming resort of Galton-next-the-Sea, but all plans for a relaxing stay are scuppered when one of the guests is found dead.

The body is found in the writing room, the victim part of a set visiting the seaside town for an engagement party, which happens to include Arbie's old friend, Val.

Familiar with Val and Arbie's previous experience in solving puzzling crimes, the bride asks the pair to investigate. They quickly discover that the victim had no shortage of enemies, and many of the guests are up to no good. But who is simply hiding a secret, and who is hiding murder?

Discover more gripping mysteries from Faith Martin with the Ryder and Loveday series.

Coroner Clement Ryder and probationary WPC Trudy Loveday form an unlikely duo when they team up to solve crimes in 1960's Oxford.

Dear Reader,

We hope you enjoyed reading this book. If you did, we'd be so appreciative if you left a review. It really helps us and the author to bring more books like this to you.

Here at HQ Digital we are dedicated to publishing fiction that will keep you turning the pages into the early hours. Don't want to miss a thing? To find out more about our books, promotions, discover exclusive content and enter competitions you can keep in touch in the following ways:

JOIN OUR COMMUNITY:
Sign up to our new email newsletter: http://smarturl.it/SignUpHQ
Read our new blog www.hqstories.co.uk

X https://twitter.com/HQStories
f www.facebook.com/HQStories

BUDDING WRITER?
We're also looking for authors to join the HQ Digital family!
Find out more here:

https://www.hqstories.co.uk/want-to-write-for-us/

Thanks for reading, from the HQ Digital team